D1624337

DO YOU HAVE
THE COURAGE TO PLAY?

CHAMPION'S QUEST

ROLL THE DIE OF DESTINY.

YOUR ADVENTURE AWAITS.

CHAMPION'S

QUEST

THE DIE OF DESTINY

BOOK ONE

FRANK L. COLE

SHADOW
MOUNTAIN

Visit us at shadowmountain.com

Library of Congress Cataloging-in-Publication Data

Names: Cole, Frank, 1977– author. | Cole, Frank, 1977– Champion's quest; bk. 1.
Title: The die of destiny / Frank L. Cole.
Description: Salt Lake City : Shadow Mountain, 2021. | Series: Champion's quest ; book 1 | Audience: Grades 4–6. | Summary: When Lucas Silver, who is trying to run away, and his friend Miles and two girls they know, Jasmine and Vanessa, step out of Hob and Bogie's Curiosity Shoppe, they discover that they have agreed to play a match of Champion's Quest, a role-playing game—played from inside the game with goblins, trolls, witches, and a three-headed monster.
Identifiers: LCCN 2021011957 | ISBN 9781629728506 (hardback)
Subjects: CYAC: Friendship—Fiction. | Self-confidence—Fiction. | Monsters—Fiction. | Magic—Fiction. | Fantasy games—Fiction. | Role playing—Fiction. | LCGFT: Fiction.
Classification: LCC PZ7.C673435 Di 2021 | DDC [Fic]—dc23
LC record available at https://lccn.loc.gov/2021011957

Printed in the United States of America
Lake Book Manufacturing, Inc., Melrose Park, IL

10 9 8 7 6 5 4 3 2 1

FOR CAMBERLYN—HERE'S A WHOLE BOOK DEDICATED
JUST TO YOU. YOU HAD BETTER READ IT.

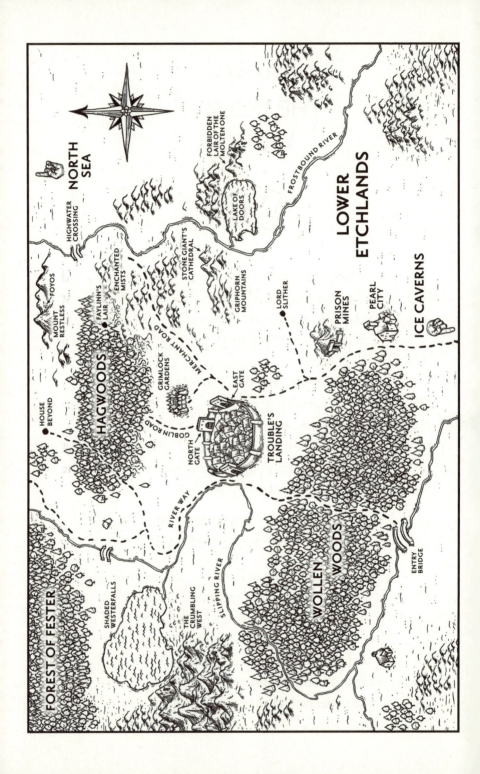

CHAPTER I

THE BLINKING WINDOW

It seemed like every kid in Bentford, West Virginia, had shown up to the Greenwillow Aquatic Center for the first day of summer vacation. Well, not every kid. I happened to be hiding in an alley, waiting for the coast to clear, behind a dumpster full of beets.

The dumpster belonged to the Debrecen Diner, a Hungarian restaurant known for their borscht, which apparently means beet soup, and I was having a terrible time ignoring the smell. Pinching my nose closed, I pulled the train ticket out of my pocket and reread the catchy phrase printed at the top for what had to be the fiftieth time.

YOUR LIFE IS YOUR ADVENTURE,
BUT WE CAN HELP YOU ON YOUR WAY.

Over the years I'd bounced around various foster homes, I'd been on plenty of buses and taxis and had even flown on a couple of airplanes, but not once had I ever ridden on an actual train. They weighed millions of pounds, their cars could stretch for miles, and they even traveled on massive tracks bolted to the ground. You couldn't just turn a train around and head back because someone had changed their mind.

Trains were permanent. Their destinations were permanent. And my ticket on the Carrington Express would take me on a thirteen-hour journey to New York City—the perfect place for a kid like me to disappear. Make no mistake about it, I would be on that train—and this time, I was never coming back.

"Oh, man, this thing really stinks." A voice startled me from my daydream. "What's in it?"

Turning around, I saw a small boy wearing a tank top, swim trunks, and a fanny pack, gagging at the smell from the dumpster. A faded patch of sunscreen glistened on the tip of his nose, and his dark-brown skin shimmered from chlorinated pool water.

"Miles, what are you doing here?" I asked, blinking in confusion and a little startled by his sudden appearance.

Miles Maldonado flashed a mouthful of crooked teeth and rubber-banded braces. "I'm having second thoughts about you leaving," he said.

Realizing it was only Miles, I managed to relax a little and strained my neck to look out at the road. "We've talked about this. Are you sure no one saw you?"

He shook his head. "No one ever sees me, Lucas. You know that."

Miles's size made it nearly impossible to guess his age, but just last month, he had turned eleven and would be entering the sixth grade after the summer. He was just waiting for a growth spurt to kick in—or so he liked to point out to anyone who would listen. Miles had been at the pool earlier when I had snuck away, and he was *supposed* to still be there.

"You agreed to stand guard at the aquatic center. I don't want anyone else to know I'm leaving."

Mr. and Mrs. Crowe, the caretakers at my latest foster home, the Sunnyside Group Home for Foster Children, had dropped us off at the aquatic center thirty minutes earlier, placing us in the care of Vanessa, their annoying sixteen-year-old daughter. It had only taken Vanessa ten minutes to abandon her post to go splash a boy at the side of the pool, and she'd never noticed me slip away. I had given Miles the assignment of keeping an eye on Vanessa. If she suspected for one second what I was trying to do, she would crush my plans for good.

Miles shuddered, catching another whiff of rotting beets. "I *am* standing guard. I mean, I was. But you wanted me to let you know if I saw something suspicious, right?"

A gurgling sensation instantly filled my stomach. "Why? Who saw me?"

"No one, but there was a fight just now between Tugg Roberts and Jasmine."

I frowned for a second but then raised my eyebrows. "You mean Jasmine Bautista?"

Miles nodded. "Yeah, Jasmine had Tugg and his buddies all backed up against the wall of the concession stand. I think most of them are scared of her."

"That doesn't surprise me," I said.

Jasmine Bautista fought . . . a lot. She had moved to Bentford about the same time as I had. She lived with her grandmother in the townhomes just down the road from Sunnyside. We were both the new kids at school and had been paired in a couple of our seventh-grade classes. Jasmine was nice enough—until you crossed her. Tugg Roberts was *not* nice, and he was always looking for a chance to make someone else's life miserable.

"It was way intense." Miles swallowed and gave a nervous

laugh, as though he had just witnessed something traumatic. "And then they threw her out."

"What do you mean?" I asked. "Tugg threw her out?"

Miles's eyes locked on my travel bag stashed behind the dumpster. He refocused on me and shook his head. "No, the manager of the aquatic center did. He said Jasmine had caused all sorts of problems and told her she couldn't come back. If you ask me, she was just standing up for herself." He glanced at my travel bag again.

Maybe it was because we had similar histories with our parents—mine had died when I was only eight, and Miles's parents had passed away when he was just a baby—or maybe it was because he had treated me like an older brother when I first arrived at Sunnyside seven months ago, but whatever the reason, the two of us had always clicked. I really liked Miles, but when I realized he had just finished his pointless story and it had absolutely nothing to do with me, I could've pummeled him with my suitcase.

"*That's* the suspicious something you wanted to tell me about?" I asked.

"I . . . I just thought it was kind of cool, you know?" His countenance withered. "Those boys were a lot bigger, but Jasmine really had them worried."

At that moment, I could feel my chest starting to constrict, as though a troll had wrapped its huge paws around me and begun to squeeze. Some people called them panic attacks, but I had a better name for them: the Creepers. On stressful days, the Creepers could almost knock me out cold.

"That's cool," I said, patting Miles's shoulder, my chest heaving, "but can you go back to the aquatic center now?"

"Um . . . I don't want you to leave anymore. Well, I never

wanted you to leave. You can't leave me all by myself with Vanessa. She'll eat me alive!"

"Miles, be quiet," I pleaded. "Someone's going to hear you."

Unzipping his fanny pack, Miles pulled out the tin of Magic: The Gathering playing cards I'd given him as payment for acting as lookout.

"I wouldn't feel right about helping you run away," he said, lowering his voice and pushing the box into my hands. "Why do you want to leave?"

"I told you why."

"You don't like the Crowes?" Miles looked bewildered. "But they're so nice. And we have the best setup in our room. We have a TV, a PlayStation, *and* we're on the third floor." He had always had this weird theory about upper-level bedrooms. The higher the floor, the better. It meant luxury.

"I *do* like the Crowes," I admitted.

Most of the time the Crowes gave me plenty of space, but they weren't looking to adopt a bunch of strangers. They had Vanessa—and she was enough trouble by herself. The state had hired the Crowes as the caretakers at Sunnyside, and I didn't need a caretaker anymore. I was twelve and a half years old, nearly a teenager, and almost old enough to drive—if you rounded up.

"But they're not my family," I said. I didn't *have* a family, not anymore, at least, and if there was one thing my time in the foster program had taught me, it was that I would never have a proper family again.

Miles threw his hands up in exasperation. "But its *summer vacation*. At least wait until fall."

Snapping my attention back to the entrance of the aquatic center across the street, I had to concentrate on each breath, as though my lungs had forgotten how to work on their own. The wave pool churned in the distance, loud music blasted from speakers like there was a rock concert going on, but so far, no one had noticed me missing.

"We can't talk about this anymore," I insisted. "We made a deal."

As I tried giving the cards back, Miles twisted out of the way, acting like the box was molten hot. The lid tumbled off and cards scattered everywhere, a few of them landing in a puddle.

My vision went fuzzy.

Miles immediately dropped to his knees to help, but while pawing at the cards beneath the dumpster, he grabbed one by the edge and creased the corners.

"Just let me!" I shouted. That card happened to be one of the rarest ones I owned, and Miles was bending it.

No—it was one of the rarest cards *Miles* owned. Whether they stayed in mint condition or not, this wasn't my collection anymore. If I never played *Magic: The Gathering* again, that was fine by me, so long as I made it on that train and far away from Sunnyside.

"I'm . . . I'm sorry, Lucas," Miles said, scrambling to his feet. "I didn't mean to drop them. Please don't freak out."

"I'm *not* freaking out," I snapped. "I'm fine." But I could feel myself spiraling out of control.

"Don't let the Creepers in," he pleaded.

Just hearing him utter those words was enough to make me want to crawl into a cave filled with starving troglodytes and die. My last real doozy of a panic attack had been almost three months ago at an afterschool art-show event. The Crowes had taken all the fosters from Sunnyside to watch me stand in front of more than a hundred people and talk about the silly clay serving platter I had painted in ceramics class. I had tried getting out of my part, had begged the teacher, but there had been no way around it. The presentation accounted for a big chunk of my final grade. So when Tugg Roberts had tossed the notecards for my speech into some kid's homemade volcano, covering them in goopy sludge, I'd just lost it. Tugg claimed it had all been an accident, but even if nobody believed him, it didn't matter. Everyone had seen my collapse. My screaming. The tears. That had been one of the worst attacks ever—and also when Miles had learned about the Creepers.

"Take deep breaths, remember?" Miles rubbed my shoulder. "You can beat it."

Wheezing, I flinched away from his hand. It wasn't like I was transforming into a werewolf. That would have been way cooler. I needed to force my lungs to obey. I just needed to focus on something else. Something not involving my impending doom. Something like . . . like the enormous, bloodshot eyeball looking at me through a window at the back of the alley.

"What is *that?*" I asked, catching my breath.

It wasn't a real eyeball, of course. The thing was almost the size of a beach umbrella. But it *was* moving, its eyelids blinking rapidly.

Tingling with curiosity and no longer bothered by the Creeper in my chest, I walked toward the window and squinted up at the wooden sign hanging above the door next to it.

HOB & BOGIE'S CURIOSITY SHOPPE

Red paint had chipped away from the emblem of a two-headed dragon carved into the wood. Stuck within each of the dragons' mouths was a pair of six-sided dice.

"Curiosity Shoppe?" Miles asked. He had followed me down the alley. "What does that mean?"

How should I know? Maybe they sold gag gifts, or better yet, board games. I loved board games. I was kind of shocked I hadn't noticed the store before. That eyeball certainly should have caught my attention.

A neon sign blinked in one corner of the window, buzzing with an electric hum.

HOB & BOGIE'S CURIOSITY SHOPPE
HOURS OF OPERATION: THE WITCHING HOUR UNTIL DAWN

A handwritten placard under the sign said:

ALWAYS CLOSED SUNDAYS, DIRECTLY AFTER A FULL MOON AND
DURING THE TOURNAMENT OF THE URCHIN MINOTAUR.
ABSOLUTELY NO SOLICITORS WHATSOEVER—
WITH THE EXCEPTION OF MADGE CROCKERY

Miles eagerly jiggled the doorknob, but it didn't budge. "Is it closed?" he asked.

Pressing my face against the window, I peered into the shadowy dark. Dust motes drifted through the air. I could see bookshelves lining the walls, but I had no clue when the Witching Hour began, and I didn't have a phone to google it.

"Too bad," I said, pulling back from the glass and glancing down at Miles. "Can you go back to the pool now?"

Miles looked at me in shock. "You don't want to see if someone will let us inside?"

"Sure, I do, but I don't think it's—"

Before I could finish the sentence, the doorknob made a soft click and the latch suddenly gave way. The door's rusty brass hinges gave a teeth-clenching, unoiled screech as it slowly peeled open. I almost caught a glimpse of the inside of the shop before Miles screamed bloody murder. A monster appeared in the opening, twirling a razor-sharp dagger within its gnarled fingers.

CHAPTER 2

HOBSEQUIOUS
ODDENTRY & BOGIE

Miles belted out at the top of his lungs for almost ten straight seconds before his scream became a whimper, blubbering out like a deflating balloon. I had to snag him by the arm just to keep him from falling over. Having played oodles of role-playing games since I was old enough to read, I knew what the monster was—it was a goblin. Yellow eyes gleaming, the goblin's lips wriggled back, revealing a mouth filled with fangs.

"Oh, right," the goblin said, noticing our sheer panic, "I always forget."

After hiding the dagger in a leather sheath strapped to his belt, the goblin stuck his thumb into his mouth and, with a swift popping motion, pulled out his teeth. Miles wobbled as though he might faint.

"Miles, they're fake," I said.

The goblin ran his tongue across the row of normal teeth that had been hiding behind the fangs. "Look, kids, I didn't mean to scare you, but my shift just ended, and if you don't mind, I'd like to get home before my next one starts."

"What's it talking about?" Miles demanded, yanking desperately on my elbow.

"I think he just works here," I said, realizing how ridiculous the two of us must have looked. This guy was just an employee. I spotted the name tag pinned to his shirt. "His name's Barry."

"So it's not really a monster?" Miles asked, refusing to look directly at the goblin.

"Well, that depends on if you ask my ex-wife." Sucking his breath in sharply, Barry gave an awkward laugh, then stared down at Miles sympathetically. "How old are you, kid?"

"Eleven." Miles's voice cracked, and he cleared his throat. "I'm eleven. How old are you?"

Barry pocketed his fake fangs and puffed out his cheeks, no longer amused. "Old enough I shouldn't still be working here," he said. Barry brushed past us and hurried away down the alley.

Sticking my foot out, I caught the door before it could close and pulled it back open. Earlier, when I could only see shadowy fixtures through the window, I'd been slightly interested in looking around. Now, having just encountered Barry in full goblin garb, I simply had to explore the store.

Inside, the air was thick and stuffy and carried the smell of a long-overdue library book. Candles in brass holders flickered on either side of the doorway. The store seemed to be about the size of a small apartment. A couple of rows of tall bookcases loomed on either side of the center of the store, stuffed full of manuals, maps, old skulls, pieces of armor, a variety of hooded cloaks, and many other interesting items. The center aisle seemed almost like a path through the dark archway the bookshelves created. Two heavy wooden tables sat in the middle of that path, game boards set upon them and colorful cards strewn about as though someone had only recently stopped playing.

A low growl rumbled from the giant eye still staring out the window. Bright green, gold, and pink feathers sprouted from the back side of the eye like wild writhing hair, and though I couldn't see where it was plugged in, I figured it was electric.

To the rear of the shop, past the bookshelves, an ancient-looking cash register sat on a glass showcase lit by fluorescent bulbs and in front of a door with a weathered sign that read "Office." Approaching the case, I felt my skin prickle with excitement. Rows upon rows of hand-painted barbarians, wizards, and rogues gleamed beneath the lights.

"They have mini figurines." I pulled my wallet from my back pocket.

Mini figurines made role-playing games so much more fun. I had always wanted to buy some. Peering into the case, I noticed they weren't priced, which in my experience meant they probably cost a fortune.

"Miles, check these out," I said.

Having wandered over to examine another section of the store, Miles was staring at a large scratching post bolted to the end of a bookcase. The Crowes had a similar but smaller one at Sunnyside, and their two cats loved sharpening their claws on it when they weren't using my ankles.

"It's a *sloth*." Miles pointed at the creature hanging from the scratching post.

The sloth's glassy eyes seemed to twinkle in the faded light of the shop as Miles reached a finger out to poke it.

"I don't think that's a good idea," I warned. Miles liked to poke things. It was just his nature.

"It's not real," he said. "It's just stuffed."

As soon as Miles finished saying that, however, the sloth began inching toward the ceiling. Mesmerized, we watched it slowly pull itself toward a potted plant on the top shelf of the bookcase next to the post. Then a jingling bell from the doorway announced another customer. I spun around in time to see Jasmine Bautista storming into the shop. Her long black hair whipping around, she looked like the illustration you'd find in the dictionary under the word *infuriated*.

"Lucas?" she asked as she spotted me standing across the room, her scowl brightening a little. "Is that you?"

For the briefest of moments, I considered ducking behind a bookcase. Not that I had done anything wrong to her, but Jasmine had entered the store on a mission—and she appeared to be holding rocks.

Jasmine's eyes narrowed as she noticed Miles. "You were just at the pool, weren't you?" she asked.

Hiccupping and nodding, Miles waved back timidly.

"Well, I'm looking for someone," she said, holding up her rocks. "You see Tugg Roberts come this way?"

"No one's come this way," I answered. "It's just us."

"You sure about that? I thought I saw him sneak down this alley." Lowering her hand, Jasmine glanced sideways at the bizarre feathered eyeball snarling in the window. "What *is* this place?"

"It's a curiosity store," Miles said. "They sell all sorts of curious things. Like sloths."

As Jasmine wandered over to where Miles was trying to muster up enough courage to tickle the sloth, the door to the back room office opened. A man with long black hair, a goatee, and a gold rope necklace spilling out from the collar of his burgundy button-down shirt stepped into the shop. Stretching, he smacked his lips as though he'd just been roused from a satisfying nap.

"Excuse *me*," the man barked out in surprise when he

noticed me kneeling on the floor in front of the case. "Little boy, what are you doing down there?"

"I was just looking at your collection," I said. "They're super cool."

"Yes, I can see that you're looking. But how did you get in here?"

I nodded at the door, still open a crack, a corner of the floor mat wedged in the opening.

"Barry, you complete waste of space." The man clucked his tongue. "I'm sorry, but we're not open. Not for several hours, actually."

"Why do you open so late?" Jasmine asked, making her way over to the glass counter.

The man's frown deepened. "Goodness. How many of you are there?"

"Just three." Miles poked his head out from behind a bookshelf, holding up a long, sheathed sword with a bejeweled hilt.

"That . . . that is *not* a toy!" the man shouted, flabbergasted. "We don't just pick things up without asking. And you're what? Seven? Eight?"

"Why does everyone keep asking me my age?" Miles asked, returning the sword to its shelf. "I'm eleven, I'll have you know."

"Okay, little ones, fun's over. Contrary to popular belief, the aquatic center is on the opposite side of the road, but I suppose I can see how you made the mistake. What with the locked door and the utter absence of swimming pools and barbecue grills . . ." The man twisted the corner of his mustache. "This is not a children's store. Off you go."

"What kind of store is it?" I asked, puzzled.

"It is a *gaming* store," he replied, forcing a smile.

Jasmine crossed her arms. "A gaming store—and it's not for children?"

"We play different kinds of games here," he said, quirking an eyebrow. "Most aren't suitable for the likes of children. And I don't know how you got into my shop. Perhaps our door needs to be fixed, but I have a jam-packed schedule. I'm very, very busy."

"Yeah, I think you just woke up," Jasmine said.

"So what if I did?" the man fired back. "What's it to you? We don't run normal business hours here. Now, Sheba and I have loads of things to do before we open."

"Sheba?" Miles asked.

"Sheba." He nodded toward the sloth, who unblinkingly observed the argument from across the room.

At that moment, the door opened again and another figure entered the store. Old and balding, patches of stiff white hair poking out above his ears, the man wore sunglasses and a long trench coat bundled up around his chin as though he had just stepped in from a blizzard and not the hottest day of the year.

"The lines at this hour. Bogie, you wouldn't believe it," the older man said, tossing his coat onto an empty chair while balancing two paper sacks of foil-wrapped sandwiches in the crook of his elbow. "I thought for sure I would be in and out. But I had to wait nearly thirty minutes just to place my order. You would think it was a holiday or . . . some . . . thing . . ." His voice puttered out as he noticed us standing by the counter. "Oh my, Bogie, we have visitors." Eyes brightening, he glanced at his wristwatch. "And . . . they're early."

"They're *not* early, and they're *not* visitors," Bogie grumbled. "These children are trespassing."

"Trespassing?" Jasmine scoffed. "Hardly. We were just looking around."

"Yes, and I've told you several times now that we are *closed*," the man called Bogie replied, his voice even but beginning to show strain. "We don't open until . . ."

Clearing his throat, the other man interrupted Bogie before he could finish. "Oh dear, you do remember as I was heading out earlier how I mentioned I was considering changing our operating hours? Just for the summer, of course. You remember that conversation, don't you, Bogie?"

"Conversation?" Bogie looked down as though seeing the three of us for the first time.

Hurrying over, the older man pressed two sandwiches into Bogie's reluctant hands. "Would you be so kind as to deliver one of those to the back for me? He'll be famished by now," he said before placing the remaining sandwich in a bowl with the name Sheba etched across it. "Sheba, chop-chop. Try to get to it before it spoils."

Turning her head, the sloth noticed the sandwich and—her expression unchanging—began slinking down the pole like hot glue. At that speed, it would take her all day to make it to her meal.

Eyes sparkling in the dim candlelight, the older man rubbed his fingers together and stepped behind the display case, nudging the younger man out of the way. "My dear guests, my name is Hobsequious Oddentry, but I prefer you call me Hob. Easier to pronounce. You've already been introduced to my somewhat disgruntled partner in crime." He held his hand out toward Bogie. "We are co-owners of this curiosity shop, and there's no point in beating around the bush any longer. I'm certain you're all wondering why we've called you here today."

"Don't drag *me* into this," Bogie muttered, disappearing into the back with the extra sandwich. I heard something squeaking just beyond the door.

Who *were* these strange people, and what was Hob talking about? No one had called us there. We'd just stumbled on the store by accident. Glancing at Miles and Jasmine, I checked to see if they had an explanation, but they appeared equally confused.

Hob dipped his chin, pressing his fingers against his chest. "It's by no mere happenstance that you are gathered here this afternoon. I have just come into the market for a brave Band, and I have the utmost confidence you'll do nicely."

"A brave band?" Miles asked, scrunching his nose. "We don't play instruments. I mean, Lucas and I don't. I don't know about Jasmine."

"Not a *marching* band," Hob said. "I need a brave Band of Champions, of course."

Ducking behind the case, the ancient shop owner rummaged about momentarily before resurfacing, clutching a bulky leather sack with both hands.

"What do you say, friends?" he asked. "Care to join me for the game of a lifetime?"

CHAPTER 3

THE ROLL
OF DESTINY

Hob cleared a game table, scattering the playing cards from one of the previously occupied spaces.

"Have you lost your mind?" Bogie asked, reemerging from the back room. He looked as though he had just swallowed a bug. "Your Band is set to depart on a Quest this evening."

As he peeled back the wrapper from one end of his sandwich, the spicy aroma of Italian meats, cheeses, and spices instantly filled the room, and my mouth watered. I hadn't eaten lunch yet and had planned to grab something on my way to the train terminal.

"I'm choosing to place my arrangement with my previously intended Band on a temporary hold," Hob said.

"This feels oddly like sabotage," Bogie said through a mouthful of sandwich.

Hob waved his hand impatiently toward Bogie. "It's not sabotage. It's an awakening. That Band had no imagination, *and* they were a bunch of bumbling slowpokes. I've said this before, and I'll say it again: age does not automatically equal experience."

Lowering his sandwich, Bogie stared at Hob quizzically.

"May I remind you the Band of Biting Blades were Sapphire Level, were they not?"

"Don't you think it's weird?" Jasmine asked, leaning close to me as the two shop owners continued their discussion. "That guy acted like he knew we were coming here."

"Yeah, I guess it's a little weird," I agreed, but it was obvious what was going on. Even a twelve-and-a-half-year-old could see they were trying to get us to buy something. They had a fully decked-out goblin employee, a robotic eyeball (that as far as I could tell served no real purpose other than to shock people who happened to be walking by), and a *pet sloth*, for crying out loud. Luring customers in to play a game was probably one of Hob's better sales tactics. Get us playing and cut the game off right when things got interesting. No better way to make some-one want to spend their money.

Glancing up from the table, Hob pointed to the empty chairs. "Young Champions, if you'll kindly take a seat."

Miles wasted no time in scurrying over and plopping down in one of the chairs.

"What kind of game is it?" Jasmine asked.

"An RPG, I think," I said. "A role-playing game. Each of the players creates a character and then they're taken on quests."

"Sounds kind of boring," she whispered.

"If it's like the ones I've played before, it's super fun," I assured her.

Role-playing games were the only way I had survived my awful stint at the McMurdie Boardinghouse, my previous fos-ter home before Sunnyside. I had joined an online campaign with a team of complete strangers. No one cared about my age, and the website kept the party anonymous. I would never have given my personal information out to complete strangers, but the great thing about the website was that they never asked. I had played my all-time favorite character—a gnome sorcerer with a dark history. Then the website crashed, and the owners had yet to start it back up again. I really missed those days.

"It's kind of like playing a character in a movie," I explained.

"Then why aren't you going over there?" Jasmine asked.

"What time is it?" I eyed the table as Hob hefted the leather sack onto the counter and loosened the drawstring. I hadn't been exploring the shop very long, but time had a way of slipping by when I wasn't paying attention.

Jasmine checked her cell phone. "It's one-thirty." Her phone screen was splintered, and the case looked scuffed and damaged, but at least she had a phone. I had never owned my own piece of electronics.

"I think I actually have to go," I said.

My train was scheduled to leave at four-thirty, and it would take me at least an hour and a half to walk to the terminal, so long as I avoided any further distractions, like getting captured by Vanessa. That didn't give me much time to try out a role-playing game. Some campaigns took hours to play, while others could carry on for weeks.

"Go?" Hob's head shot up. "But you've only just arrived. You don't have school, do you?"

"No," I said, awkwardly shifting my weight and realizing every pair of eyes was now trained on me.

"Well, what could be so important that has you off in a rush?" Hob pressed.

"I'm sure the boy needs to check in with his parents," Bogie suggested. "He's a young child, after all. It's probably for the best, Hob. You're not thinking clearly."

"Lucas doesn't have parents," Miles said. "He's an orphan. Just like me."

Immediately, Bogie let out something between a loud snort and a choking cough, and chunks of half-chewed bread shot across the room. Shaking his head, he gestured to Jasmine with the wrapped end of his sandwich.

"You, girl. Are you an orphan as well?" he demanded.

"I'm not an orphan," Jasmine snarked. "My parents are back home."

Bogie paused in thought, then held up his index finger. "And where is *home*, exactly?"

Jasmine studied him for a moment before answering. "In the Philippines . . . but I've lived with my grandmother here for most of my life. So I'm not an orphan."

Bogie made an exaggerated sigh. "I don't know why you planned this, Hob, but you've tried this before and it's never worked. The wandering war party with nothing to lose?" He scoffed. "Don't think I don't remember. Mark my word, you've stepped in it this time. Royally."

"What does he mean by that?" I asked. "Stepped in what?"

"Pay him no attention," Hob said. "Bogie's just upset I secretly snuck onions into his sandwich."

"I am not upset . . ." Peeling back the top layer of bread, Bogie frantically searched his sandwich, tossing aside lettuce and tomatoes. After a few tense moments, he rolled his eyes, evidently not discovering any onions, and turned his back to the counter, muttering under his breath.

"Why do you have to leave?" Jasmine asked me.

"I just have somewhere I need to be." I flashed a look of warning at Miles, but he was too preoccupied with gazing longingly at something in Hob's hands to give away my secret.

"Is that, like, the rule book?" Miles asked, his breathing becoming more rapid.

"This is the official *Champion's Quest Field Guide*," Hob said. Licking his thumb, he peeled open the cover, revealing thick, waxy pages. "Would you care to take a look? You seem like the type of fellow who follows the rules to the letter."

"You have no idea," I said.

Miles reverently took the old book in his hands.

Hob then produced a feathered quill and a small inkwell from the bag, which he handed to Miles. "Be sure to add all your names to the Participant Log."

Nothing made Miles happier than gobbling up instruction manuals. I knew he would now be dead to the world for the foreseeable future, which would definitely make sneaking away easier for me when the time arrived.

"At least stay long enough to set up your Quest," Hob said, staring pointedly at me, pulling out a chair from the table. "We are open most evenings, which will give you plenty of opportunities to check back in and resume once you've gotten to where it is you're going."

If only it were that easy. If things went exactly as planned, there would be no returning. Not to Hob & Bogie's Curiosity Shoppe and definitely not back to Bentford.

"Miles, is it?" Hob scanned Miles's handwriting.

"Yes, sir," Miles replied. "Miles Maldonado."

"Oh, I like that." Hob stroked his chin. "A name like Miles has deeper meaning to it. I dare say this companion will go the distance. Don't you agree, Bogie?"

Bogie harrumphed, chewing disinterestedly behind the counter.

"Then we have Lucas *Silver*," Hob read adding emphasis to

my last name as Miles continued writing. "That name has value to it. Most definitely. And lastly, Jasmine . . ." Hob waited for Miles to finish, but Miles only shrugged.

"I don't know how to spell her last name," he said, holding out the quill to Jasmine.

Jasmine shot a sideways glance at me before crossing the room. Sliding into her seat, she plucked the feather from Miles's outstretched hand and scribbled her name on the line. Hob grunted as he lifted a heavy box out of the leather sack. The box looked like it was covered in alligator skin, and it had solid brass hinges and latches keeping it shut. The latches made a satisfying pop as the box opened, and Hob began setting stacks of colorful cards on the table.

Oh, all right. What did it matter, anyway? It wasn't like we were going to start a full campaign. As long as I was out the door in thirty minutes, I had enough time to learn the basics of a new game.

"This is so awesome," Miles squealed as I crowded in next to him. "I've never played anything like this before."

"Is this a deck-building game?" I asked, tilting my head to try to read one of the upside-down cards.

"Not exactly." Hob hurriedly flipped the cards over and then gave them a quick shuffle with his nimble fingers. "These aren't for you, actually. Uh, I mean, they're not for the Champions."

Next, Hob removed a square wooden bowl from the box and placed it at the center of the table. Colorful gemstones lined the outer rim; images depicting four, faceless warriors were carved into the outside of the bowl.

"What's that for?" Jasmine asked, grabbing for it.

The old man promptly moved it out of her reach. "Not so fast, Ms. Bautista," he said sharply. "One does not just handle the Champion's Catch so willy-nilly. First, we must select the leader of your fearless Band. Shall that be you, then?"

Jasmine chewed the inside of her cheek. "You mean, like the one in charge? Does it matter that I don't have a clue how to play?"

"It matters not," Hob replied. "You shall all have opportunities to make key decisions during your Quest, but the Band Leader, of course, will have the final say."

Jasmine shrugged. "I mean, I guess I could . . ."

Miles cleared his throat, cutting her off. "Um, no offense, but I think I'd feel better if Lucas was our leader." He looked at Jasmine but then dropped his eyes.

"No, it's fine, Miles," I said. Actually, I preferred to not be the one in charge. That was way too much pressure. Through all my role-playing game adventures, not once had I ever been the leader.

"But you've already played," Miles reasoned. "You have more experience."

"I've never played Champion's Quest before," I said, glancing at the unfamiliar box.

"Miles is right," Jasmine agreed.

"Seriously, it's no big deal," I insisted. Besides, in less than twenty minutes, I would be sneaking off for good.

"Yeah, but I'd rather not have that kind of responsibility." She looked back at Hob. "Lucas will be our Band Leader."

His eyes flitting back and forth between the three of us, Hob waited for someone to change their mind. Then, when no one spoke up, he slid the unusual bowl in front of me.

"Would you care to take the Destiny of your Band into your hands?" he asked, holding out a dark-gray object.

Over my years of collecting, I had gathered quite an

assortment of dice, stowed in my suitcase, which was still tucked behind the dumpster out in the alley. Varying in size, color, and shape, they served a variety of purposes during game play. The caretaker at the McMurdie Boardinghouse had tried to get me to throw away my collection. She told me they were just taking up space and that I shouldn't waste my time hoarding junk, but I didn't listen to her. I loved the clattering sound of rolling dice during a role-playing game. It meant something important was about to happen, and I believed with the right roll, my situation could always change for the better.

The die Hob handed me, however, was unlike any I owned in my collection. At about the size of a golf ball, the twelve-sided orb had to weigh close to half a pound. The die quivered unsteadily in my palm, as though it were filled with some sort of liquid, but it was the color that made it the most peculiar. Murky smoke swirled beneath the surface, like a violent storm cloud on the verge of a thunderclap. As the smoke churned, each number on the die briefly lit up with a glowing, white light.

"How is it *doing* that?" Miles whispered.

"Magic," Hob replied.

"Or batteries," Jasmine said with a smirk.

Hob sniffed indignantly. "Do you not think batteries are magical, young lady?"

"What's inside it?" I asked, shaking the die close to my ear and listening to its soft swishing. "Is that water?"

"I don't know," he said. "The Die of Destiny just came with the box. Each number is linked to a Quest, and each comes with its own set of difficult challenges. Some Quests have never been completed to this day. The roll determines which quest you will play together."

"Aren't you forgetting something?" Having finished his sandwich, Bogie now stood beside us, looking down at the table disapprovingly.

"No, I believe I have everything ready to go," Hob said, blinking up at the other man.

Bogie stroked his beard with his long fingers and shook his head. "This is your last opportunity to back out, old friend, before you make an unfortunate mistake."

"Why would I back out now?"

"I'm just offering a desperate man a rope. Besides, who will be their fourth?"

"What on *earth* are you talking about?" Hob asked.

"Stop acting as though you're just now hearing the rules," Bogie snapped. "I'm trying to do you a favor. A Band of Champions is made up of four participants. One, two, three, four. No more, no less. It says so in the manual."

"He's right," Miles chimed in, pointing to a page in the Field Guide. "Game play only begins when all four characters have been selected. It's the rules."

"And I count three less-than-qualified players at this table," Bogie said. "Unless they intend on recruiting Sheba, they are one companion shy." He held his hand out toward the sloth, which had collapsed at the center of the room and fallen asleep.

Hob leaned back in his chair. "I'm fully aware of the rules, thank you very much. After all, this isn't my first rodeo."

"I suppose you've thought of a way to bypass it, then?" Bogie asked, raising his voice. "That after countless campaigns, you've somehow figured out a loophole to the age-old rule. Is that it?"

"No need to shout, Bogie," Hob said, remaining calm despite Bogie's agitation. "They're not officially starting tonight, remember? I just want them to have a little taste of the fun before Lucas leaves."

"A 'taste of the fun'?" Bogie blurted out. "Of *Champion's Quest?*"

Raising his eyebrows as though annoyed, Hob pursed his lips as the two men engaged in a gripping staring match. The room fell into almost complete silence—the only sounds coming from the window, where the eyeball continued to growl in the background. Miles fidgeted about nervously, and even Jasmine seemed shocked by the weird argument. I wondered why Bogie had become so aggravated and figured he must really hate children.

After several tense seconds, Bogie turned his head away and ran a hand through his hair. "If this is indeed what you want," he said, his volume returning to a normal level. "I will not press the issue any further. But I promise I shall not go easy on you. This changes nothing."

After kneeling to pick up Sheba from the floor and carry her the rest of the way to her bowl, Bogie slipped behind the counter and exited into the back room.

Hob gave a dramatic sigh. "My word. I'm so sorry about that, my friends. Don't trouble yourselves with his behavior. Bogie always gets a little persnickety before nightfall. Now, where were we?" Leaning forward to check his game setup, Hob snapped his fingers. "Ah yes, the Roll of Destiny. Lucas, if you would be so kind."

Gazing down at the twelve-sided die, I ran my thumb over its smooth, marble-like texture—the mystical smoke churning and the strange liquid fidgeting inside. Then I tossed it into the Champion's Catch. Bouncing sharply against the wood, the die tumbled end over end into the center of the bowl and came to a stop.

"Quest number eleven," Hob's voice boomed, as he peered back into the box.

Shifting a few items out of the way, he rifled through a sheaf of loose papers and handed a page of parchment with burnt edges over to Miles.

"Mr. Maldonado, would you read right there at the top?" he asked. "Please inform the other members of your Band the result of Lucas's Roll of Destiny."

"Quest number eleven," Miles read, clearing his throat. "The Tale of the Aged and the Ageless. Three hundred years ago . . ."

Something buzzed in Jasmine's pocket, startling Miles from reading, and she pulled out her cell phone.

"Hold on. It's my grandmother," she groaned, sticking the phone to her ear. "Hello, Lola."

A raised voice chirped back at her from the phone's tiny speakers.

"I know. No, I left the aquatic center a little while ago," Jasmine said, wincing. "Just barely. Not even . . ."

More shouting, but I couldn't understand what was being said because Jasmine's grandmother was apparently speaking in another language. Suddenly, Jasmine bolted up from the table, knocking over her chair.

"That's a lie!" she yelled. "Who told you that? I didn't punch those boys."

"She's telling the truth," Miles whispered. "I only saw her kicking them."

Less than a second later, Jasmine's shoulders hunched over as her grandmother really laid into her. "Yes, Lola," she muttered weakly. "I'll be out on the curb in a minute." The call ended, and Jasmine stared at the floor. "I have to go now," she said, glumly turning toward the door.

"Uh . . . well . . ." Flustered, Hob held up a hand to stop her. "I . . . I understand, but it's not wise to separate so early in the game. You still need to choose a Character Role and . . . uh . . . we need to go over . . ."

"I'm sorry." Jasmine interrupted him. "I don't have a choice. I'm probably going to be grounded forever." Glancing at me, she smiled half-heartedly. "See you later, guys."

Then, despite Hob's objection, Jasmine briskly crossed the room, and the doorbell jangled as she exited the shop.

Scratching the back of his head, Hob blew out his cheeks. "Unquestionably a little unorthodox, but I suppose it will be all right. She'll just have to wait while I fill the rest of you in on the rules of the game."

"We have to go too," I said, scooting my chair back from the table.

"We do?" Miles whined in disappointment.

"You what?" Hob looked simply flabbergasted.

What had I been thinking? Vanessa wasn't that awful of a babysitter. At some point during the past hour, she would have at least checked to make sure we weren't floating lifeless in the pool.

"Miles, you've been away from the pool for a really long time now," I said, dragging my fingers down the sides of my face. "Vanessa's going to know something's up."

"Now, I must insist," Hob called out, "it's imperative we discuss a few things."

At that moment, Bogie resurfaced from the back room and started applauding in amusement.

"Quest number eleven?" he asked, leaning across the counter and smugly clapping his hands. "You sly little cheating wolverine."

"Not now," Hob snapped. "And I did *not* cheat."

Bogie grinned. "Such desperation. But you know it doesn't matter, Hobsequious. Did I not say you had stepped in it royally this time?"

The doorbell jangled for the fifth time that afternoon, and my worst nightmare came true as Vanessa Crowe burst into the shop.

Bogie erupted with laughter. "And in walks the loophole," he cheered, vigorously drumming his hands on the counter. "Ladies and gentlemen, we have our fourth."

Excerpt from THE CHAMPION'S QUEST FIELD GUIDE

Welcome, Brave Heroes!

For untold centuries, daring volunteers seeking fame and glory have entered the game of Champion's Quest. Thus, congratulations are in order. As you embark on your first campaign, you now join the ranks of legends. Be wary and vigilant, for Champion's Quest is not like other role-playing adventures and will present challenges never before faced. After your stalwart Band has been assembled and your Quest randomly selected, the real adventure begins. To complete your campaign, you must gain experience, depend on one another, and learn from your mistakes, as there will be many.

While some of your good fortune will rely upon strategic rolling from the Den of Dice (see pages 6 and 7 of this Field Guide for instructions), your Fate and Destiny are not ultimately contained within the palm of your hands. Opportunity will always be within reach of those clever enough to claim it.

Upon your Character Selection, each hero shall be properly outfitted for the Quest terrain, provided with basic provisions within the Champion's Dispenser, and bequeathed an Advancement Medallion (see pages 14 and 15). Pay close attention to these crucial items as they are of the utmost value to your success or failure in Champion's Quest. You already have all you need to win. Good luck!

Warning—Game play in Champion's Quest only ends upon successful Quest completion.

CHAPTER 4

THE KOBOLD
CONFRONTATION

There was no way I could have hidden from Vanessa. She spotted me the moment she entered the shop in a whirlwind of screeching fury.

"I've been looking for you *everywhere*," Vanessa chided.

The candles flickered, and books toppled off their shelves as she slammed the door behind her—and for the first time since I had stepped into the building, the eyeball in the window stopped growling.

"Where's Miles?" she demanded, her eyes darting around the room.

Leaning his head past my arm, Miles shakily raised his hand. "Here," he said meekly.

"Oh," Vanessa growled, stamping her foot, her face bright red and her blonde hair a tangled mess. Not from swimming, of course—Vanessa didn't swim. "All my friends left the pool without me to go to the mall, and *now* I have to *waste* the rest of my afternoon driving you two *home*."

I wanted to apologize to Hob for Vanessa's barging in, but both Hob and Bogie were gone. The box of Champion's Quest remained right where he had opened it along with the swirling Die of Destiny—the number eleven glowing ominously in the bowl. Even Sheba had somehow snuck away, leaving her untouched sandwich jutting up from her food bowl like a massive cigar. I noticed the several stacks of playing cards Hob had laid out on the table. Some looked well-worn and crinkled; a few had been ripped in half and pieced back together with masking tape.

"Let's *go!*" Vanessa belted at the top of her lungs.

"Okay, okay," I said, clamping my hands over my ears. "Come on, Miles. We should have left awhile ago."

"I really wanted to play, though," Miles said glumly. "Do you think we can come back?"

"Probably not." Playing a round of Champion's Quest was the last thing I wanted to do now.

Vanessa gripped the doorknob but stopped before opening it. Turning to the side, she squinted at an area on the floor beneath the window where the now-silent eyeball hung lifelessly.

"What's that supposed to be?" she demanded. "Did you write that?"

"Write what?" I asked, approaching the door.

Grabbing my sleeve, Vanessa pointed at the floor where four footlockers with wooden slabs and leather bindings had been lined up in a row. Equal in size and shape, the four chests had each been labeled with a different name: Lucas Silver, Miles Maldonado, Jasmine Bautista—and Vanessa Crowe.

"Do you think you're being funny?" Vanessa asked.

"I didn't write that," I said, looking at Miles.

Miles threw up his hands defensively. "Don't look at me."

"You know what? I don't even care," she said, yanking the door open.

Warm afternoon sunlight spilled through the opening. I could smell the smoke from the barbecue grills over at the aquatic center and hear the throb of the wave pool whipping itself into a froth. I could also feel my chest beginning to tighten. No doubt about it. The Creepers were coming. Could I make a run for it? Could I somehow lose Vanessa and make it all the way to Carrington Station before she caught me? My heart pounded, and I wanted to scream. Why had I been so careless? This had been my best chance—my only chance—to escape Sunnyside. I may not be much of a planner, but I *had* planned for this.

Today, the Crowes were meeting with a potential family. A family for someone at Sunnyside. There was a pretty good chance I could be swapping homes soon, and I simply had to escape before that happened. With the Crowes at their adoption agency meetings all day, filling out paperwork and taking care of a bunch of other foster stuff until late into the evening, there was never going to be a more perfect opportunity to run away. Now I had a worthless train ticket in my pocket and nowhere to go. I felt furious at Vanessa for ruining everything and at Miles for tempting me to check out the shop, but mostly, I was just furious at myself. But just like what had happened earlier, when I'd noticed the eye peeking out of the window, something unusual forced the Creepers back into their hole.

The alley outside Hob & Bogie's Curiosity Shoppe, with its brick walls and beet-filled dumpster, had completely disappeared. One moment it had been there, and the next it was gone. Instead of sunbaked asphalt, my feet slopped through wet, suction-y mud. A grove of crooked trees stood in the place of the Debrecen Diner. There were no cars or buildings, no more smells of barbecue or sounds of stereo music. The Greenwillow Aquatic Center had vanished as well. Dumbfounded, I gawked at a roaring river splashing over rocks and sweeping off in either direction less than a hundred yards away. It had been barely afternoon when I had started the game with Hob, and now a dusky sky filling with blinking, shimmery stars loomed above me.

"Don't just stand there," Vanessa seethed, marching forward, oblivious to the massive changes in scenery. "Why do I always have to babysit? You'd think you would be old enough to take care of—" Stopping midsentence, she swung around. "Um . . . where's my car? Where are we?"

"It says here, the first step for beginning our Quest is choosing our Character Roles," Miles said, nibbling his lower lip, his face buried in the Field Guide. He gasped and snapped the Field Guide shut. "Hob's going to think I stole this." He immediately wheeled around, but then his expression turned muddled. "Did we accidentally go out the back door?"

"You two turned me around in there," Vanessa said, whirling on her heels and tromping back toward the store.

The door creaked as it scraped against a stone floor, but instead of candlelight spilling out, a dim gleam from blackened logs smoldering in a fireplace lit up the opening. The bookshelves and tables and the glass counters with the mini figurines on display were missing. The room looked almost empty except for a large mound covered by a blanket at the center of the floor.

"This isn't the curiosity shop," Miles said, stumbling into my back as the three of us stepped through the doorway.

Immediately, I clamped a hand over Miles's mouth. "Someone's over there," I whispered, nodding at the mound suspiciously.

"Hello?" Vanessa called out.

"Vanessa," I hissed.

"What?" she fired back.

The sleeping figure never made a sound, but I did hear a scratching noise coming from just beyond the outer wall. At first distant, the scratching grew louder until it reached a crescendo. Then the wall burst open, and amid the flurry of dust, a figure with the head of a lizard and a long, whipping tail scrambled through the hole.

Without any hesitation, the creature pounced, plunging its claws into the lump of blankets and ripping off the cover. Instead of a person lying there, however, it discovered only a scarecrow curled up, with two gaping punctures in its straw-stuffed head.

"This isn't real, is it?" Miles snagged hold of my sleeve "That's just Barry, right?"

"I don't think that's Barry," I said, my pulse quickening.

Barry may have looked like a real goblin when we first met him, but after closer examination, I could tell he had only been wearing a really cool costume. The beast crouching on its two hind legs across the room looked nothing like Barry.

"What is going *on?*" Vanessa demanded. "Am I losing my mind? And what are you supposed to be? A toad? Could someone please tell me how to get to the parking lot?"

Snapping its muzzle, the creature looked over, croaking in surprise. To my amazement, Vanessa stepped toward it, her hands clenching into fists.

"There's a chapter about monsters in the back," Miles said, feverishly shuffling through the Field Guide. After sifting through a few pages, his eyes widened and he hooted triumphantly. "A kobold!"

"Let me see that," I said, snatching the book from his hands.

KOBOLD—OPAL OPPONENT

A persistent hunter, burrower, and cave dweller. When pro-voked, kobolds pursue their enemies relentlessly, and they always travel in packs.

7—STRENGTH, 9—SPEED, 6—WISDOM, 8—VITALITY.
SPECIAL SKILL—BONE DAGGER

Holding up the illustration, I squinted at the figure across the room. The book had captured every detail, right down to the kobold's raggedy trousers and menacing shard of bone tucked in its belt.

"Let me give you a piece of advice, okay?" Vanessa con-tinued, her sassy voice snapping me back to reality. She had already crossed the room and now stood directly in front of the kobold. "I know what this is." She wiggled her fingers close enough to graze the creature's glistening snout. "It's called larp-ing—and it's pathetic."

Larping stood for live-action role-playing and, contrary to what Vanessa thought, I wished I could be a part of a group like that. There were clubs of larpers that spent the weekends jousting, playing music on lutes, and acting as though they were taking part in actual quests.

"I've seen your little group hanging out in parks, hitting each other with sticks," Vanessa said. "Nobody thinks you're cool."

She may not have been paying any attention, but I was. Despite its cowering appearance, the kobold had wrapped its fingers around the handle of its dagger. Before I could warn Vanessa, the creature unleashed a shrill, ear-piercing cry and leapt to its feet. Screaming, Vanessa fell backward, but at the exact moment of the attack, everything in the room . . . stopped.

Neither Vanessa nor the kobold had moved an inch. The monster's unblinking eyes gleamed ferociously, but they could've been made out of glass. Even Miles, cowering midsquat near the floor, his hands clamped over his ears, was frozen in place. It was as though someone had grabbed a magical remote control and pressed pause on everyone in the room.

Everyone, that is, except for me.

"Roll for your Fate!" A chilling voice filled my ears, sending a tremor through my spine.

Panicked, I scanned the room, fully expecting to see a giant towering above the ceiling. Instead, sparkling glitter suddenly appeared, swirling and fizzling around me. The hut looked like the inside of a snow globe.

Something warm and tingly appeared in my hand, and when I looked down, I was holding a new game piece. Shimmering like a pearl, this die felt much smaller than the one I had rolled back at the shop—the one Hob had called the Die of Destiny. The numbers one through four had been etched into the six-sided die's glossy surface, along with an X occupying the other two sides.

Was this magic? A spell? The die hadn't been there moments before, but the twinkling dust grabbed my attention, as the swirling mass of sparkles gathered around a familiar object.

"No way," I whispered, mystified.

The Champion's Catch, the same ornately carved bowl Hob had pulled from the box not even thirty minutes ago, now hovered in the air a few feet away.

"This is a game," I gasped in astonishment. "I'm in the game!"

I didn't know how or why it had happened, but somehow, we had magically entered the game of Champion's Quest.

Gnawing on the inside of my cheek, I glanced over at Vanessa, still glued to the floor, her mouth open wide enough to swallow a football. It was kind of nice not hearing her grating voice, but also super weird. Why was I the only one not frozen?

"Roll for your Fate," the haunting female voice boomed once more, snapping my focus back to the floating bowl.

"Yes, I know," I said. "I get it."

Feeling the strange die feverishly tingling against my palm, I stepped toward the Champion's Catch and tossed in the die. I watched it flip over and over until it came to rest on the number one.

"Oh, man," I griped. That was a horrible roll.

Then the Champion's Catch, the die, and the floating glitter vanished and Vanessa's scream cut through the silence. Falling back into the wall, she raised her hands as the unfrozen kobold lunged, its dagger outstretched. To my amazement, the blade clanged noisily against something bulky and metal. Clutched in Vanessa's hand was what looked like a large, circular pan with a long handle. Hissing in pain, the kobold pulled back as the blunt surface of the pan knocked the dagger free and it whirled across the room and stuck into the wall, well out of reach.

"How did you do that?" I asked, baffled by Vanessa's impressive dodge. She may have been a high school cheerleader, but no amount of acrobatic skill should have saved her from the kobold's point-blank attack.

"Don't ask me questions," Vanessa ordered. "Just hit it already."

"Hit it with what?" Maybe if I had my suitcase, I could've knocked the monster over the head, but that was back behind the dumpster, which was now a bazillion miles away.

"What's that you're holding?" She pointed to my side and the silver cylindrical contraption that extended from my hand.

First the die and now this. Why did weird things keep appearing from out of nowhere? Right. Magical game.

The metal contraption was pill-shaped and about a foot long. I lifted my hand, feeling the cool metal beneath my fingertips. It weighed next to nothing, as though it were made of some sort of lightweight aluminum.

"Uh . . . what *is* this thing?" I asked. Rotating the object, I noticed a dark-gray button positioned next to my thumb.

"I have a whip," Miles exclaimed, swinging around a clinking leather strap. Much smaller than my metal contraption, Miles's strange whip had several beaded tassels dangling from one end. "At least I think it's a whip."

"Great. A whip, a weird mail tube, and this frying pan," Vanessa said, holding up her new weapon. "We don't stand a chance!"

"Yeah, we must have rolled very poorly," Miles said.

My eyes suddenly widened. "Wait. You rolled too?"

He nodded vigorously. "Just now. I rolled a four on that die. That's a good number, right? It was the highest one." He tried brandishing his newfound accessory, but the whip flopped around, looking more like a limp shoelace instead of a dangerous weapon.

"I didn't have a choice," Vanessa grumbled. "I tried running out of this stupid hut, but I couldn't go anywhere, and that creepy voice kept saying '*Roll for your fate.*'"

"But how?" I asked. "You guys were all frozen in place."

"No, *you* were frozen in place," Miles said. "And so was Vanessa, and so was—" The kobold roared deafeningly, stopping Miles before he could finish.

Somehow the three of us had forgotten all about the lizard standing in the room.

"Now, wait just a second," I said, stumbling backward as the kobold turned toward me, saliva dripping from its fangs. "I don't want to hurt you."

"I don't think it's too worried," Vanessa said.

"You better do something," Miles warned as the kobold crossed the room, rapidly bearing down on me.

I had nowhere to go and no chance of getting out of the way. Squeezing the strange contraption tightly, my thumb grazed the protruding button, and I pressed it down out of instinct. I heard a ratcheting *plink* as the device suddenly vibrated and a twelve-inch blade popped out from one end of the tube.

"It's a sword!" I exclaimed, sucking in a breath and marveling at the razor-sharp blade gleaming in the darkness.

A real sword. Well . . . actually, it was more like a knife but definitely more useful than what it had been only moments before.

"How did you do that?" Miles asked.

"I pushed a button," I replied.

Out of the corner of my eye, I noticed Miles frantically turning his tasseled whip over and over in his hands, searching for a button.

"So, stab it already!" Vanessa demanded.

I had never used a sword in battle—for that matter, I had never been in a battle before. I wasn't even sure the blade would stay extended or if it would just retract into the tube when I tried to use it, like a safety measure. The kobold wasn't about to give me any time to think up how to use my new weapon. It charged toward me.

Holding my breath, I shrank away from the creature's attack

and then, my eyes partially closed, I swung the blade toward the kobold's skull. With one scaly claw, the monster easily blocked my attack and ripped the knife free from my hand.

"Oh, darn," I heard Miles say.

Then the kobold laughed. Not the maniacal laughter of a movie villain, more like the throaty hacking sound of a lawn mower.

As it flung back its hand preparing to strike me down, a section of the floor suddenly gave way beneath its feet. With a yelp, the kobold dropped out of view and into the newly formed hole with an explosion of debris. It all happened so fast I hardly had time to blink. Coughing desperately, I batted away the cloud of dust as a cloaked figure leapt out of the hole, swapping places with the monster, and landed catlike on the floor. Clutching a mysterious spade-like weapon, it dumped a shovelful of dirt back down into the hole, and then an eerie, greenish light bloomed up from the floor. As the hut lurched into a sort of tense, unnerving silence, I gaped in shock at the stranger standing in the middle of the room.

It was an actual warrior, just like the ones I had created on paper in my role-playing games. A rogue, maybe, probably of elvish descent, and a skilled one at that. It was like *Lord of the Rings* and we'd just been saved by Aragorn. I wanted to whoop with excitement, but I could barely catch my breath.

"Thank you for helping us," Miles squeaked, sounding as though he had just sucked in helium.

Turning, the hero straightened to his full height, which wasn't actually that tall, making me rethink my initial assessment. That was no elvish rogue. Perhaps a gnome. I did love gnomes. But when the figure pulled back his hood, my smile instantly wilted as a lock of long black hair tumbled across a young girl's shoulders.

"Oh, you've got to be kidding me," I said, blinking in disbelief at Jasmine Bautista.

"It's about time you got here," Jasmine said, her angry eyes locking with mine. "I've been waiting for you guys for almost two days, and we have *loads* to talk about."

CHAPTER 5

THE ROOM BEHIND
THE FIREPLACE

I t's nice to know my decoy worked," Jasmine said, kicking the scarecrow aside and sitting on the floor.

"Is the kobold gone?" Miles leaned forward cautiously, staring at the spot where Jasmine had previously emptied her shovel. "I mean . . . did you really kill it?"

Jasmine shrugged. "That's usually what it means when the weird flashes of light appear, but there will be more. There's always more. That one was probably just a scout or something. They've been after me since I got here."

I stared at Jasmine in bewilderment. "You're joking, right? How long have you really been here?" She had only barely left Hob and Bogie's to smooth things over with her grandmother.

"Do I *sound* like I'm joking?" Crossing her legs, Jasmine balanced the shovel on her knees, its spade gleaming in the dimly lit shack. "What took you so long?"

"We left right after you," Miles said, glancing sidelong at me. "A couple of minutes later at most."

For a second, she eyed Miles skeptically, as though she might call him out for lying. Then she rested her chin on a fist and released a frustrated sigh. "Time must move differently here. Can't say it surprises me."

"Where is *here,* exactly?" I wondered out loud. There was no point in trying to pinpoint our location with regards to Bentford. The four of us had been transported to another world. That much was certain. But what *was* this other world, and how would we get out of it?

"I don't remember what this place is called. It has a weird name, but I forgot," Jasmine said, staring at her dirty fingernails. "There are no people out there, though, and this is the only house I've been able to find."

"How do you know this person?" Vanessa asked. Standing next to the door trying to use her cell phone, Vanessa had been silent since the attack, and her unusual weapon lay discarded next to her on the ground.

"That's not going to work," Jasmine said. "There's no cell service here."

"Uh, thanks, but I think I'll keep trying," Vanessa replied. "And who are you, exactly?"

"This is Jasmine Bautista," I explained. "She goes to my school."

"And she was at the aquatic center today before they kicked her out for fighting," Miles added.

"That was you?" Vanessa looked stunned. "With that Tugg boy?"

"I forgot all about that," Jasmine said, cracking a smile. "I was going to find out where Tugg lived and pay him back for getting me into trouble. I didn't think I'd ever let that go. I guess when you've been busy hiding from a pack of lizard monsters for two days, you end up changing your priorities."

"Kobolds. They're called kobolds," Miles said, holding up the Field Guide. "It says so in the 'Compendium of Monsters' section. Kobolds are cave dwellers and always travel in packs."

"You have the Field Guide?" Jasmine asked, leaning forward. "That would've come in handy at least once or twice."

Had she really been trapped here alone that long while hardly any time had passed in Bentford? It didn't make any sense, and yet Jasmine certainly looked different than she had when she left Hob & Bogie's. Missing was the brightly colored outfit she'd been wearing—blue jean shorts, a pink T-shirt, and flip-flops. Now, a pair of tall leather boots covered the bottom of her mud-stained pants, lacing up just beneath her kneecaps. She wore leather half-finger gloves, and partially hidden beneath her cloak was a gray, padded shirt covered with metal studs. Her eyes were sunken and exhausted, and I could see twigs and leaves snarled in her hair.

"Hey, I know what that is," Miles said, pointing at the golden chain dangling around Jasmine's neck. At the end of the chain was a brass medallion with an oval, cream-colored stone throbbing faintly like a pulse at the center.

"You know what *this* is?" Jasmine asked, frowning.

Nodding vigorously, Miles flipped open the cover of the Field Guide. "It's on page five. It's called the Advancement Medallion, right? It has all sorts of important stuff to let you know your status, like your Progression Stone—that's the white one in the middle. When did you get it?" he asked.

"A couple of hours after I got here," Jasmine said. "Right after the first monster attacked me and then went back for the others. I'm guessing you'll get a medallion too. But I don't really know what it does."

"It's not so much what it *does* but what it *tells* you," Miles explained. "It's like an alarm of sorts, or a warning signal." He held up the manual and showed us a picture of a medallion identical to Jasmine's.

I looked at Jasmine, my eyes narrowing. What did she mean when she said we would get a medallion too? How would we get one? What was she not telling us?

"I still need to read more about it, but the row of red circles along the top is your Vitality Meter," Miles continued, then his grin suddenly faltered. "Oh. Um, why is your Vitality Meter so low?"

"That's what happens when you get stabbed over and over with one of those bone knives," Jasmine replied.

"You were *stabbed?*" Vanessa asked, lowering her phone and looking concerned. "Like stabbed for real?"

"There's no blood or anything like that, which I thought was weird at first," Jasmine explained. "I kept thinking those creatures had somehow missed me, but I couldn't be that lucky. This game, even though it's real, it's not *entirely* real, if that makes any sense."

"It doesn't," Vanessa said. "I don't know what you're talking about. What game?"

"Champion's Quest," I answered. "We started it back at Hob and Bogie's."

"Yeah. Right before you stormed in, we had just opened the box and were learning all the rules," Miles said.

"I don't care!" Vanessa shouted. "How do we go home?"

"We can't," Jasmine said. "Believe me—I've tried. I thought living with my Lola was hard, but I'd gladly go back to her if I could. This place is *not* fun for kids."

"There has to be a way back." Vanessa nodded at Miles's Field Guide. "Look in there and find out how to quit the game."

"There's just a warning right at the beginning," he said, flipping to the inside cover. "Your game play in Champion's Quest only ends upon successful completion of your Quest."

Whirling around, Vanessa suddenly bore down on me. "*None* of this would have happened if you had just stayed at the pool like a *normal person!*" she said, seething with anger. "But no, you had to go sneak away and make me late for the mall."

"Well, I'm late for something too," I fired back.

Then again, maybe I wasn't. If five minutes of regular time equaled a couple of days in Champion's Quest, I still had a chance to make it to my train before it left. Maybe I *did* have time to play the game.

"Hey, what do you guys have to eat?" Jasmine asked.

"Nothing," I admitted. I had only brought a bag of gummy worms and they were in my suitcase back in the alley. Come to think of it, I may not have gone without food for as long as Jasmine had, but I was hungry too.

"Well, I'm starving," Jasmine said. "I haven't eaten anything since yesterday." Climbing to her feet, she moved over to the fireplace and grabbed one of the still-smoldering logs.

Miles gulped. "Why are you doing that?"

"It doesn't burn," she said. "It's a trick log."

"And you just figured that out on your own?" I would have never thought to grab a burning piece of wood with my bare hands.

"No," she replied flatly. "Someone showed me. You'll see."

I felt so confused. Who showed her—and how did grabbing a burning piece of wood accomplish anything?

Removing the log from the fireplace started a chain reaction. The sound of grinding gears filled the ramshackle hut as the floor vibrated and the wall began to move.

"You actually know this girl?" Vanessa whispered. "Like, she's your friend?"

"Yeah, I mean, . . . sort of," I said. *Friend* wasn't the word I would have used to describe our relationship. More like mutual acquaintance, forced to endure middle school together as the new kids on the block.

"It'll make more sense once you get in there." Stepping to one side and gesturing inside, Jasmine gave us a full-on view of what had become of the fireplace. The meager log burning beyond the hearth had been replaced with a doorway, its warm golden light spilling from the opening.

Miles frantically skimmed the manual. "I don't see anything in here about a secret room."

"I'm not going in there," Vanessa said. "I didn't sign up for any of this."

"Suit yourself," Jasmine replied. "But I'm leaving with or without you, and believe me, you're going to wish you had once more lizard guys show up."

"Where are you going?" I asked.

"To the Entry Bridge." Tossing aside the log, Jasmine rubbed her hands together, dusting away the ash. "That's where we're supposed to go."

Exasperated, Miles snapped the Field Guide shut, surrendering his search. "How do you know that?"

Jasmine opened her mouth to answer but then looked at the ceiling as though searching for a better reply. "I don't know how to explain it. I just know, and you will too in a few minutes. Anyway, there's a bridge over the river an hour or so away from here, and then Trouble's Landing is about a two-day journey past that, I think. Until *you* showed up, I haven't been able to get across the bridge." She jabbed a finger at me.

"Me?" I blinked at the others, confused.

"You're the Band Leader, aren't you?" she asked.

The memory of Hob handing me the Die of Destiny came

surging back, and I felt my knees turning mushy. That *had* been an important decision, after all. The position of Band Leader seemed way more involved than what I had originally guessed.

"If you don't mind, could you kind of speed things up?" Jasmine jutted her chin toward the doorway as a chorus of terrifying screeches rang out in the distance. "I'm pretty sure there are more lizard monsters heading our way."

Miles smiled at me nervously and, for the first time in the seven months since I had met her, Vanessa looked as though she wanted me to make a decision for her. Taking a deep breath to steel my nerves, I walked toward Jasmine and stepped into the secret room.

CHAPTER 6

A BASKET
OF CROCKERY

Moving through the doorway, the warm light dimmed, and I realized I had stepped into a crazily colorful room. Purple and red curtains hung along the walls, covering what I assumed were windows, though I couldn't actually see beyond the dense fabric. The floor was covered with a thick, shaggy pink carpet that felt like a pillow-top mattress. At the center of the room, encircled by four orange-and-green polka-dotted chairs, a wicker basket rested on the floor.

"Are we going the right way?" I asked, turning back to check with Jasmine, but the doorway had vanished. There no longer appeared to be any way in or out of the bizarre room.

For someone who had played a ton of adventuring games, I wasn't feeling very confident anymore.

"Jasmine? Miles?" I called out. I would have even settled for Vanessa, but my voice merely echoed in the room. My chest constricted, and I started to sweat. *Now what?* I wondered.

Stepping into the circle of chairs, I nervously eyed the basket and nudged it with my foot. When nothing out of the ordinary happened, I knelt on the floor and cautiously removed the lid.

"The Champion approaches," a high-pitched voice called out from inside the hollow container.

Yelping in surprise, I leapt back and smacked my shoulder against one of the polka-dotted chairs.

"Ow." I grimaced as I slid onto the ground, my legs sinking into the fluffy carpet.

Two hands no bigger than cotton balls wriggled above the lip of the basket, followed by a tuft of yellow hair like a mangled dandelion. Finally, a bright-pink face appeared with a pair of black, pinprick eyes.

"What did you do that for?" the miniature face huffed, eyes darting about the room. "Did you think you were under attack or something?"

"Uh . . . well, yeah, maybe," I said, rubbing away the dull throb in my shoulder.

"In *here?*" the strange fairy-like creature clarified, jabbing a thumb at the ground. "In my personal lodgings?" She snickered and shook her head in bafflement.

"Well, you kind of snuck up on me," I said. "And what are you supposed to be, anyway?"

"What am I 'supposed to be'?" The creature gazed thoughtfully at the ceiling. She appeared to be female and spoke with what might have been a British accent. "I once wanted to be a scientist, but that was when I was little and didn't realize Crockerys don't make good scientists or alchemists or . . ." —she grunted, gripping the edge of the basket and swinging her legs over the edge—"any -ists, for that matter. So I had to settle on just being a plain ole Crockery. Madge's my name. At your service."

With her red pants and clunky boots, Madge looked like a garden gnome statue minus the beard and plus an oversized winter coat.

"And what might *your* name be?" she asked.

"Lucas Silver," I said.

"Yep, that sounds about right. You're the Band Leader. The one in charge. The big cheese. Honcho poncho." Shivering, Madge cinched her coat collar up around her chin. "Chilly night, isn't it?"

"I guess," I said, despite starting to sweat. "What kind of creature is a Crockery?" Was she some sort of sprite—or pixie?

The wee woman blinked as though trying to solve an impossible equation scratched upon a chalkboard. "Uh, no, sorry. A Crockery's not a creature," she said, speaking much slower. "It's my last name, of course. Madge Crockery? Ring any bells?"

I shook my head.

"Ah, well, I do have a tendency to pop up now and then." Leaning an elbow across one knee, she jabbed a finger at the floor. "What I do *here* is help Champions get kitted up for their Quest. Now, would that be you?"

"A Champion?" I asked, my voice cracking. "I . . . I don't know. Maybe?" How was I supposed to answer that? A Champion sounded like someone important. A soldier or a warrior. The name just didn't seem to fit me.

"Look, you either are or you're not," she said, slapping her leg. "No in betweens. No maybes. Because if you're not, you really shouldn't be in here and I shouldn't be talking with you. I could bundle up and go back to my nap. Crockerys do love naps."

"I'm a Champion," I said. It sounded weird saying that, but if this was how the game was to be played, I'd just roll with it.

"Well then, approach." Madge somersaulted backward into the basket.

Crawling on my knees, I leaned forward, peering down into the basket. Lying at Madge's feet was a stack of clothing, a leather pouch with a brass snap, a piece of parchment rolled tightly and tied with string, and lastly, the object Miles had called an Advancement Medallion, identical to the one around Jasmine's neck.

"Listen closely, Lucas. We have loads of things to go over, and you'll be wanting to start right away, of course," Madge said. "First and foremost, you are to play the role of Artisan."

"I am?" I had never heard of that type of character before.

"Excellent choice. Both reliable and resourceful. Clever with setting and disarming traps. Are you any good with tools?"

"Nope," I answered almost immediately. I wasn't even sure I could use a screwdriver correctly.

"Yikes," she snorted. "Well, no better time for learning than the present. Am I right?"

"Can I choose something else?" I asked. What about a barbarian or a wizard or a paladin? If I was supposed to face down monsters throughout this Quest, I'd feel more comfortable playing something other than a glorified handyman.

"You rolled the Die of Fate earlier. You remember that?" Madge asked.

"Kind of." I recalled the moment when time had come to a standstill just as we were about to be attacked by the kobold. "When I rolled a one?"

"Yep, that would be it. Well, that was the Die of Fate—and rolling a one makes you the Artisan. The choice was made, I'm afraid. Now, normally, your character choice would have been made prior to stepping into the game, in a more peaceful and relaxing setting, but you didn't do that now, did you? You hopped right in and therefore had to roll."

"I didn't know I was going to be playing for real! Otherwise, I would've prepared better. I would've picked something else."

Quirking an eyebrow, Madge dug her hands into her hips.

"And I suppose all the other Champions had a clue what they were really getting themselves into when they agreed to play? Is that what you think?"

My shoulders slumped. "Probably not."

"Oh, cheer up, Mr. Silver. I've been at this a long time, and if there's one thing I've learned, it's that falling boulders don't just make waves in lakes." She beamed at me proudly.

"What's that supposed to mean?" I asked.

Puffing out her cheeks, Madge shifted her weight from one leg to the other. "It means . . . it means that nothing in the world is just *all* random. Dirt and rocks crumble, rain falls and collects. Everything happens for a reason. Including your Roll of Fate. You have a chance to experience something truly remarkable here, or it could be a real rotten time, and it depends entirely on you." Stooping over, she lifted the stack of clothing toward the top of the basket. "Right, here are your things. We can't have you standing out like a sore thumb in those fancy digs."

As she started to place the items in my hands, the pile turned into glittery sparkles, and I made a desperate swipe at the clothing as it dissolved.

"What are you doing?" Madge asked, snickering. "Trying to catch flies?"

"Did I do something wrong?" I asked, searching the floor for the missing clothes. I hadn't reached the point of frustration, but I was rapidly approaching it.

Clucking her tongue, Madge jabbed a stubby finger at me. "You're already wearing them."

My entire outfit had magically changed. Similar to Jasmine, I now wore a dark-green robe, a padded shirt, leather pants, and a belt with a brass buckle. Scratching her nose with her thumb, Madge handed over a circular necklace.

"Always keep your eye on this," she said. "Everything you need to know is contained on this Medallion. Those stones aren't just for decoration. All Champions start their first Quest at Level Opal with ten Bloodstones on their Vitality Meter. Do try to not lose all your health at first." She gestured to the top semicircle of red stones. "Each of the creatures you encounter have some form of Vitality, but you won't know just by looking at them because they won't be wearing an Advancement Medallion like you. As you may have already figured out, they have other attributes too. Strength, Speed, Wisdom. You have the same." She pointed to three other rows of pale green stones.

"Ten Bloodstones, rows of other stones, and we start at Level Opal. Got it," I said, even though I didn't have it and Madge's explanation hardly made any sense at all.

Madge tapped the center stone on my Medallion, trying to get my attention. "Lucas, please stay with me. At Level Opal, it doesn't take much to bleed you dry."

"Okay, I think I understand." Basically, we were beginners, and until my overall level increased, I should stay away from danger, lay low, and steer clear of enemies. No more kobold confrontations for me.

"But you can't just avoid getting into trouble either," she added. "Else what kind of adventure would that be?"

"Can you read my mind?" I asked.

Madge smirked. "Only when you spell everything out for me. Now, you already have your Gadget, right?"

"My what?"

She puffed out her cheeks. "Your Gadget. Your Hero's Device, of course. The first thing you claimed upon arrival."

An uncomfortable pit formed in my stomach as I remembered

the metal tube. "I don't have it anymore," I said. "That kobold took it from me."

Madge's narrowed eyes made me want to wither out of the room. "Try to be more careful."

My belt was suddenly somewhat heavier as the cylindrical contraption from earlier reappeared at my waist.

"You and your Gadget are connected. It has a way of making it back to you . . . most of the time," she said. "It *is* possible to lose it, and when that happens, it's quite difficult to replace, but that item is very much a part of who you are. Oh, don't beat yourself up. There's always *someone* who goes and loses the most important item in their inventory right from the start. Not usually the Band Leader, but . . ."

"Thank you," I said, relieved. Gazing down at the unusual weapon, I was just about to once again press the button when Madge cleared her throat.

"Not in here, Lucas," she said, her tone turning annoyed. "If you poke a hole in one of my chairs, I'll poke your eyes out."

"Gosh, I'm sorry." I immediately lowered the Gadget.

"Nah, I'm just playing with you. I would never do such a thing," she said with a grin. "But those chairs *are* expensive and imported from Bangladesh, so please try to be careful."

"Okay, I will." I crinkled my eyebrows. *Imported from Bangladesh?* But then I shook away the thought of asking her about that. "So, it's a knife, right? I push that button and stab monsters with it." Easy enough, in theory. Though, based on my recent encounter with the kobold, actually using the Gadget wasn't going to be a breeze.

"Oh, ho! It's more than that, my boy. The Gadget is whatever you need it to be. Once you learn how to trust yourself, you'll use it the right way."

"And how do I learn that?" I asked.

"Maybe you should ask the Gamekeeper. He's the one with the Field Guide, and something tells me he has no plans of giving *that* up anytime soon."

"Gamekeeper?" I asked. "Are you talking about Miles?"

She nodded. "Yeah, the little squirrelly fella."

"Miles is playing the Gamekeeper?" That sounded way cooler than the Artisan. "I thought I was the one in charge." Not that it mattered, but hadn't we all agreed upon that in the beginning?

"Doesn't mean what you're thinking," she said. "This isn't like other games."

"Tell me about it." There was so much to learn and not enough time to process everything.

"Now, let's go over the details of your Quest, shall we?" Removing the string, Madge unfurled the rolled piece of parchment and started reading from it. "A long time ago, Foyos, a monstrosity unlike any other known throughout the realm, appeared in the Lower Etchlands. That's the land you're standing on right now, in case you were wondering," she said, nodding at the floor. "Driven by his insatiable greed for power, Foyos terrorized the countryside, taking whatever he wanted and destroying anyone who attempted to stop him. When all hope of having peace throughout the land seemed completely lost, the monster brought about his own demise, sheerly by mistake.

"One fateful evening, Foyos entered the lair of the immortal witch, Faylinn, determined to claim her magical talisman—the source of her immortality—as his own. A talisman as powerful as that, however, could not be taken by merely killing Faylinn but could only be bestowed as a gift, which she had no intention of doing. Enraged by her stubbornness, Foyos decided to slay her anyway, but Faylinn, evil and cunning in her own right, convinced him to make a deal with her instead. In exchange for sparing her life, Faylinn would willingly surrender her talisman. And that is where the mighty Foyos erred, for the witch altered the magic and, instead of granting immortality, the talisman cursed the wearer with endless aging. Transformed by her spell, Foyos fled to his mountain hideout, where, in his weakened state, he drifted into a deep sleep. Fearing his eventual return to power, Faylinn imprisoned the beast in a tomb, and there he has remained to this day.

"But all spells, even those as powerful as the one cast by Faylinn, must eventually come to an end. After three hundred years of slumbering, the magic has begun to wear off, and as each day passes, Foyos grows in strength. Your fearless Band of Champions has been chosen to journey to his mountain tomb and defeat the monster once and for all before he returns to rain terror across the land."

The crisp parchment crinkled as Madge's tiny fingers effortlessly rolled it back into a tube and tied its string around it. Then she tossed the rolled paper at me, which I succeeded in catching after clumsily fumbling about. "You're going to need help to get close to Foyos. That talisman might be wearing out, but it's still powerful. Without a spell from Faylinn, you might suffer the same fate as the monster himself. At the bottom of that scroll is your Active Quest Log, which will tell you the steps necessary to complete your Quest." She scrunched her eyes shut and quoted apparently from memory:

"Cross the Entry Bridge;
"Traverse the perilous Wollen Woods;
"Pass through the city of Trouble's Landing;

"Chart a course to the Hagwoods and seek out the
    help of the immortal witch, Faylinn; then
"Journey to Mount Restless and slay the mighty Foyos.

"Trouble's Landing is about a twenty-mile trek from the Slipping River," she continued. "Once your Band has crossed the Entry Bridge, your Quest officially begins."

"It hasn't started already?" I asked, searching around for a pocket in my leather pants to carry the scroll but not finding any. "What about that kobold?"

"What, *that?*" Madge smirked. "That was just giving you a little taste of the action. You weren't even the target, but you did act as a decent distraction. Poor kobold probably thought it had found a hearty meal. Little did it know, the Harvester had learned a trick or two with her Spade."

"Harvester? That's Jasmine then, right?" I asked, beginning to piece things together.

"Yes, sir! Lucky gal, got to spend two whole days acclimating herself to the environment. Poor thing would've been in deep trouble had I not grown bored of waiting around for the rest of you lot to show up, and took the liberty of getting her outfitted. Though it's difficult to say who she was more alarmed by—me or the kobolds." Madge snickered. "Nah, Jasmine will be a wonderful Harvester once she gets control of that stubborn streak of hers."

Miles was the Gamekeeper, Jasmine the Harvester, and I was playing the role of Artisan, whatever that meant.

"Don't look so confused," Madge said. "You'll figure it out as you go. Remember, you're the leader of your Band. You should trust each other, but you'll need to be the one to make the tough decisions when they matter most."

"You know, I'm not really the leader type," I admitted.

Leaning back, Madge gave me a stern looking over. "I'm sure you'll do just fine. For now, Miles has been given the task of researching all your questions in the Field Guide."

"He has?"

"Of course he has. I just told him to." When I screwed up my face even more, Madge just chuckled. "I *can* be in more places than one. I'm not exactly a normal character, if you catch my drift?"

"What are you, then?"

"A friend," she said. "Your only friend, and I do mean *only*. Here's your Dispenser." She handed me the last item from the bottom of the basket—a leather pouch, its top flap snapped into place with a brass button. "You only get one of these, and space is limited, so don't go filling it with random garbage."

Madge gestured to my belt, and the Dispenser latched onto it as though it was attached with magnets.

"You've got one ration pack, which, in theory, should be enough to get you all the way to Trouble's Landing, barring you don't take any unnecessary detours," she said. "Once you get there, I suggest you stop by Madame C.'s Armory and Potion Parlor at the north end of the city. It's not on the main road, but you'll find it easy enough. Excellent selection and fair prices. She won't lead you astray like the others. Now—do you have any other questions before you go?"

The tiny woman had just filled my head with so much information I could've asked a hundred questions and still had plenty more to fire off. But before I could open my mouth to ask the first of many, I found myself standing outside the secret room, staring down at the dwindling fireplace. I heard Madge's echoing voice fading away softly in the distance:

"Good luck, Champion . . ."

Excerpt from THE CHAMPION'S QUEST FIELD GUIDE

CHARACTER SELECTION

Choosing your Character is one of the most important steps to having a successful Quest. By rolling the Die of Fate, willing Champions choose their Level Opal Character from one of four core roles:

The Artisan

In need of a blade, or a trap, or a winch?
The Artisan's Gadget always helps in a pinch;
For the Artisan is wise and may know a few tricks
To battle your foes when you're stuck in the mix.

> *Hero's Device—the Gadget of Necessity.*

The Harvester

Should your Band face the grim of the gathering thick,
The Harvester's Spade might just do the trick;
Through earth and through soil or by fruit and with seed,
The Harvester reaps what the Champions need.

> *Hero's Device—the Sower's Spade.*

The Luminary

What's better than hope when failure brings grief?
Let the Luminary's charm be your source of relief;
The Luminary's skill may hold claim as the best
When faced with despair on a perilous Quest.

> *Hero's Device—the Spark of Spiriting.*

The Gamekeeper

In your Quest should you venture where evil has hatched,
Then the Gamekeeper's Tether is truly unmatched;
Are your foes far too great, have your plans gone awry?
When the Gamekeeper calls, friends are always close by.

> *Hero's Device—the Beckoning Tether.*

CHAPTER 7

THE WILD
CROWS

After getting our Character assignments, we headed out from the shack. The rest of our morning passed without any other excitement. No more kobolds or magic dice rolls or tiny, gnomish women hiding in baskets. I figured it had to do with the Entry Bridge. That was the first official checkpoint, according to Madge. After we crossed over, the real adventure would begin.

As we walked, I discovered that as Band Leader, I was in charge of the ration packs. No one else had been given any, so I took three of the four in my Dispenser pack and handed them out. Each of the ration packs contained a few sections of beef jerky as well as a small package of six wafers wrapped in waxy paper.

Jasmine tore open her wafer packet, munching on a couple and groaning with satisfaction as she wiped her mouth with the back of her hand. I'd have done the same if I hadn't eaten in that long.

"Why aren't you eating?" she asked me. "Aren't you hungry?"

"A little, I guess," I admitted.

It *had* been a while since I had eaten. It seemed like forever ago that I'd gone to the aquatic center with Miles. I stared down at the cracker in my palm and frowned. I sniffed it. It had a weird, oily smell to it, almost like gasoline. I wasn't that hungry.

"I'm not really a fan of beef jerky *or* crackers," Miles said.

Jasmine grinned. "Try it. Trust me, you'll like it."

Shrugging, I broke off a corner of the cracker and placed it in my mouth. At first, I gagged, unsure of what I was expecting it to taste like, but as I began to chew, I instantly changed my mind.

"What *is* this?" I asked, swallowing the bite and crunching into a much larger piece of the wafer. "It tastes like . . ." No, it couldn't taste like *that*, could it?

"It tastes like your favorite meal," Jasmine explained, her smile widening.

"Cheesy enchilada casserole?" I blurted as the full flavor of Mexican spices hit the back of my tongue. It was the one good thing that had come out of the McMurdie Boardinghouse— Mrs. Turnbuckle's enchilada casserole. I didn't think I would ever taste it again.

"Mine tastes like a PBJCPS delight!" Miles exclaimed.

"A *what?*" Vanessa asked, opening her package of wafers, her eyes narrowing suspiciously.

"A peanut-butter-jelly-cheese-puff sandwich," he said. "It even tastes like the puffs are smushed into the grape jelly, just how I like it."

"That's disgusting." Vanessa glowered. She nibbled on her wafer and then walked on in silence, enjoying several crackers of her own favorite meal.

Over the next little while, I ended up eating two more wafers and half a piece of beef jerky before I finally called it quits. Each piece tasted different. Along with cheesy enchilada casserole, I munched on a bacon cheeseburger, a garlic alfredo pizza, and a strawberry-and-vanilla ice cream sandwich. It was the best meal I had eaten in quite some time.

"I don't understand how this works," Vanessa mumbled, looking down at the open Dispenser pouch attached to her belt.

"You just have to focus your mind on an item, and it will . . . uh . . . dispense," Miles said, stifling a burp.

"I get *that*." Vanessa looked at him sharply as her large pan, which turned out to be called the Spark of Spiriting, whooshed as it magically materialized in her hand, appearing out of thin air.

Gasping, she shook her head in astonishment. "But *how* does it work?"

I had been wondering the exact same thing. The Dispenser wasn't heavy; it was hardly noticeable attached to my belt, and yet it held my food and my Gadget easily.

"Magic, I guess," I replied. "It's all part of the game."

"Part of the game," Vanessa muttered under her breath.

Despite her sour attitude, I was honestly surprised by how well she had handled everything. I fully believed Vanessa would have had the most difficulty accepting the fact she wouldn't be hanging out with her friends at the mall anytime soon. I don't know what Madge had said to her to calm her down, but since stepping out from Madge's weird room as the Luminary, the fourth and final member of our Band, Vanessa had yet to raise her voice at anyone. Even though Madge had taken her phone away when she swapped her clothing out with the standard issue outfit, Vanessa had gone along without much complaining.

"Does anyone know what a Luminary is supposed to do?" Vanessa asked.

"As Luminary, you are charged with enlightening, inspiring, and encouraging the other members of the Band," Miles explained, reading from the manual. "You shall find power in words, music, and upliftment of the soul."

I snickered, and Vanessa steered an angry glare in my direction.

"What's so funny about that?" she demanded.

"Nothing, I just . . . uh . . . can't think of a better person for the job," I said.

"According to the Field Guide, our Dispensers are indispensable," Miles announced. "Each one contains fifty slots of storage space. Seems like a lot."

Wrapping my leftovers in a piece of cloth, I opened my pouch. My vision became cloudy as the inside of my Dispenser suddenly blipped before my eyes, floating in the air like a holographic image. I could still see my surroundings, which was probably a good thing since I definitely didn't want to be surprise-attacked by an enemy while checking my inventory. With the remaining food in my ration pack and a waterskin, everything I now owned took up thirteen slots in my Dispenser.

A loud chittering sound rose from beneath Miles's robe, and a glistening snout nudged its way out from under the furls of fabric. The snout belonged to a bright orange armadillo named Goon. The name seemed odd for the tiny armored creature, but that was the name stamped on its collar when the armadillo had first appeared on Miles's shoulder in Madge's secret room. As Gamekeeper, Miles had been given a Familiar, his very own animal assistant.

"I just love Goon." Miles beamed, wiggling a finger at the small creature. "Vanessa, do you think we could get one once we get back home?"

Vanessa scowled at Miles. "I'm allergic to most animals,"

she reminded him. "And it's not like armadillos are sold in pet stores."

"Oh yeah," Miles said with a huff of sadness. "Well, I'm allergic to chocolate."

"You're allergic to chocolate?" Jasmine smirked. "How's that even possible?"

Miles shrugged. "Chocolate makes me itch. I'm also allergic to Vaseline and seafood. Though I guess I'm not technically *allergic* to seafood. It just makes me barf. I always wanted my own pet. My parents had a dog named Nancy. She was a cocker spaniel, but when they died, Nancy was given up for adoption." Miles had a tendency to ramble when he was nervous or excited, and I could tell he was both at the moment.

"I don't think Goon's an actual pet," I explained. "He's supposed to help in battle."

At least that's what Familiars did for heroes in normal role-playing games. So far, the only thing Goon had been good for was breaking Miles's concentration. Miles giggled and wiped his ear as the armadillo affectionately nibbled his earlobe. Then Goon gave a loud screech and dove back under his robe.

"There it is," Jasmine announced, flicking her chin toward the outline of a bridge arching over the river. "We should probably get ready, just in case."

"Just in case of what?" I asked.

"Madge said there would be some sort of monster guarding the Entry Bridge," she said, gripping her shovel.

"What kind of monster?" Miles hastily flipped to the section at the back of the Field Guide where he had spent the past hour reading up on all sorts of creatures.

But there was no need to search the book. As soon as we walked within twenty feet of the bridge, the monster scrabbled

out from the riverbed, kicking up dirt with his boots. The oaf-
ish creature was easily ten feet tall, with gray, sagging skin,
drooping bloodshot eyes, and tusks jutting up from his lower
lip that could have poked holes in a steel door. His head looked
like a misshapen watermelon, and he wore woolly pants and the
smell . . . well, the smell was almost too much for me to take. It
smelled like mystery casserole sealed in a Tupperware container
and long forgotten in the back of the refrigerator. The kind
covered in green fuzz.

"Who dares approach Jugger's bridge?" the monster demanded in a thundering voice.

I looked at Jasmine and then back at the monster. Man, he
was humongous.

"Jugger wants to know. Did you not understand Jugger?" he
asked, pounding his chest. "Who goes there?"

He sure did like to use his name a lot, but I couldn't
help but feel goose bumps forming on my arms at his classic
bridge-monster question.

Jasmine nudged me with her elbow. "I think you have to
answer him."

"Oh, right. Uh . . ." I swallowed, still shocked by the massive size of the monster. "*We* goes there?" I replied, chuckling
awkwardly.

"Ogre," Miles whispered, crowding close and pointing to the
picture in the manual. "He's an ogre. 'Mountain folk known for
their incredible strength,' but apparently they're also really dim-
witted," he added a little louder than he probably should have.

Jugger's eyes bulged from his melon-shaped head. "Who says
that? Where does it say that about Jugger?"

"Er . . . not you," Miles nervously backpedaled. "I didn't
mean you, of course. I just meant ogres in general."

THE DIE OF DESTINY

"Well, I have ten Wisdom, thank you very much. And fourteen Strength." Shifting his tusks back and forth, Jugger dislodged a piece of bone the size of a salami from between his teeth and spat it into the river.

"Maybe you shouldn't talk anymore, Miles," Jasmine suggested.

"Jugger votes for that too," Jugger said, folding his beefy arms. "Right. What will be the name of your Band, then?"

"Our name?" I asked, scrunching my nose.

"You have to have a name before you may pass," he grumbled.

"That seems pointless," Vanessa said. "Why?"

Opening his mouth to reply, the ogre puffed out his cheeks before nodding at Miles. "Page eight. Third paragraph."

Miles hurriedly sifted through the manual. "Here it is. 'No Band of Champions is complete without a proper name. As you embark on your first Quest together, you shall henceforth be known and honored by this name. Imbued with powerful magic, it shall give you direction, purpose, and, most importantly, hope during the darkest moments of your adventure.'" Miles wiggled as the tiny mound of Goon worked his way around the inside of his robe. "It also says this is an essential rule of Champion's Quest and that there's no getting around it."

"As Jugger said," Jugger replied, leveling his bloodshot eyes on me. "So, what's it going to be?"

Looking at the others, I shrugged. "What do you guys think?"

"I vote for the Misfits," Miles suggested. "Because we're all kind of misfits in our own—"

"That's lame," Jasmine said, interrupting him.

"This is *just* like larping," Vanessa muttered, her voice rising as she glanced over her shoulder and sighed. "We're going to turn into a bunch of dorks . . ."

"What about the Bentford Four?" I offered but instantly regretted it.

"*I'm* not from Bentford," Jasmine said, disgusted by the suggestion. "And neither are you."

"It was just an idea."

Jasmine's nose twitched. "My Lola always calls me a little Aswang whenever I get into trouble. It's Tagalog for a really creepy monster in the Philippines."

"Not bad," I said. Monster names were fairly common in role-playing games. My online group had been called the Howling Hydras. We were awesome.

"Yeah, absolutely not," Vanessa added. "I'm not going to be called an Aswang for as long as I have to play this ridiculous game."

"Then what?" I asked.

Rolling her eyes, Vanessa stared up at the ogre. "We'll be the Crowes. That sounds like what something larpers would call themselves."

"But I'm not a Crowe," I said. That name had nothing to do with me and it never would.

"You live at my house. You eat my food, and I drive you two around everywhere. Whether you like it or not—and believe me, I don't like it—you're a Crowe." Her eyes flitted over to Jasmine. "And you? Well, the voting's three against one."

When I started to complain, Vanessa held up a finger, the nail of which had been painted lavender before but now looked dull and dirty. "This is not open for discussion, Lucas. Okay? I'm the oldest one here. I'm in charge, and what I say goes. But if it'll make you happy, we'll drop the *E*."

"The *Wild* Crows," Miles piped in.

Vanessa smirked, her expression brightening. "The Wild Crows. Does that satisfy you?"

The Wild Crows. I had to admit the name had a nice ring to it, even if Vanessa had been the one forcing it down our throats. I glanced over at Jasmine, who stood off to the side, nibbling on her lower lip.

"That works," she said with a shrug.

Jugger gave an unimpressed grunt. "Brilliant. Jugger approves."

A shrill, awful screech rose from beneath the bridge as an enormous spider scurried out and up the riverbed. Red with yellow spots and coated in spiny fuzz, the spider was about the same size as a small horse—one with a billion eyes blinking at us from its hideous face. It was also missing a couple of legs; I could see the gnarled stumps where they had fallen off a long time ago. I had never been a fan of spiders, and those were only the ones small enough to smush with my shoe.

"Oh, disgusting!" Vanessa shrieked, leaping back behind Jasmine, who looked equally grossed out by the spider.

Miles seemed to be handling the appearance of the spider for the most part, but if he hadn't had the Field Guide to distract him while he searched for the arachnid's stats, he probably would've passed out.

"Spish ain't disgusting!" Jugger snapped. "Spish is Jugger's pet. And if there's one thing Spish knows, it's how to properly welcome a bunch of measly little crows to our neck of the woods." Putting his hand around his back, the ogre pulled a nasty-looking battle-ax off his shoulder. "Now, which one of you are we gonna stomp first?"

"Why didn't we see *this* coming?" I asked as the world around me froze and the Die of Fate once again appeared in my hand.

CHAPTER 8

AN OPPORTUNITY
CLAIMED

Pixie dust swarmed around me like a cloud of mosquitoes. It tingled against my skin, cool and fizzling, like some sort of magic golden ginger ale, and I was suddenly covered in goose bumps. Still holding his book, Miles stood beside me. He hadn't been frozen. None of us had. Well, Jugger and the horrifying Spish had stopped moving, but this was way different than what had happened in the shack when we'd gone up against the kobold. Amid the sparkles, the Champion's Catch appeared, floating in the air. The row of gemstones lining the outer edge of the catch glowed and flickered as the magical dust gathered beneath it like a mini tornado.

"Roll for your Fate," a voice whispered from inside the Champion's Catch.

"Who does that voice belong to?" Vanessa demanded. "And why does she get to tell us what to do?"

Stepping up to the floating rectangle, I peered over the edge, squeezing my hand tightly around the Die of Fate. I showed it to the others, and Jasmine frowned.

"Why did it just appear in your hand?" she asked.

I shrugged, and Miles cleared his throat.

"It's because he's our Band Leader," he said. "Lucas controls the fate of our party throughout the game."

Just as it had during the kobold attack, the Die of Fate's numbers flitted about randomly across the surface of the die. I was just about to toss it into the Catch when Miles anxiously called out to stop me.

"Maybe we should think about this," he said.

"What's to think about?" Jasmine asked. "You heard what Jugger said. We have to fight."

"You know, violence isn't always the answer," Miles said.

"I'm not a violent person," Jasmine snapped, even though her knuckles had turned white around the handle of her Spade, "but if we don't roll, we'll be stuck here forever. Or do you know another way out of this?"

"Let's just see what happens," I said. The swirling pixie dust felt like it was trying to pull me into the funnel as I tossed the die into the catch.

The die came to a stop on the number four. Miles's Advancement Medallion began to glow, and he cried out in panic. "Now what?" he demanded as a new multisided die appeared in his hand. The die fought and fidgeted like an angry insect, and he almost dropped it twice.

"The Gamekeeper now wields the Die of Opportunity," the disembodied female voice announced.

"I do?" Miles squeaked. "That's cool. I—I think." Having already flipped to the page in the manual, Miles struggled to balance the open book in the crook of his elbow while the new game piece tried to break free of his hand. "The Die of Fate determines who receives the opportunity," he explained. "Each of our characters is linked to a number; the first one we rolled back at the shack. Number four is the Gamekeeper. Which is me."

"Then what does *that* do?" Vanessa asked, nodding at the new game piece straining in Miles's hand as though it was trying to punch him in the face.

Miles gasped, still struggling to contain the tiny, angry die. "I don't know yet. Oh, stop squirming, please!"

"Rolling the Die of Opportunity must give you a better chance," I guessed.

Vanessa frowned. "A better chance of what?"

"Of beating Jugger." I pointed at the frozen Jugger, his ax towering above us in the air.

"Those things?" Vanessa laughed cynically. "That's a troll and a giant spider. We're a bunch of kids. We can't beat them."

"But we're not just kids here," I said. "We're Champions." It still sounded weird calling ourselves that, but here, that's what we were. *Champions.* "I'm the Artisan. Jasmine's the Harvester. You're the . . ."

"The Luminary," she replied dryly, holding up her heavy pan. "Which means what, exactly? Am I supposed to cook for the troll?"

"Ogre," Miles whispered.

"No one cares, Miles," Vanessa snapped.

"Well, there's only one way to find out." Pressing her hand into the small of Miles's back, Jasmine pushed him toward the Catch.

Miles sucked in a deep, nervous breath and then rolled. The game piece ricocheted against the walls of the Catch, howling like a tiny wolf, and Miles clenched his eyes closed, whimpering until the die came to a stop.

"This is it for me, isn't it?" he asked.

"Yes!" I cheered, pumping my fist.

"What?" Miles gawked at me in panic.

"No, Miles, that was an awesome roll. Look." I pointed into the Catch. "A sixteen is solid gold. You can't get better than that."

If we had been playing a normal game sitting around a table, our chances of defeating our enemies would have been pretty much guaranteed.

A playing card suddenly appeared at the bottom of the Catch. I recognized the image from one of the cards stacked on Hob's table back at the shop.

"Daroon's Ever-Expandable Armor," Miles read, his voice trembling.

Then a gust of wind blew through the center of our group, whipping through our hair as the pixie dust tornado shot out from underneath the Champion's Catch and gathered around Miles. Miles's Dispenser opened, and his Tether, the frayed, tasseled whip he had received when he became the Gamekeeper, rose from the opening. Miles yelped as the card vanished and his Tether looped around, twisting in the air and forming into a spiky, circular object that attached itself to his wrist.

"Is it a bracelet?" Jasmine asked, once the whirlwind of dust had settled.

"I guess so," Miles gasped. "But how am I supposed to fight a monster with a bracelet?"

The strange spiky bracelet didn't look like any normal armor. It barely covered his forearm. Would it even be able to block a blow from Jugger's massive battle-ax? I seriously doubted it, but as I leaned over to examine Miles's arm, the mysterious, disembodied voice returned.

"Prepare for battle," it announced.

Then the Champion's Catch and the multisided dice disappeared and just like that, the real fight began.

CHAPTER 9

THE WORLD'S
BIGGEST GOON

As time sped up, Jugger bellowed, and he swung his ax at Jasmine. Somersaulting out of the way like an acrobat, she expertly stabbed her Spade into the dirt and hurled a large clump of mud right at Spish. Squealing and hissing, the enormous spider scuttled after her.

"Um, a little help here would be nice," Jasmine pleaded, zigzagging back and forth. While she may have been confident at first, that spider was right on her tail.

I could feel my heart beginning to race as panic settled in, but I had to tell myself it was just a game. If in any other situation I'd found myself going up against an ogre and a giant spider, I would have run away screaming. But this wasn't a normal situation. None of this was actually real.

"I guess I'm on it," I said. Snatching my Gadget from my Dispenser, I stepped toward the spider but had to duck as Jugger took another swing, this time at my head.

"Not even across the bridge, and I'll be ending your little campaign," the ogre spat. "Not cut out for questing. Not even fit to carry that bite-sized doohickey."

His ax swished again, close enough to split a gaping hole down the middle of my shirt.

"Ah, come on," I complained, staring down at my pasty, freckled chest peeking out through the rip.

That was a new shirt. My only shirt. Luckily, I could still move because the next time Jugger attacked, I stepped out of the way—no ripped shirt this time—and the ogre buried his ax in the ground. As he grunted, trying to pry his ax loose, I pressed the button on my Gadget and the blade shot out from one end. For just a moment, the sight of the gleaming knife mesmerized me. Was I really about to stab an ogre with a sword?

"Careful there, little man. Don't you go shaving my arm," Jugger warned.

Holding my breath, I raised my Gadget and swung the blade down on top of Jugger's beefy, hairy forearm. I heard the sound of a gong going off somewhere in the back of my head, and my whole body shook. Teeth rattling, I had no choice but to drop my Hero's Device, which felt like a tuning fork.

"Nice try," Jugger grunted, mud slopping from his blade.

No armor, my weapon out of reach, and no way to help my friends. I had to be the worst hero ever. Blinking up at the ogre, I hopelessly awaited Jugger's final blow just as Jasmine plowed into my side, knocking me out of the way. We rolled through the dirt, and I heard Spish scrabbling as he skittered past.

Utterly winded from failing to capture Jasmine, Spish turned toward a new target. Miles hadn't moved from his original spot and was just standing there staring at me with a distant, bewildered look in his eye.

I snapped my fingers. "What are you looking at, Miles?"

Spish pounced. Miles clamped his eyes shut as the spider's fangs clanged harmlessly against his spiky metal wristband. When Miles realized he hadn't been bitten and his special armor had actually blocked the attack, he puffed out his chest like a superhero.

"Not today, you dumb bug," he said, panting breathlessly.

"Look out," Vanessa gasped as Jugger's ax came out of no-where, hitting the small boy squarely in the side.

It all happened in a dizzying blur. One moment Miles had been standing there, the next he'd taken flight. Horrified, I watched his limp body launch through the air, toppling end over end like an action figure before landing in a large bush with a thud.

"No way that just happened," I said, covering my mouth in shock.

"Oh, my parents are going to kill me," Vanessa groaned. "Miles, are you dead?"

He had to be dead. No one could have taken the full brunt of Jugger's ax and survived.

"I'm fine," Miles's chirping voice announced from inside the bush. "I thought you said rolling a sixteen was awesome. It's definitely not awesome."

"Are you hurt?" I asked, baffled he could still be alive, let alone able to speak.

"I don't think so," he replied, sounding irritated. "I'm just going to sit here, if that's okay."

"Good idea," Jasmine said, twirling her Spade like a baton and squaring off with the ogre.

"Not sure you even know how to use that properly," Jugger growled with a menacing chuckle. "Think spraying me with dirt is going to save your little necks?"

"Probably not," Jasmine answered, jutting out her chin de-fiantly. And then, as though finally understanding something about her weapon, she made a sly grin and hurled her Spade right at Spish, striking him in his bulbous belly.

A burst of greenish light erupted as the spider reared back, his body blurring. Then, staggering to one side, he exploded into a firework of multicolored sparkles. Huffing with annoyance, Jugger stormed over and shoved Jasmine into the mud with one meaty paw.

"There, that settles it," Jugger said, glaring down at the girl.

Instead of finishing her off with his ax, however, the ogre heaved a sigh of disappointment. "You'll need to do better than that," he said. "Much better. Think I'm the strongest or the meanest or the most dangerous opponent you'll ever face? Lucky for you, I'm just here to test you."

"Test us?" I asked, climbing to my feet.

Jugger nodded. "And you didn't do so hot, now did you?"

Breathing heavily, Jasmine stood up from the mud. "Hey, I killed your spider."

Shoulders bobbing up and down, the ogre began to snicker. "What, Spish? He's ninety-nine years old and only has five legs. What did you expect? He wasn't even supposed to be here today, but Loogey called in sick and I had no choice but to drag him along. Now, Loogey's a proper spider. Not a chance in the world would you have dodged Loogey had she been here."

I may have been rattled from the fight, but I did manage to raise an eyebrow. "Your spiders' names are Spish and Loogey?"

Jugger scowled. "Spiders name themselves right after they hatch, and they don't exactly have much of a vocabulary."

"This isn't our fault," Vanessa said. "We didn't know you were going to attack us."

Jugger heaved a sigh. "You're the Champions, aren't you? Of course it's your fault. You didn't fight smart, you stood clumped together like a bowl of soggy dumplings, and you got bested by a five-legged spider and an ogre with nothing better to do than guard the Entry Bridge."

"I don't understand," I said, feeling my frustration bubbling to the surface. "What was the point of rolling those dice if they didn't do anything to help us?"

Jugger clucked his tongue. "The Die of Opportunity does tons of things, depending on how you use what it gives you."

"But Miles rolled a sixteen," I said.

"Yeah, so? The higher the number doesn't matter. A sixteen selected Daroon's Ever-Expandable Armor, a fancy prize unless you have nothing but a spider's brain in your noggin. Who's the dimwit now?" Jugger yelled over at Miles's bush. "Wearing it on his wrist like a dolt. That boy should've started the fight in the bush instead of ending it there. The Die of Opportunity gives an opportunity to one Champion, but you have so much to learn. And you would have known how to use the armor had you read the clue on the back of the card. Weapons and armor come and go, but they're just a bonus. You can't rely on such things to be your only advantage. You were given the tools you needed, but only the Harvester had enough sense to use it." He jabbed a finger at Jasmine. "And you got lucky, my dear. Spish isn't as quick as he used to be. Had Loogey been here, you'd be spider chow right about now."

"I tried using this thing," I said, retrieving my Gadget from the ground. The blade had retracted into the device. A lot of good that had done. "I stabbed you, and it didn't work."

"Because I have iron skin, obviously," Jugger explained.

Iron skin? I stared at the ground, running my hand through my hair. Then having a knife always at the ready was completely worthless.

"You need to think differently, boy," Jugger said. "You've got yourself quite a weapon there. The Gadget provides what the Champion needs, but if all you want is a blade, that's all you'll get from it."

"You're not going to kill us, then?" Jasmine asked him.

"No one actually dies in this game. Even Spish, all popped and glittery, will be back eventually. Won't be happy about it, but he'll be back," Jugger explained. "No, you can't die, but Champions can get knocked back to the beginning of the game, depending on who thumps you. And you don't want that, believe me. Because you can't ever get out of here until you deliver on your promise."

"What promise?" Vanessa demanded.

"The one to rid the Lower Etchlands of Foyos," Jugger said. "The promise you made at the beginning when you rolled for your Destiny."

"I never rolled for anything," Vanessa huffed. "This isn't fair."

"No, it isn't, but I don't make the rules." The ogre licked his lips, his tongue like an enormous pimple-covered slug poking out of his mouth. "Now, what should I do with you? Should I show mercy? Should I step aside and let the fabled Wild Crows pass through?" Stiffening his shoulders, Jugger sucked in a deep breath. "Nah, I think I'll finish my lesson and send you back to that little shack."

"Please don't do that," Vanessa begged as Jugger swung his ax off the ground.

A rumbling noise like the sound of a galloping pony started tromping the ground, loud enough to distract even Jugger from pummeling us. We all turned to locate the source of the sound just as Miles burst out from the bush, riding in the saddle of an enormous animal. Goon had grown ten times his usual size and resembled a miniature orange tank covered in savage-looking armor. Squealing hysterically, Miles clung desperately to a leather strap around the armadillo's neck with one hand while the other flailed behind him. Within seconds, the charging duo covered the distance and the three of us leapt out of the way as Miles and Goon rushed past, galloping right up to Jugger.

Blinking in bewilderment, Jugger tried swatting at them with his ax, but the armadillo simply jumped over the weapon, scrabbled up the handle, and climbed onto the monster's bicep. Then, with Miles hanging on for dear life, Goon lowered his skull and plowed straight into Jugger's chin like a battering ram.

Excerpt from THE CHAMPION'S QUEST FIELD GUIDE

THE DEN OF DICE

While weapons, skills, and creative ingenuity provide an advantage, it is your rolling from the Den of Dice that shall give you a fighting chance. Make no mistake about it, the dice are no ordinary game pieces. They are tricky, have a mind of their own, and may present themselves to you whenever they wish and certainly on more than one occasion.

The Die of Destiny—All Quests are chosen for a Band of Champions when the Band Leader rolls the Die of Destiny. But that is not all. Whenever Destiny calls throughout your adventure, this twelve-sided marvel may provide you with a bevy of possibilities.

The Die of Fate—Six-sided and ever changing, the Die of Fate may be used to determine the Character you shall play on your magnificent Quest. Though it might seem such, random it is not. And perhaps the magic of the Die of Fate is not in the way it selects your Role or even how it reappears when you least expect it, offering a chance to alter your fate. The real magic is in its ability to bring out the Hero within all who cast it.

The Die of Opportunity—With sixteen sides and well-worn edges from use during countless confrontations, the Die of Opportunity gives Champions a fighting chance. Oh, but do try not to put all hope in the luck of your roll, as there shall always be more than one pathway out of a pinch.

The Die of Wonder—Ten-sided and cloaked in mystery, not much is known about the Die of Wonder or what it will offer at the beginning of your Quest. One thing is for certain, how-ever—no matter the prize unwrapped from the Gifting Meadow, a successful outcome depends entirely upon the choices of the Champion who claimed it.

CHAPTER 10

THE GILDED GARGOYLE

As Jugger, the mighty ogre, collapsed to the ground and exploded into a fountain of green sparkles, Miles leapt down from the saddle, a jubilant smile stretching from ear to ear.

"Miles, that was awesome!" I exclaimed, wrapping my arm around his shoulders. I didn't know how he had transformed his armadillo into a freakish war machine, but he'd done it in the nick of time.

"How did you do that?" Jasmine asked, nudging him with her elbow.

"The idea came to me while I was sitting inside that bush," Miles said, panting as though he had just run a marathon. "And that's when Goon started talking to me."

"He did *what*?" Vanessa cocked an eyebrow.

"Apparently, I can communicate with him. Because he told me to give him the armor." Miles beamed, his eyes wild with enthusiasm.

At some point following Jugger's epic explosion, the armadillo had shrunk back to normal size. Chattering excitedly, Goon scurried onto Miles's leg and then dove beneath his cloak once more.

"My Tether hadn't turned into a bracelet after all. It was a *saddle*," Miles said. "An armadillo saddle, I guess? Because the moment I put it on Goon, he grew really big and then he said, 'Hop on.'"

Vanessa smirked. "You're just making that up."

"Okay, maybe he didn't say those exact words, in fact, I don't think Goon can actually talk out loud, but he definitely wanted me to ride him. So I did."

"Not to break this up, but I think you might want to move away from those mushrooms," Jasmine warned. Grabbing me by the arm, she pulled me away from a patch of grass with triangular-shaped mushrooms that had begun to stretch like colorful balloons.

A mighty clap of thunder suddenly boomed overhead, and I shielded my eyes as a fork of lightning struck the ground. When I opened my eyes again, a fat, winged monster with charcoal-colored skin stood at the edge of the bridge.

"*Coucou*, my Champions," the monster called out in a deep, guttural voice. Decked out in jewelry from head to toe and wearing what might have been a shimmering toga, the creature wildly waved a handkerchief through the air.

"Welcome to my Gifting Meadow," he said, speaking with a French accent. "I see you have bested that filthy ogre. Well done, I say. *Bien joué*."

"Do we really have to fight another monster?" Vanessa complained. "Don't we get a break?"

The winged creature gasped, appearing to take offense at Vanessa's words. "You're not comparing *me* to *Jugger*, are you? *Non, non*, my cupcake, I am not here for fighting. I am Gilner, the Gilded Gargoyle, and this, my friends, is your lucky day."

Tossing his handkerchief high above his head, the gargoyle

gave a majestic bow, his bracelets banging together. Even his stone-like wings were plastered with baubles as though he was some sort of living Christmas tree. Once the handkerchief touched down in the grass, the mass of quivering mushrooms burst with one glorious pop.

The first thought entering my mind—as globs of gooey mushroom showered down upon our heads, smelling worse than Vanessa's most fragrant shampoo—was that we had just survived a battle with an ogre and a giant spider only to be buried alive by this gargoyle's mushroom grenades.

"*Ooh, la, la!* There is a reward here for each of you," Gilner the Gilded Gargoyle announced.

It was like waking up to the most bizarre Christmas morning ever as at least a dozen brightly wrapped packages now occupied the spaces where the fungi had exploded.

Wiping the slime off his face, Miles took a shaky step forward. "These presents are for us?"

"But of course, brave Gamekeeper. And since you were the one who toppled the mighty Jugger, you may be the first to roll the Die of Wonder." Extending his hand, Gilner gestured to the Champion's Catch, which had appeared and now floated over a fresh pile of mushroom goop. A new golden game piece with ten sides sat in the bowl.

"Is it normal to receive gifts like this?" Jasmine asked, keeping her voice low and her eyes glued on Gilner.

"Not exactly," I said. "But none of this is exactly normal."

Winning rewards may have been part of role-playing games, but I couldn't remember a time when an animated statue wearing enough costume jewelry to open a boutique had let me roll for my prize.

"What's in them?" Miles held up a narrow, rectangular package with shiny green wrapping paper.

"*Désolé, mon amis*, I cannot say." Clucking his tongue, Gilner waggled a finger. "Because that would just spoil the fun. I *will* tell you that you shall not be sorry with any of these prizes. Each special item has the potential to drastically help you along your way."

As we each took turns rolling the Die of Wonder, a random present would drift over from Gilner's Gifting Meadow, floating lazily in the air like a balloon. Miles went first. After checking for the gargoyle's approval, he ripped the polka-dotted wrapping paper off and removed the lid. I caught a glimpse of what looked like a trading card resting inside the package, but as soon as Miles touched it, the card dissolved and a small cube appeared in its place.

"That is the Revolutionary Die of Change," Gilner announced, hovering above.

Miles's fingers quivered as he held up the object. "What does it do?" It looked just like any other basic game piece with one exception—all six sides of the die were blank.

"Should you ever feel a dice roll has not delivered to your highest expectations, simply cast this Die of Change on the ground and demand a reroll," Gilner said.

"*Any roll?*" Miles asked, glancing at me.

"Yes, any," the gargoyle replied. "And on any Champion in the game."

"Awesome," Miles whispered. He opened his Dispenser and put it in carefully.

Though my present had been quite large, covered in checkerboard wrapping paper and decorated with peacock feathers, once the strange playing card disappeared, I was holding only a small red coin.

"Brilliant!" Gilner cheered. "Simply drop Zabor's Coin of Interrogation into water, and a character of your choosing shall instantly appear and be compelled to answer two questions. All you have to do is state the phrase, 'I, insert your name here, of the Wild Crow Band, wish to ask you my first question, *et ainsi de suite*.'"

To be honest, I had thought vanquishing an ogre should have won us something a little fancier—like a pouch of gold or a magical potion. Still, I could probably find a use for the coin at some point in the game. Opening my Dispenser, I deposited Zabor's Coin of Interrogation into one of the available slots.

"The Unlocker's Skeleton Key of Unlocking," the gargoyle's voice boomed when Vanessa had opened her present. Gilner explained that no matter how complex the lock, Vanessa's key would open any door she ever came across along her journey.

"So where's the door out of this place?" Vanessa asked, acting as though she couldn't care less about her prize.

"This is the biggest box I've ever opened," Jasmine said, carrying on the unwrapping frenzy.

"The Grains of Persuasion." Gilner shook his head in amazement as Jasmine pulled a tiny glass vial filled with a white, powdery substance out of the giant box.

"Is this good?" she asked, rotating the stoppered bottle in her fingers.

"*Mais, bah oui!* Is it good?" Gilner tutted. "A Champion fortunate enough to come across this magical crystalline powder will discover they have the power to convince any foe to change their mind."

Standing in the pile of torn wrapping paper, we glanced

around at each other, all still slightly bewildered by all that had happened.

"Please remember these gifts are single-use only. Once you choose to activate them, they cannot be accessed again," Gilner explained after we'd all added our prizes to our Dispensers. "Now, you must make haste and head for the city of Trouble's Landing. The horrid Foyos awakens—and all that stands in the way of his inevitable return is your fearless Band of Wild Crows. And now, I bid you *adieu*!"

Having said this, the Gilded Gargoyle waved goodbye as we crossed over the bridge into the Wollen Woods.

CHAPTER 11

DWINDLING
BLOODSTONES

Aand there's plenty more where *that* came from, ya laddies and lasses," an angry dwarf called out from high above us in the treetops.

It had been two days since the Gilded Gargoyle had sent us over the bridge. Only two days, but it felt like months. The first day it had been fine. Hardly any trouble at all. We wandered through the forest along the trail, which had been easy enough to follow. Then, later that evening, when we stopped beside what we thought was a peaceful lake, we discovered that we'd made camp next to a nest of oversized scorpions and had to deal with them the rest of the night.

During that encounter, Vanessa had earned a roll of the Die of Opportunity, but all it had given her was a bunch of weird, metal strings dangling from the narrow handle of her Spark. They were called the Strings of Spiriting, but she had no idea how to use them. Luckily for us, Miles was still able to use Daroon's Ever-Expandable Armor on Goon, and the armadillo fearlessly chased away the scorpions.

I had hoped today would be a little more low-key, but at a fork in the road, just as we were trying to figure out which path to take, three dwarf bandits in camouflage jumped us. I mean literally jumped *on us* from an overhanging tree. Jasmine took care of the first two, but the third one was making a nuisance of himself.

"Make it easier on yourselves," the last dwarf demanded from his perch in the top branches of a tree. "Give up the treasure or face my wrath." He started to pelt us with darts from a wicked blowgun, shooting me three times in rapid succession. This was getting old fast. My left arm went completely numb. The tree began to sway as the dwarf leapt from branch to branch overhead, preparing for another attack. There had to be something about his red knee-high boots that gave him special leaping abilities because for being a squat, bearded man about half the size of Miles, that dwarf could practically fly.

"We've already told you," I shouted through my cupped hands. "We don't have any treasure." I barely dodged another dart that whooshed through the air and stuck in a tree stump with a loud twang.

"A likely story, but I'm not buying it," the dwarf replied in his Scottish brogue. "You'll pay for me brothers and you'll pay dearly."

"Here he comes again," Miles warned as a flurry of leaves and twigs fluttered down from above.

"Well, sic Goon on him," Vanessa said.

"These dwarves are too nimble for Goon. Plus, he's still tired after battling those scorpions." Miles stared down at his mammoth armadillo, who appeared exhausted.

Goon had been a ton of help against the scorpions even though they'd batted him around a bunch with their stingers.

"Just draw him out like we did with his brothers," Jasmine said. "Miles, you be the bait. I'll take care of the rest."

"I don't want to do that again," Miles begged.

"But you didn't really do it last time, Miles," Jasmine said. "You ran back under the trees before I had a chance to attack."

"Yeah, but it was so scary," Miles said.

"Well, I'm not going out there," Vanessa insisted, folding her arms.

"You're the only one who hasn't even tried," I said. "Everyone needs to take their turn."

Pursing her lips, Vanessa glowered at me. "Don't talk to me about taking turns. It's your fault we're here in the first place. And besides, I'm not crazy. I don't have a death wish."

"Fine, I'll do it. Again." I tossed up my hands in frustration.

"Face it, Lucas. You're just good at being the bait," Vanessa said.

I desperately wanted to argue with her, but with the dwarf bounding around above us, I knew it wasn't the right time. Taking a deep breath, I nodded at Jasmine.

After rolling a seven on the Die of Opportunity at the beginning of the dwarf attack, Jasmine had drawn the card of Blaridor's Branch of Barricading from the Champion's Catch. None of us knew what it was really supposed to do, but it had transformed her Spade into a long bō staff–like contraption. Maybe she had trained in mixed martial arts back in Bentford or something, but whatever the case, Jasmine knew how to wield it expertly. She had already taken out the other two dwarves with her skilled attacks.

While the dwarf whistled gleefully, bouncing around from branch to branch, I stepped out into the clearing, covering my head with my Gadget. It was the only thing my Hero's Device seemed to be good for. Oh, sure it glowed and buzzed and shot a knife out of one end every time I pushed the button, but it had been too small to use against the scorpions, and the dwarves never stood still long enough to allow me to poke them with it. For all it had been worth so far, I could have tossed my Gadget into a nearby pond.

The swaying tree grew still, the calm before the storm, and then the dwarf cackled and hollered and cannonballed from the top branch, swooping down like a skydiver, his arms outstretched and ready to pummel me to death, but then Jasmine swatted the dwarf out of the air with a loud crack. Squealing and caterwauling like a stray cat, the dwarf popped just as the others had done in a flash of purple and blue sparkles.

I heard jingling near my feet and stooped over, noticing a small pile of silver coins where the dwarf's sparkles had just evaporated.

"Is that *money?*" Vanessa asked, joining me in the clearing. "From the dwarf?"

"'Vanquished monsters leave behind treasures for the victorious heroes,'" Miles read from the manual. "This can include coins, weapons, and artifacts."

"What about the scorpions?" I asked. "Did they leave us anything?"

"We didn't wait around long enough to find out," Jasmine said, leaning on the Branch.

"And Goon just chased them away," Miles said. "The scorpions might still have their treasures if we wanted to go back and finish them off. Er . . . but, just to clarify, I don't," he added quickly. "I'm fine with leaving them alone."

"Me too," Vanessa agreed. "So how much money's there?"

I silently counted the stack of coins. "Twenty pieces."

"Great. Five for each of us," she said.

"Or all for Jasmine." I closed my hand around the coins

before Vanessa could snatch them. "She was the one who defeated the dwarves, after all."

"With our help," Vanessa said.

"It's fine." Jasmine sniffed and smiled, gripping her Branch confidently. "I say we split the loot."

· ◆ ● ◆ ·

An hour later, I stumbled through a clearing in the trees and found a boulder that looked like a perfect resting place. I collapsed next to it with a painful "Oof!"

I slowly realized I'd sat in a mud puddle as my pants started soaking. "Well, that's just wonderful. I don't think I like this place anymore," I muttered.

Jasmine emerged from the forest and poked at the ground with her new weapon, checking for traps. After all we had been through, it was a good idea. Miles wandered into the clearing next, followed closely by Vanessa.

"I'm starving," Miles said. Hands drooping at his sides, he kicked off his boots. "Does anyone have anything left to eat?"

"Nope," I said. My Dispenser was clean out of snacks. "I ran out of food just before those dwarves attacked."

Heaving an annoyed sigh, Vanessa began digging the dirt out from underneath her fingernails. "I always thought dwarves were supposed to be friendly."

"You can't keep basing everything you think you know about this place off cartoons," I said. Getting tired of being wet, I removed my rear end from the puddle and moved to a patch of relatively drier ground.

"The dwarves in the *Lord of the Rings* were friendly, weren't they?" Vanessa asked, sneering at me. "I saw those movies too."

Of all the people in the world who could've been our fourth companion, why did it have to be Vanessa Crowe?

Puffing my cheeks out in frustration, I gathered some nearby branches and within a couple of minutes had a decent fire blazing. It may have been a warm, muggy evening, but the heat from the flames gave me a teensy bit of comfort.

"Does anybody know how we can fill these back up?" Jasmine asked, pulling out her Advancement Medallion.

More than half of her Vitality Meter stones had winked out, but at least hers were still red. Mine had all turned pink and had been blinking nonstop since I'd been jabbed with poisoned darts. From what I knew about games like this—which was turning out to be basically nothing—my health meter wasn't doing too hot.

"I think my name should be changed to ax-magnet," Miles griped. He was in the worst shape of all. After his run-ins with Jugger, the scorpions, and those divebombing dwarves, Miles only had one Vitality Meter stone that hadn't gone dark.

"Well?" Vanessa gave my leg a sharp kick.

"Ouch! Hey, why'd you do that?" I asked, wincing in surprise.

"What are we supposed to do, Mr. Expert?" she demanded, glaring at me. "We're all dying here."

"Why am *I* the expert?"

"You're the one who dragged us into this mess, and you're the one with all the dice. Yeah, I've seen them on your dresser," she said. "We're not going to last much longer if we don't figure out a way to heal ourselves."

"First off, I didn't drag *anybody* into this," I said. "And second, you seem to be doing just fine."

Vanessa's eyes narrowed. "What's that supposed to mean?"

I tried biting my tongue, but it was no use. "You still have all your health," I said, nodding at her Medallion. "Maybe if you helped during battles, we wouldn't be in this mess right now!"

"Keep your voice down," Jasmine cautioned. "Something's going to hear you."

Vanessa cocked her head as though checking her hearing. "Excuse me? Oh, I get it. You're jealous because somehow I'm better than you. Or have you forgotten who it was who tripped up that first dwarf?"

"No, you were just hiding behind a tree when the dwarf ran after me and you accidentally tripped him with your Strings of Spiriting." I may have been having trouble catching my breath, but I refused to let her take credit for that victory.

"Well, it's not like I know what to do with these things," Vanessa fired back, shaking the cluster of metal strings drooping off the end of her Hero's Device. "You have a sword. Miles has a jumbo armadillo. Everyone's got actual weapons. What do I have? A frying pan!"

"It's not a frying pan," I said, rising to my knees and feeling my blood turning into barbecue sauce. "And it doesn't matter anyway because all you do is run away. You don't do anything to help."

Not once during any of the attacks had Vanessa willingly contributed to the fight. I may have been absolute garbage at fighting, but at least I was giving it my best shot.

"Maybe you should calm down." Miles pressed his hand against my shoulder, trying to settle my nerves.

"Yeah, cool it," Jasmine added. "Arguing isn't helping us."

Digging at the corner of my eyes with my thumbs, I swallowed the lump in my throat. I wasn't crying, not yet at least, but I had to calm down before the situation got out of hand.

The last thing I needed was an attack from the Creepers. Vanessa already thought I was a weirdo, and I didn't need Jasmine figuring that out as well.

"You're right," I grumbled. "I'm sorry about getting so mad."

"You should be," Vanessa said, though the edge had left her voice. "Because what I do is called 'dodging.' Maybe you should try it sometime."

"Anyway, about this?" Jasmine held up her Medallion. "If another monster surprises us in the night, we won't make it."

"May I see the Field Guide, please?" I asked Miles. He eagerly handed it over.

After flipping through the pages and finding the section labeled "Becoming Familiar with Your Advancement Medallion," I began reading out loud:

"As ancient as the game of Champion's Quest and filled with mystical power, the Advancement Medallion acts as both a beacon and a warning. Each stone represents an integral component to the success or failure on your Quest. The Soul Stone, the centerpiece of your Medallion, announces your rise to greater levels of glory as the color changes from Opal to the eventual Diamond—the highest level of Champion's Quest . . ."

Vanessa snapped her fingers, jolting me from the book. "Skip to the important part, please," she said, forcing a smile. "We don't need to go full dork right now."

With a reluctant nod, I skipped to the part about Vitality Meters at the bottom. "Pay careful heed to your Vitality Meter, which may dwindle due to injury, witchcraft, or even poison. Each Champion must not let the last Bloodstone darken, indicating their unfortunate demise and a restart to the beginning. While not all items may be lost, some important artifacts may be removed from the Champion's Inventory and the Band must once again work their way through the original challenges of their Quest."

"What?" Jasmine asked. "We'd have to do everything all over again? Like every battle?"

"Apparently," I said.

"But I don't want to do any of that again," Miles griped. "I don't like getting chased by dwarves."

Dragging her fingers down the sides of her face, Vanessa released a desperate groan. "Are we seriously doing this right now? Is this really happening? I was supposed to be spending my summer vacation at the mall."

"Keep reading," Miles urged, shaking his Advancement Medallion as though trying to force a little life back into his Bloodstones.

"Potions, spells, or much-needed rest can greatly aid your return to full health. Never underestimate the power of the Luminary. The magic they possess shall do wonders for any Hero down on their luck." As I finished reading that paragraph, the three of us looked over at Vanessa.

"Chad Maverick was going to take me to the movies," Vanessa continued, paying no attention. "Now I'm sitting in the dirt, wearing circus clothes, and my hair feels like a bird's nest." Pausing from her rant, she looked up and scowled. "Why are you all staring at me?"

"You're the Luminary," Jasmine said.

Vanessa folded her arms. "And your point is?"

"The book says you can help heal us," Miles replied.

Vanessa waited about five seconds before throwing her head back and growling. "With what? My super special frying pan? You're all disturbed." Standing up, she dusted off her knees and turned toward the trees. "I need to get away from you people for a while."

"I think it would be better if we stuck together," Jasmine said.

"I'm not going that far away," she snapped. "If you hear me getting eaten by an ogre or a troll, or whatever you want to call it, just come running and save me, okay?"

And she headed for the forest.

CHAPTER 12

BANGALOO BERRIES
AND VIPER PODS

"Seriously, what are we going to do for food?" Miles asked after Vanessa had wandered away. "I miss my wafers. We ate those so fast, and I'm seriously hungry now."

Getting pounded by monsters had definitely worked up my appetite, but we had emptied all the food from our Dispensers. There was nothing left.

"Maybe we could find something," I suggested. "You know? Like in the forest."

The familiar whooshing sound of a Dispenser dispensing drew my attention to Miles, who was holding handfuls of bright-orange berries.

"Like these?" he asked.

"I thought you were all out of food," Jasmine said.

"Oh, I'm definitely out, but I picked these berries earlier." A couple of the tiny berries slipped through his fingers, bursting in the dirt and oozing golden syrup. "The Field Guide says Champions can collect different sorts of plants from the forest to make potions or even food."

"For all we know, those could be poisonous," I said.

"These are Bangaloo Berries." Jasmine plucked one from Miles's overstuffed hands. "They're not poisonous."

"And how do you know that?" I asked. I may not have been a fruit expert, but I felt fairly certain the berries Miles had collected could only be found in the Lower Etchlands of Champion's Quest.

Jasmine's lips parted, but then she paused. "Uh . . . I'm not sure," she said. "It's kind of weird, isn't it?"

"Not weird at all for the Harvester," Miles said, wearing a goofy grin and diving into the Field Guide. "*Through earth and through soil or by fruit and with seed, the Harvester reaps what the Champions need.* You must know things about fruits and seeds and all plant life. It says so in the manual."

"What about this?" Miles asked when another item emerged from the pouch. "Can we eat this too?" It looked like a watermelon, only it had black-and-silver stripes and was pocked with dimples.

I started laughing. "Geez, Miles, how much did you collect?"

"A whole bunch," Miles admitted, handing the melon to Jasmine for inspection. "I filled up almost all my Dispenser slots."

"This is a Kakarind Gourd," she explained. "It's also not poisonous. But the berries and the gourd aren't that great if you eat them raw. They're only edible when you cook them."

An ember popped out of the fire, landing on Vanessa's Spark of Spiriting, which was lying in the dirt.

"Did you say cook them?" I glanced at Miles.

"Vanessa does keep calling it a frying pan," he said and immediately dumped the berries and the gourd into the Spark.

As we began heating the fruit over the fire, Vanessa finally returned from her time alone in the forest.

"What's that smell?" she asked, sniffing the air.

"I picked a whole bunch of stuff, and now we're cooking it," Miles explained. "Boogerloo Berries and . . . um . . . um . . ."

"Bangaloo Berries and Kakarind Gourd," Jasmine said.

Miles nodded. "Yeah, those."

Frowning, Vanessa stared at the sludge swirling in her Spark. "And are you purposely trying to burn them?"

"We're not burning them," I said. At least, I hoped we weren't, but the smoke had grown thick and started to smell like burnt hair.

Shoving me out of the way, Vanessa grabbed a twig from the ground and began stirring the ingredients. With deftly moving fingers, she scraped the charred parts from the bottom of the pan, and within a few moments, the sloppy berry-and-gourd concoction transformed into a golden sponge cake.

"I think I saved most of it," Vanessa said, wafting her hand across the surface. She removed the pan from the coals and sliced the cake into four even sections.

"Vanessa, this is really good," Jasmine said through a mouthful. "Seriously, guys, try it."

"It's a little overdone," Vanessa admitted. "Maybe if you had told me you were going to try baking, I could have come and helped sooner."

Taking a bite, my mouth instantly exploded with flavor. "It tastes like pineapple upside-down cake," I said, devouring my piece.

Miles moaned with delight. "Boogerloo Berries must be sent straight from heaven." Then he nearly choked as he gestured wildly. "Look at your Medallion!"

Looking down, I half-expected to see a tarantula crawling up my shirt, but I discovered that the stones on my Vitality Meter had stopped blinking and turned red instead of pink. My

Bloodstones weren't the only ones changing. More than half of Jasmine's and Miles's meters had begun filling back in as well.

"We're healing," I said, astonished.

"Because of the cake?" Jasmine asked.

"No, because Vanessa is the Luminary." Miles slapped his knee. "She has the power to heal us. That's what it says in the Field Guide."

"What are you guys talking about?" Vanessa glanced up from nibbling on her piece of cake.

"We're now realizing that each of us has special talents," I explained. "Miles can communicate with wildlife. Jasmine knows everything about plants and trees. You can cook . . ."

"I could always cook," Vanessa corrected. "My brownies are the bomb."

"Yeah, but could your food ever heal people?" I asked.

She didn't answer, her eyes narrowing as she appeared to let the possibility sink in.

"We all have something we can do," Jasmine said. "And it's not just for fighting enemies."

"Except I'm not quite sure what I can do yet," I said. "But I'll figure it out as we go."

"What about the fire?" Jasmine drew my attention to the smoldering embers.

"What about it?"

"You made it, didn't you?" she asked. "How did you do that?

"I just . . . you know?" I shrugged. "I just struck a rock against my . . ." My voice trailed off as I held up my Gadget. To everyone's shock, instead of the familiar blade, a rough steel rod jutted out from the end of my Device. "When did this get here?" Come to think of it, I couldn't even remember making the fire. It had happened so naturally, as though I had built a million fires out in the woods—but I'd hardly ever been camping. The rest was all a blur.

"I think that's a ferro rod," Miles explained. "A fire-starter. I used one once in Cub Scouts."

"But what happened to my knife?" I asked.

"You didn't need a knife," Miles said. "Jugger told you to think differently. Your Gadget can be used for more than just a weapon."

"You're the Artisan," Jasmine added. "You build things. And I bet fire is just one of many things you can build."

"That settles it." Climbing to her feet, Vanessa headed for the trees again.

"Where are you going now?" Jasmine asked.

"I don't know about you guys, but I'm still hungry. If Miles found those berries, there has to be more. Aha!" she exclaimed, kicking at a pile of dead leaves. Reaching down, she plucked a veiny, brown bulb about as large as a volleyball from the pile. "This may look disgusting, but with my Luminary skills, who knows? Maybe I could turn it into a pie."

As Vanessa separated the bulb from its thorny stem, a spray of foul-smelling vapor began pouring out from the bottom.

"Vanessa, stop." Jasmine tried to warn her as the cloud of gas expanded, filling the air.

Gagging, Vanessa chucked the bulb into the forest. "What is that?"

"Viper Pod," Jasmine said, covering her nose with the top of her cloak. "Don't breathe in the fumes."

But I had already breathed in the fumes and was growing dizzy. Staggering away from the fire, I watched in horror as Vanessa stopped coughing, her eyes bulged, and she collapsed to the ground.

Then everything went black. It was like someone had covered my head with a sack, only this felt much worse. I couldn't see or hear anything.

Moments after blacking out, my sight and hearing returned, and I sucked in a breath. The hideous gas from the Viper Pod was gone, and I filled my lungs with cool, clean air.

"Is everyone all right?" I asked, sitting up.

"I don't think so," Jasmine said, sounding agitated.

"Oh, please, no," Miles whined. "I had just started to heal."

"This is officially the worst game ever," Vanessa added.

Then I took in my surroundings and realized where we were—sitting on the splintery wooden floor back inside the hut at the beginning of the game.

Excerpt from THE CHAMPION'S QUEST FIELD GUIDE

THE CHAMPION'S DISPENSER

Each Quest comes with its own specific challenges and, though timelines vary drastically, some Campaigns may take weeks or even months to complete. You never know where the road may lead or how long it may be until you are fortunate enough to wander upon a traveling merchant. Thus, once your Destiny has been chosen, preparing for the long haul is an absolute must.

Bequeathed to each member of your Band is their trusted Dispenser. Food is essential, as are medicines, potions, maps, tools, and weapons. One should make wise decisions with what they choose to occupy the available slots, for space shall always be limited. And while it is possible to collect the most peculiar items along your way (see pages 37 through 72 for the list of offerings from the Gifting Meadow), storing a hefty artifact such as a giant's enchanted femur may not be the most practical on your Quest.

Take heed, brave Champions, for while the Dispenser is an essential tool, it is not foolproof. The incantations making it possible to store supplies on the ethereal plane are powerful, but your Dispenser is directly linked to the progression of your Advancement Medallion. It is not unheard of for some valuable items to mysteriously disappear due to some ill-fated and unforeseen circumstances.

CHAPTER 13

THE GRAINS
OF PERSUASION

Grumbling under her breath, Vanessa marched toward the fireplace and yanked harshly on one of the burning logs. "Which one was it?" she demanded.

"What are you looking for?" I asked.

"The log that opens the secret room?" She tried another, but the fire only popped and crackled. "I'm going to grab that little Madge by the throat and demand she send us home. She knows the way out of here, and she just doesn't want to tell us." After removing every log from the fireplace and finding no secret room, Vanessa unleashed an angry snarl. "You can't blame this on me."

"No one blames you," I said, though deep down inside, I did.

Vanessa's impulsiveness had poisoned us all. If she had just waited until Jasmine had identified the Viper Pod, we would still be alive and that much closer to our destination. Starting over was the last thing we needed. It wasn't like a video game where you could return to a checkpoint. We had spent two days traveling toward Trouble's Landing, and now we'd have to spend the next two days doing it all over again.

"Look on the bright side," Jasmine said. "I do have all my health back."

It definitely wasn't much of a silver lining, but each of the Bloodstones on my Advancement Medallion had returned to full strength. Opening my Dispenser, I began browsing through my slots, which didn't take long, seeing how I hadn't collected anything along the way. I still had my Gadget and Zabor's Coin of Interrogation. I had hoped my ration pack would have returned with the reset, but that still looked to be empty.

"All out of food, but I have everything else," I said.

"Me too," added Jasmine, pounding her Branch of Barricading against the floor.

"I think I'm good too," Miles announced after checking his Dispenser. "Everything seems to be . . ." His eyes suddenly widened in panic as he began pulling items out of his Dispenser rapidly, dumping them on the floor. "No, no, no," he groaned.

Bunches of Bangaloo Berries smashed beneath his feet, along with at least a dozen other odd trinkets. At some point, Miles had collected rocks and pieces of bark and even a few rusted forks and spoons I remembered the dwarven bandits had left behind. Miles kept searching and tossing until he'd emptied everything from his Dispenser. He dropped to the floor in a heap of sadness.

"What's wrong?" I asked, tripping over his pile of knick-knacks as I crossed the room and knelt next to him on the floor.

"The Field Guide," Miles whispered, his eyes glistening with tears. "It's gone."

· ◆ ● ◆ ·

It had been afternoon when we had been poisoned by the Viper Pods out in the Wollen Woods, but now it was early morning, the sun just barely starting to poke up in the horizon. The reset back to the shack must have cost us several hours even though it had felt like we'd been unconscious only moments. Madge hadn't given us a time limit to finish our Quest, but we didn't want to wait around for the kobolds to return. Instead, we immediately headed out from the shack. Feeling horrible for having lost the Field Guide, Miles moped along at the rear of the group, Goon perched on his shoulder, until we spotted Jugger near the Entry Bridge. Unlike before, when he'd been dressed for battle, the ogre now wore a raggedy gray smock over his shoulders as well as some sort of skullcap pulled down over his pointy ears.

"The Wild Crows lasted longer than I would have guessed," Jugger said, glancing up from carrying a couple of crates down toward the river. "Still, here you are, and I can't say I'm surprised. You made it, what? Two days?" Moving his head from side to side, he unleashed a barrage of loud pops. "What finally did you in?"

"Viper Pods," Jasmine replied glumly.

"Poisoned yourself, eh? Yeah, it can happen to the best of them, though I'm not really talking with the best of them right now, am I?" Digging a finger into one of his ears, Jugger gazed toward the horizon.

A loud commotion of clattering metal snapped the ogre's attention to the river, where a large raft had been moored to the bank with gnarled rope. Two enormous spiders wrestled with each other at the rear of the raft, their long limbs entangled, sending a current of waves lapping against the shore.

"I told you to sit there and stop squabbling," Jugger growled. "I haven't been gone but five minutes and look at you. Who knocked over my kitchenware?"

One of the spiders stared guiltily up at the ogre, several dented pots and pans scattered beneath his feet.

"Loogey, you know better." Jugger grumbled something under his breath. "No, Floyd, don't try stacking them back up, you nitwit." More pots fell over, and the spiders nearly toppled into the river.

"Are you going somewhere?" Jasmine asked.

"As a matter of fact, I am," Jugger answered, snapping his head back. "I'm due for a little vacation. So my brother Gurgle is coming to relieve me for a few days. He's going to temporarily take up my duties as Guardian of the Entry Bridge so I can go to the festival."

"What festival?" I wondered.

Jugger glowered at me. "Two days should have been plenty of time to read the Field Guide cover to cover. There's a blooming glossary in the back, for crying out loud."

Out of habit, I looked over at Miles but remembered he no longer had the Field Guide, and he blubbered miserably.

"The Festival of Bonnie Barters always takes place this time of year in Trouble's Landing," Jugger explained. "People from all over the countryside gather for a week of merriment and to peddle their goods. There are new shops to visit, and the food . . . " He whistled blissfully. "Most of the delicacies are only available during the festival."

"This festival's in Trouble's Landing?" I asked, even more curious.

Both spiders began hissing at each other again, and the ogre slapped his forehead. "No, stay there, Floyd. Right there—don't move. Loogey, stop poking him. You're only making it worse. I'll be down in a minute."

As he stooped over, setting down his crates, I spied the gleaming edge of Jugger's battle-ax strapped to his back beneath his smock. Maybe it was because we were so tired from being beaten down so much, but for some reason, Jugger looked even bigger and nastier than when we had fought him before.

"Right, let's make this quick, shall we?" Jugger said, removing his skullcap. "Obviously, I've got a mess to clean up before I shove off. So, if you don't mind . . ."

Just as the ogre removed his ax, extending it high above his head, poised to strike, Jasmine uncorked a glass tube and blew the contents into Jugger's face.

"What the devil?" Coughing in surprise, the ogre sucked the powdery substance up through his nostrils. "Oh, you'll pay for that, missy, I assure you. Jugger does not like . . ." Sputtering, he caught himself, shaking his head, and then, to my surprise, lowered his ax.

"Did you just use the Grains of Persuasion on me?" Jugger asked, dragging a finger under his nose and inspecting the white powder.

Grinning sheepishly, Jasmine held up the bottle. "I figured since you were already heading to Trouble's Landing, maybe we could catch a ride with you. It's like you said before." She glanced at Miles. "Maybe violence isn't always the answer."

"I did say that," Miles admitted.

"Clever girl," Jugger said, picking up his ax. "As long as the four of you can keep a couple of troublemaking spiders from strangling each other for the duration of our trip, it would be my absolute pleasure to take you."

"They're not going to try to eat us, are they?" I asked, warily eyeing the massive spiders.

"Eat you?" Jugger scoffed. "Why? You part fly or something?"

I just shook my head.

"Then you should be fine." Wobbling woozily, Jugger hefted the crates into his muscled arms. "Mind your step, friends. It can get a bit slippery on deck."

CHAPTER 14

TROUBLE'S
LANDING

"And do you see that right there?" Jugger nodded to a dome-shaped structure rising up above the wall. "That's Maradoom's Arena. Named after the great warrior Maradoom, of course. The same what bested the Sickled Sorcerer in a battle of wits more than two thousand years ago. That's where the Tournament of the Urchin Minotaur takes place every year after the last harvest and, if all goes as planned, where I shall be claiming my prize by tournament's end."

Shifting awkwardly on Jugger's raft, I tried getting comfortable, which was proving to be extremely difficult with two of Floyd's legs draped across my lap. The enormous spider had fallen asleep more than an hour ago, and I didn't know the best way of sliding out from underneath his knobby appendages without waking him up. Floyd was Spish's replacement until Jugger's five-legged spider companion could respawn, which could take quite a while to happen. When some of the game's creatures were slain, it was possible it could be more than a year before they regenerated. Jugger was one of the only exceptions. As Guardian of the Entry Bridge, whose main assignment was testing new Champions before they set off on their Quest, it was necessary for him to respawn almost immediately.

"Can anyone enter the tournament?" Miles asked, sitting cross-legged next to the ogre and eagerly gobbling up every bit of information he graciously offered.

Jugger's head bobbled. "More or less, but they usually cap the entries at fifteen participants, otherwise the tournament could likely last until winter—and who would want to wait around for that? Oh, over there, that building with the tower that looks like it's made of dragon's teeth?" He pointed, and we all followed his finger. "That's the Observatory. On a clear day, you can spot the Stone Giant Cathedral on the eastern peak of the Griphorn Mountains from there. Normally, the Observatory is free to anyone who wants to take a look, unless, of course, the warlock Boodrick Bodriggle happens to be back in the city. Then it'll cost you at least one blood sacrifice."

The journey to Trouble's Landing should have taken us more than two days and would have been filled with more monster encounters, and the first time around, we'd barely eked by with our lives. As passengers on Jugger's raft along the Slipping River, however, we covered the distance in less than six hours and arrived on the outskirts of the city midafternoon. The only monsters we saw were those prowling along the shoreline, and they wanted no business with an ogre and his two giant spiders.

The clinking of silverware almost startled Floyd awake as Jasmine stooped over the side of the raft and cleaned our dishes in the river. Jugger had fed us a meal of stewed beef and cabbage. At least I hoped it was beef. It had been a little chewy, but it tasted decent. Not as good as cheesy enchilada casserole or an ice cream sandwich would have been if I still had any magical wafers in my Dispenser, but I was grateful for the meal.

"You don't have to wash mine," I insisted, unsuccessfully

trying to move as Floyd snuggled down, his full weight pressing against my legs. "I'll get them eventually."

"It's fine. I don't mind," Jasmine said. "I actually like washing dishes."

"You do?" Vanessa smirked. "Please tell me you're joking."

"It's the only time my Lola isn't nagging me," Jasmine admitted. "The bigger the load, the longer I have peace. I usually just put in my earbuds and drag it out as long as possible."

"So it's just you and your grandmother at your apartment?" I asked.

She nodded. "My parents visit every year for a couple of weeks, but they haven't been able to move here permanently yet. I'm able to stay because of the sponsorship program."

"Is that a good thing?" Vanessa handed her bowl to Jasmine. "No offense, but you seem like you don't really like Bentford."

Jasmine shrugged. "It's just another place to live," she said. "My parents just think living in the States will be better for me in the long run, but it's not like it's my real home."

"I totally understand," I said. "That's how I feel too."

"Hey, you three, are you not listening to Jugger?" Jugger asked, glancing over his shoulder. "We're nearly there now, and you should pay attention. Trouble's Landing's normally a neutral zone, which means that despite its name, 'less you're looking for trouble, you won't find any there. But don't go flashing your Advancement Medallions around," he said. "There's lots of ruffians in town during Bonnie Barters looking to best Champions like yourselves. Could earn 'em a hefty prize. If you're needin' a meal or a place to lay low for the night, I'd recommend Torbrick's Tavern, right off the city square. You can't miss it, and it's the best place for seeking information."

Deftly wielding the raft's massive oar, Jugger steered through a narrow canal way up to an unloading dock. Loogey and Floyd clambered onto its wooden planks and secured the raft to a post with their sticky spider webs.

"You there," a man wearing a wide-brimmed hat called out from behind a wooden podium. "It's four silver to park any boat on this pier. You can't just—"

An awful hissing sound erupted as Loogey bared his fangs and advanced a step forward. Yelping, the man immediately dropped behind the podium.

"You were sayin'?" Jugger stuck out his chin.

"Nothing," the man squeaked. "Nothing at all. Have a wonderful day." And then I heard him grumble. "I really do hate Bonnie Barters."

"Well, this is goodbye, then, and good luck," Jugger said after hoisting Vanessa off the raft and placing her gently on the dock. "I would get a map at Pavio's Pathfinder Pavilion first, if I were you. You'll find it behind the Eel and Salamander Market at the end of Satyr Street. And don't forget what I told you about your Hero's Devices. Those will determine the difference between a real Champion and any other wannabe. You got that?"

"Thank you, Jugger," I said, unsure if I should offer to shake his hand. When he wasn't trying to bash our skulls in with his ax, the ogre could be quite pleasant. I was actually going to miss his company.

"No hard feelings, right?" Jasmine asked with a sly grin.

Jugger's lips pulled wide, his tusks gleaming menacingly in the sunlight. "No hard feelings, my dear, none at all. Of course, when this tricky powder fades in an hour or two, I wouldn't want to stumble upon the likes of Jugger again if I were you."

Then, with Loogey and Floyd trailing behind him like

obedient dogs, Jugger meandered past the man cowering behind the podium and slipped down a side street.

· ◆ ● ◆ ·

There was only one way to describe the city of Trouble's Landing: jam-packed. Shouldering our way through the crowd, we were bombarded by the sights, smells, and sounds of what felt like an outdoor carnival. Countless shops butted up against each other, rising up along the gentle slope of a hill, offering everything from freshly picked apples to tombstones. We heard music, children laughing, and what sounded like growling animals from a noisy zoo close by. I had never seen so many people and creatures crammed into one location. There had to be hundreds, maybe even thousands, weaving up and down the narrow walkways.

We saw more ogres like Jugger and orcs wearing spiky armor. Elves with golden hair nibbled on grapes and leaned over balconies, mocking every other creature passing by. Miles accidentally bumped into the back of a horse in the road, and as he sputtered an apology, we realized it wasn't a horse at all but a centaur carrying a trumpet. Agitated, the centaur yelled at Miles about halflings needing manners and clomped away.

"How many more centaurs do you think live here?" Miles asked after I pulled him to safety.

Before I could answer, two more exited the blacksmith shop near us, the shrill clang of hammering metal echoing inside. Chomping on hay and sporting new, gleaming horseshoes, the centaurs walked between us into the road and met their buddy a few shops down.

"Who are all these people and these . . . things?" Vanessa asked. "Are they just made up for the game?"

"I read something before . . . well, you know, before I lost the manual," Miles said, looking away in embarrassment. "Many of these characters are here to give us an opportunity to go on a side quest or two."

"Why would we want to do that?" Jasmine asked.

"To earn experience," I said. "Sometimes miniquests are a way to level up. You can earn money, skills, or even information."

As if on cue, a shifty-looking man clutching a chicken close to his chest shoved his way through the crowd. Following several paces behind him, a woman screamed for help.

The woman snagged my sleeve. "I am but a humble peasant widow. That man has stolen my last chicken. I have no food to feed my starving children. Whatever shall we do to survive?" Feeling my cheeks flush, I tried pulling away, but she held on tightly, staring into my eyes. "If you teach that man a lesson and bring back my hen, I shall pay you handsomely."

"I thought you were poor," Vanessa said. "If you have money, why don't you just buy another chicken?"

Whirling around, the woman bore down on Vanessa, her upper lip curling into a snarl. "Do you not care about hungry children? Have you no soul?"

"Come on, Lucas," Jasmine said, prying the woman's fingers from my sleeve. "We should keep moving."

"Fine, go," the woman called out. "We'll just starve, thanks to you."

"See?" I asked after we had put a safe distance between us and the peasant woman. "She offered to pay us. That's how this works. If we needed more money, we could probably do a bunch of side quests."

"Yeah, but why would we need . . ." Vanessa began to ask,

but then she grew distracted by a nearby vendor. "Those can't be real diamonds, can they?"

"Yes, ma'am, quite real. Quite rare," the peddler announced, depositing coins from a recent purchase into his cashbox. "Collected them myself from the Ice Caverns and brought them straight here for you. Can I interest you in a beautiful brooch or a lovely pair of earrings?"

"We don't have time for this," I said. "We have our Quest, remember?"

With a snap of her fingers, Vanessa shushed me. "How much?"

"Two silver for the earrings," the peddler replied. "But I'm always willing to offer a discount."

"I still have that money in my Dispenser," she said to no one in particular. "From defeating those dwarves."

"But we should use that for supplies," Jasmine insisted.

Vanessa scoffed. "Supplies?"

"For food," I reminded her. "So we don't starve."

Ignoring me, Vanessa opened her Dispenser, and a small leather change purse appeared in her fingers. Pulling open the drawstring, she poured out a pile of clinking coins—and the peddler practically began salivating.

"Judge me all you want," she said, when we were finally able to pull her away, five pieces of silver lighter. "If I have to be here, I might as well make the most of it." Along with the diamond earrings, Vanessa had purchased a ruby necklace.

"What if we needed that money for something important?" Jasmine asked after we had walked a few blocks and crossed over onto Satyr Street.

"Then I'll sell my earrings," Vanessa fired back. "Diamonds will still be valuable."

"They're probably not even real," I said.

"None of this is real, Lucas, remember?" she said, tugging on her fancy earrings. "What does it matter if I want to accessorize my character? As long as I'm stuck here, I intend to enjoy myself."

Didn't she know we were stuck with her too? I wanted to tell her I hoped she enjoyed accessorizing her character while she could because she would be sorry soon enough. But I didn't say a word. Instead, I walked in silence, choosing to ignore Vanessa as she carried on about all the other things she planned to buy as we headed toward the Eel and Salamander Market.

CHAPTER 15

TWO ETCHINGS FOR THE PRICE OF ONE

Pavio's Pathfinder Pavilion was the only shop located behind the Eel and Salamander Market at the end of Satyr Street. The meager thatch-roofed building had crumbly brick walls and dark windows. It looked abandoned. When I tugged on the door, however, it peeled open, its hinges creaking.

"Why did we come here again?" Vanessa asked, staring around the dimly lit room.

"Hushed voices only, please," announced a dark-skinned man hunched over a large square table at the center of the room.

He wore an apron with several pockets crammed full of writing utensils and a pair of goggles that magnified his eyes to the size of tennis balls. He was brushing a block of what looked like charcoal across a large piece of parchment.

"We were told you would be able to—" I started to say, but the man cut me off midsentence.

"Patience," he commanded, his voice both calm and snooty at the same time. After a few more scribbles of charcoal, he pulled back from the table, dusted off his hands, and removed his goggles. "There. Finished. How may I be of assistance?"

"Are you Pavio?" I asked.

The man offered a curt nod. "I am. And you are the Wild Crows, are you not?"

"You've heard of us?" Miles's eyes brightened.

"Naturally," Pavio replied, a smug grin stretching across his face. "Word travels fast to Trouble's Landing, even when some *Champions* do not."

"We need to find the Hagwoods," Jasmine said, leveling her eyes on Pavio. "Can you help us or not?"

Extending his palm toward the table, Pavio beckoned us over. "Indeed, I can."

The table was in fact a giant map of the Lower Etchlands made of raised lines chiseled from a stone surface. Every land-mark, including the mountains, forests, villages, and rivers had been labeled and was displayed in intricate detail. Dozens of cities, some absolutely massive, dotted the map.

"Hey, it's the shack," I announced, spotting the now all-too-familiar hut near the table's outer edge.

"And the Entry Bridge." Jasmine pointed to a tiny star sym-bol next to the words *Jugger and Company.*

We had spent two days wandering the woods trying to find Trouble's Landing, and according to Pavio's map, the city occupied a circle of space no more than six inches from the Entry Bridge. The rest of the map seemed so huge it was hard not to feel overwhelmed. There were so many bizarre names of places—the Shaded Westerfalls, the Grimlock Gardens, the Forbidden Lair of the Molten One . . .

"Might I inquire about your Quest?" Pavio asked, drawing my attention from the map.

"We're going to go kill Foyos," I said.

"Of *course* you are." Pavio cleared his throat, and I defi-nitely detected sarcasm. "Because of your noble Quest to rid our world of Foyos's terror, I can offer you one map etching free of charge." Selecting a piece of parchment from one of the baskets, he once again stooped over, his bent body casting a looming shadow, like a storm cloud gathering above the map. "As you will see, there are many paths you may take, some more perilous than others. The Merchant Road is the most prominent." Pavio ran his finger along a winding, thin groove. "However, it is a treacherous path that could take several days to traverse, depending on what sorts of nasty, foul creatures you encounter. Nevertheless, it will lead you directly to the outer edge of the Hagwoods."

Without waiting, he refitted his magnifying goggles along the bridge of his nose and began scritch-scratching his charcoal across the parchment, replicating the details of the map with mesmerizing strokes.

"What's that cloudy area near the woods?" Jasmine asked, tapping a questionable spot with her finger. "It looks like the Merchant Road goes right through it."

"That would be the Enchanted Mists," Pavio answered, without looking up. "Without a proper guide, it's doubtful, if not impossible, to pass through."

Jasmine crinkled her nose. "Can we avoid going through them?"

Pavio tilted his head to one side, his magnified eyeballs blinking up at her. "Unfortunately, no. Your destination requires passage. I am but a humble Pathfinder. It is all listed in the fine details." With a click of his fingers, he snapped a single lens off his goggles and placed it upon the area of the map containing the Enchanted Mists. Though blurry at first, tiny words began appearing through the glass:

HAGWOODS
Home of the Immortal Witch Faylinn.
Guarded by Enchanted Mists and Faylinn's undead horde.

"*Undead horde?*" Miles squeaked.

"Isn't there another way we could go?" Jasmine asked.

"The Merchant Road is the only direct path to the Hagwoods," Pavio explained. "All other roads can take weeks to cross."

"*Weeks?*" Vanessa blurted, causing Pavio to jump and drag a stray charcoal line across the etching.

Licking his thumb, Pavio attempted to remove the accidental smudge. "Yes, weeks," he muttered, annoyed.

"I don't like this guy," Jasmine announced loudly enough for him to hear.

Eyelids fluttering, Pavio snatched up the finished etching. "Will that be all, then?"

"What about there?" Vanessa pointed at an area a few inches to the west of the Enchanted Mists that looked to be a winding path connecting Trouble's Landing to the Hagwoods.

Looking both bothered and bored, Pavio glanced down. "What of it?"

"Is there any mist blocking us from going that way?" Vanessa asked.

"There is not." He pushed the goggles up onto his forehead.

"Then why can't we take that? It's, like, half the length of the Merchant Road," Vanessa said, her head bobbing mockingly.

"That's the Goblin Road," Pavio explained. Holding out our map etching, he shook it vigorously until Miles snatched it from his fingers just to make him stop.

"If it's shorter and doesn't require passing through an undead hoard, I vote we take it," Jasmine said.

"The Goblin Road is for Emerald Champions or higher," Pavio said. "The four of you are only Opal."

Vanessa heaved an exasperated sign. "Emerald? Opal? What does that even mean?"

"The Soul Stones on your Advancement Medallions are Opal." Pavio slowed his speech as though talking to a child. "The Goblin Road is meant for those who have attained a Soul Stone of Emerald or higher."

"So if we're Opal, and I'm guessing that's like level one, what level is Emerald?" I asked.

Pavio gave a tired shrug. "Six or seven, I suppose, though I'm horrible with the details. Regardless, it would be unwise of you to travel that way. You would never survive." Turning his back to us, he put an end to the conversation and began tucking loose pieces of parchment back into their baskets.

"That settles it, I guess," I said, leaning across the map and feeling the rough edges digging into my palms.

"Why does that settle it?" Vanessa asked.

"We're not the right level," I explained. "The Goblin Road is a big risk."

"Level, shmevel," she said. "This whole game's a risk."

"Well, Lucas is our Band Leader," Miles chimed in, "and I agree we shouldn't do something we're not supposed to."

Shifting her weight, Vanessa bumped against the table. "I don't care what he thinks he is in this game, I'm not about to let *Lucas* tell me what to do."

I wasn't trying to tell anyone what to do. I was just trying to play smart. Level one—Opal—players weren't supposed to take on difficult challenges. When they did, bad things happened.

We'd already gone back to the shack at the beginning once. Why risk restarting again?

Pavio, who had just finished putting all the parchments back in their places, sighed, took the last one back out, and turned around. "Who am I to try to sway your wise decisions? If you choose to travel that way, I shall not stop you. It will be one silver for the etching, please."

Cocking her head to one side, Vanessa glared at me. "Now that settles it."

"Fine," I said. If they wanted to go that way, I wouldn't stop them, but as I opened my Dispenser to pull out my money, Miles grabbed my sleeve.

"What do you *really* think we should do, Lucas?" he asked.

"It doesn't matter what I think," I said.

"Yes, it does. You're our leader." Miles looked more than panicked. Breaking rules was a big thing for him, especially when it meant possibly facing monsters too horrifying to imagine.

"Miles, don't be such a worrier," Vanessa said. "This guy's just trying to scare us."

"And I'm doing a horrible job at it." Pavio held out his palm for payment.

As my coin purse appeared from my Dispenser, I hesitated. Vanessa may have made up her mind, but poor Miles looked sick. I wasn't sure how Jasmine felt, but she wasn't saying anything. Despite Miles's pleas of desperation, I couldn't rock the boat. Losing my parents at a young age and being placed in the foster program had made me really good at avoiding conflict. My opinion had never mattered, and whenever I tried sticking up for myself, it always backfired. Plus, whenever I found myself facing an argument, there was always the looming threat of a Creepers attack.

After paying Pavio an extra silver piece for the additional map, we left the Pathfinder's Pavilion and headed toward the northern gate of Trouble's Landing, which opened directly onto the Goblin Road.

CHAPTER 16

THE GOBLIN
ROAD

Grinding gears thundered as the northern gate—a massive steel door nestled in the wall of the city—sealed closed behind us. I heard the distinct sound of latching as one of the soldiers standing guard locked the door, trapping us outside.

Miles tugged at the handle for good measure, but it wouldn't budge. "What if we change our minds and want to come back in?" he called out.

Partway up the door, a slot opened and a pair of unfriendly eyes appeared. "No return entry this way," the guard grunted. "You may only enter by way of the river. You'll have to go around if you want back in."

Jasmine pulled Miles away from the door. "It's okay," she said. "We don't need to go back."

"Right. The sooner we get to the Hagwoods, the sooner we finish this stupid Quest," Vanessa agreed.

The area outside Trouble's Landing was nothing but a barren wasteland of sandy dunes, scattered volcanic boulders, and warped, leafless shrubs growing meagerly beside a well-worn path of cobblestones. Had it not been littered with so many rotting bones, it might have reminded me of the yellow brick road from the *Wizard of Oz*.

Shielding my eyes, I squinted into the distance. Though hazy on the horizon, I could see the outline of trees poking up a few miles away. If we headed out without further delay, we might be able to make it there before the morning. After walking for about ten minutes without any sign of a goblin, I started feeling better about our decision. Even Miles's mood perked up a bit.

"You seem happier," Jasmine said, noticing the skip in Miles's step.

"I'm not *happy*," he replied, unfurling the scroll containing our Quest. "But I was thinking about our Active Quest Log just now, and you know how it says here to cross the Entry Bridge and traverse the perilous Wollen Woods and then a bunch of other stuff? If we just did everything the log told us to do, we might still be stuck in the woods. It was only after Jasmine used her Grains of Persuasion that we skipped ahead. Maybe we're allowed to make decisions on our own."

I nodded in agreement. "This is *our* Quest, after all, and we're the ones who are supposed to complete it."

"Exactly," he said, snapping his fingers. "We need to make our own decisions. And thanks to Vanessa, we made a pretty good one, right? We're already almost to the Hagwoods. If we had listened to Pavio, we might be getting attacked by all sorts of monsters right now instead of worrying about a bunch of little goblins."

The sound of snapping twigs up ahead got our attention as a small, gangly creature stepped out from behind a bush.

"You're not actually calling me *little*, are you?" Standing on his tippy-toes, the creature strained his neck to peer over Miles's head.

Watching him amble onto the cobblestone path may have been terrifying at first, but before I could stop myself, I laughed in surprise.

"What's so funny?" the goblin asked.

I covered my mouth, trying to stop. "I just noticed your name badge."

Pinned to the goblin's armor, as though he had stopped by on his way back to work, was a badge with the name Barry stamped in bright gold letters.

"Is that really you, Barry?" Miles giggled nervously.

"Who's Barry?" Vanessa mumbled under her breath.

Eyes narrowing into yellow slits, the goblin chuckled right along with us. "Why, yes, it is," he admitted. "Good ol' Barry. Back from my much-deserved break."

"You know this guy?" Jasmine asked.

"He works at Hob & Bogie's shop," I explained. "He's just wearing a costume."

"Ah, but I was getting to that," Barry said. "You see, that's where you're wrong." Tugging on his green, saggy jowls, the goblin chomped his fangs together viciously. "I'm not able to wear my costume here."

"You're not?" Miles's voice cracked.

"Most certainly not," he said, unsheathing his jagged scimitar. "And I'm truly sorry for what I'm about to do, but it's kind of my job."

Then Barry lunged.

A blast of wind swooshed in, followed by a cloud of dust, and the Champion's Catch appeared, freezing the creature in place. Whether it was actually Barry or just an odd trick played by Champion's Quest to spice things up, it didn't matter. Now was not the time for figuring that out—now was the time for slaying a goblin.

On the Die of Fate, it was my number that turned up. It was the first time it had since we'd started the game, which meant I would have the chance to roll the Die of Opportunity. Gripping the edge of the Champion's Catch, I tossed in the die and waited anxiously for it to stop rolling. The angry game piece snarled and hissed as it tumbled across the bottom, eventually settling on the number twelve as the playing card appeared. I knew there had to be more to the cards than just a picture. Flipping it over, I frantically scanned the information on the back.

BLADES OF RETURNING FURY

> When facing down droves of an impossible horde,
> A Champion mustn't only rely on the sword.
> Trust in your aim and trust in the sting,
> And keep your enemies at bay with a sword made of wings.

As the card dissolved, my Gadget rose up from my Dispenser and morphed into a flat, curved piece of metal.

"A sword?" I asked, feeling a tingle of excitement. Except my Gadget didn't look like a sword. It wasn't sharp at all and looked more like a—

"It's a boomerang," Miles said.

"Yeah." I nodded. "A boomerang." I smiled until I realized I had never thrown a boomerang. Would it actually come back to me like they did in the movies?

My thoughts swarmed as I tried to remember Jugger's advice. My Gadget would provide me with exactly what I needed—and the Die of Opportunity was supposed to give me an advantage—but the boomerang really didn't feel like much of an advantage.

"I don't know how to use this," I admitted.

"Well, neither do I," Vanessa snapped, staring down at her Spark in disgust. "What are these things? Guitar strings?"

"It's just one goblin," Jasmine said, gripping her Branch. "We've already fought bigger monsters. I'll just smack him with this."

But even Jasmine had to be missing the point. Her Spade had transformed into the Branch of Barricading, and I wondered whether it was actually intended to be used as a club. With a shrieking howl, however, Barry leapt into action, ending my frantic attempt at formulating a plan. We scattered as the goblin's scimitar carved through the air. Dodging under his swing, Miles looped his Tether around Goon's neck, and the armadillo once again transformed into a tank.

Racing with a full head of steam, Goon charged forward, but as he was about to plow headlong into the goblin, Barry blurred to one side, stuck out the butt of his scimitar, and sent the armadillo rolling. The last rays of sunlight splashed against the steel, and Daroon's Ever-Expandable Armor exploded into pieces. Instantly reduced to miniature size, Goon let out a long, despairing cry before collapsing in a heap.

"Goon!" Miles cried out, scooping up the fallen armadillo in his palms. "Are you okay?"

Goon responded by blowing a loud raspberry. As the last pieces of armor dissolved from his back, the armadillo tottered back under the folds of Miles's cloak. Then Miles's Tether reappeared in his hands, flopping down like a horse's tail.

"The bigger they are, the harder they fall," Barry announced with a satisfied snicker.

"You should have stayed in the ground," Jasmine said, blocking the goblin and swinging out with her Branch as he took a step toward Miles.

"And miss all the fun?" Leaping easily over the strike, Barry snatched the weapon from her hands.

Stunned by his blinding movement, Jasmine failed to dodge, and Barry jabbed her in the arm with his scimitar.

"Don't you have anything better to do than pick on a bunch of kids?" she groaned—and a single Bloodstone on her Vitality Meter winked out.

"But this is what I was hired to do," Barry replied almost apologetically.

Trying to drown out the distractions, I held out my new boomerang, hoping for a miracle. Then I threw it at the goblin. The curvy metal weapon swished through the air like a helicopter. It looked amazing and actually hit Barry on the arm before ricocheting harmlessly away. Why did that always happen when I used my Gadget? The kobold had blocked my stab, my teeth had nearly dislodged from my mouth when I hit Jugger's iron skin with the dagger, and now that stupid boomerang had done about as much damage to the goblin as if I'd snapped him with a wet towel.

"I give up," I said. "I'm the worst Artisan in the world!"

"If only we still had the Field Guide." Sweat dripped down Vanessa's cheeks as she whipped at the goblin with her metal wires. "Maybe we would know what to do with these worthless things."

"Stop slapping me," Barry hissed, reddish welts streaking his knuckles. At least Vanessa seemed to be aggravating the goblin with her Spark.

"Were you not supposed to throw it?" Miles asked me.

"I thought I was," I grumbled.

"But it didn't have blades," he said. "Didn't the clue say it would give your blade wings?"

"Yeah, but . . ." Suddenly my eyes widened. "Miles, that's it!" I had forgotten all about the blades!

Racing toward the goblin, I managed to duck under his swing and snatch my Gadget from where it had landed. Vanessa paused long enough from her whipping to look over her shoulder. It was just the distraction Barry needed, and he snuck in a jab with his scimitar.

"Did you actually *stab* me?" Vanessa gasped, checking her Medallion.

I felt a prickling sensation in my fingers as I searched the boomerang and discovered the button was still centered on one side of the strange contraption. When I pressed it, two blades instantly popped out either end of the weapon.

"Now we're talking!" I cheered.

Rearing back, I eyed my target. "Please work," I pleaded. Then I threw the boomerang at the goblin like a Frisbee. The razor-sharp edges passed right through him as though he were nothing more than a tall blade of grass.

"Oi!" Barry yelled, eyes spinning in surprise as his whole body beginning to fade.

Dizzy and disorientated, the goblin fixed me with a murderous glare. Before he could exact his revenge, my boomerang circled back and struck him once again before returning to my hand. Then Barry burst with an explosion of multicolored sparkles.

I wanted to celebrate, but I wasn't given any time as two more goblins immediately popped out of the ground like a pair of gophers. Oddly enough, they both wore the same dorky

Barry name badge as the first. Flinging my boomerang directly at the nearest goblin, it clipped his arm, causing a yowl of pain, but then it sailed wide and the other batted it out of the air with his club.

"No more of that from . . ." one of the Barry look-a-likes started to say before blinking his eyes in confusion at the sound of strange, strumming music filling the air.

"What's that noise?" I asked.

"They *are* guitar strings!" Vanessa announced. She had somehow stretched the wires down from one end of her Device's handle and had connected them to the outer edge of the circular pan. Her Spark now resembled an odd-looking guitar.

"It's a lute," I said, positively shocked.

"It's a what?" Vanessa vigorously dragged her fingers across the strings, which actually sounded nice, if a little off-key.

Striding forward, Jasmine snatched up her Branch where it had fallen after the first Barry had popped, and plunged it directly into the ground. At once, the Blaridor's Branch of Barricading expanded in either direction, shooting up like a rocket and weaving into a wall of spiky thorns. One of the goblins squealed as he crashed against the barrier, green sparkles showering out from his chest.

Next, Miles took his turn. Gripping his Tether tightly, he looped the leather tassels, twirling them into a long tube.

"I really don't like goblins very much," Miles grunted before holding up his modified Tether to his lips and blowing a single note through the leather tube. What happened next could only be described as absolute insanity. The ground began to shake, fissuring and rumbling as steam belched from cracks that widened into a hole. And then a massive bullfrog leapt out of the hole, instantly swallowing one of the stupefied goblins in a single gulp. A second bullfrog, heeding the call of Miles's new-fangled whistle-like contraption, took off after the other goblin. The two creatures shrank in the distance, the goblin screaming in terror and the frog hot on his heels.

"It was like there was this voice inside my head telling me how to use these," Vanessa said, still strumming her makeshift guitar. The Strings of Spiriting had turned her Spark into a magical musical instrument.

"And the moment you started playing, I knew exactly what I was supposed to do with my Tether," Miles said.

"And my Spade," Jasmine added.

"You need to play that during every battle," I insisted. With Vanessa as our Luminary, we would be unstoppable.

A shrill cry filled our ears as a thousand greenish heads with glowing yellow eyes popped up all over the place, like oblong potatoes. There must have been miles of buried trenches beneath us. These goblins seemed unfazed by their fallen comrades.

"Fresh meat, fresh meat, fresh meat!" the goblins chanted, scrambling out of the ground. From what I could tell, every single one of them wore Barry's name badge, and the sound of their chanting echoed across the barren wasteland.

"Uh . . . so do you want me to start playing again?" Vanessa shouted above their hideous cries.

"I don't think it's going to matter whether you play that or not," Jasmine said.

"Me either." Grabbing up my boomerang and cramming it into my belt, I turned toward the city.

Huffing and panting, we ran as fast as we could, all the while looking over our shoulders as the horde of Barry goblins wasted no time smashing through Jasmine's barricade.

"Please, let us in!" Miles called out, smacking against the sealed gate.

"I told you, you can't come back this way," the guard objected, peering out once again from the slot. "It's too dangerous to—" His voice sputtered when he saw the charging goblins advancing toward us. "Oh, dear," he gulped and then shouted, "You're on your own!"

The slot snapped shut, and no matter how hard we pounded; he wouldn't open it back up again.

"Lucas, what do we do?" Jasmine demanded, grabbing my arm in desperation.

The Barry horde was closing in. They looked hungry and wild, and they would be upon us in a matter of moments. Maybe we couldn't die and those monsters wouldn't actually hurt us, but if we got smashed back to the beginning a second time in a row, I knew we would never recover.

"The key," Miles breathed, pointing at the gate's keyhole and frantically looking at Vanessa. "We need your key."

Swallowing, Vanessa's eyes widened with a mixture of shock and confusion, but then she seemed to understand. Opening her Dispenser, she summoned her gift from the Gilded Gargoyle—the Unlocker's Skeleton Key of Unlocking.

Determined to buy Vanessa a little time, I turned back and unleashed my boomerang at the nearest cluster of goblins. The spiraling blade popped four of the creatures into plumes of colorful smoke. But then the weapon vanished into the mass of green bodies and dropped out of sight. I felt a pang of sadness knowing that had probably ended my use of the Blades of Returning Fury, but then I heard the satisfying click of Vanessa's key twisting in the lock as the northern gate rumbled open despite the guards' efforts to keep it closed.

CHAPTER 17

THE EXPLORATORY GUILD OF THE NORTHERN REACHES

"What did I tell you?" Angrily twisting a lever, the guard shifted the massive bolt back into place, once again sealing the gate shut. "Did I not say you would have to go around?"

"Um, we're sorry?" Vanessa fired back. "Would you rather us get eaten by a million goblins?"

The guard's eyes shifted between us as he fixed his crooked helmet. "It's the *Goblin* Road. You'd have to be an idiot not to know what you were getting yourself into."

I didn't know why he was so upset. Only a handful of goblins had squeezed through the gate before he had managed to close it, and those had been so awestruck by the city lights, the guard had easily dispatched them with his sword.

"Mark my words, I won't allow you through here a second time," he grumbled, returning to his post.

"I know that was crazy stressful, and maybe I shouldn't be so excited, but did you guys see me use that boomerang?" I asked the others. I beamed down at my Gadget, which had reappeared, along with Jasmine's Spade, just moments after we had entered the gate.

Jasmine nodded, a faint smile forming on her lips. "Turns out, I wasn't supposed to use my Spade as a big stick, huh?"

"I think we're finally figuring out how to play," I said. Sure, we had just almost gotten killed by a billion goblins all named Barry, but this felt like a huge breakthrough.

"What do you think will happen to those frogs?" Miles asked, his countenance dropping. "They're still out there, beyond the gate."

"I think your frogs will be fine," Jasmine said. "They swallow goblins in one bite, remember?"

After tossing Pavio's etching into a brazier of hot coals next to the guard post, I pulled out the second map, the one containing the Merchant Road, and stretched it across a nearby bench.

"According to this, we head east," I said, glancing around at the others. I felt invigorated. "The Merchant Road runs right alongside the city."

A single moment of silence passed before Vanessa slapped a hand down across the map. "You're not seriously suggesting we go right now, are you?"

"What else would we do?" I asked, rearing back in alarm.

Sticking out her chin, Vanessa's eyes quivered hotly, as though they might shoot lasers. "I need some time to myself. I'm tired. We haven't slept at all."

"I'm not that tired," Miles said. "I wonder if getting sent back to the beginning of the game counted as a power nap?"

"Miles, don't interrupt," Vanessa said. "The point is, I need a break. And if I don't get one, I'm going to be really difficult to be around."

"Geez, okay," I said, shrinking away. As if Vanessa wasn't already really difficult to be around.

THE DIE OF DESTINY

"I agree," Jasmine chimed in, running her fingers through her hair. "We have been going almost nonstop since we got here."

"And we could find out some important stuff right here in the city," Miles suggested. "Someone has to know more about the Hagwoods."

Folding the map, I heaved a sigh of relief. "That sounds great to me."

Taking a break to explore Trouble's Landing seemed like a brilliant idea. According to Jugger, the city was a neutral zone, and since we wouldn't be in any danger unless we went looking for a fight, we decided to split up. Miles hadn't been too keen on the idea, but we promised to stay close by, and it was the only way to cover the most ground. We agreed to separate to look for clues and gather information and meet up later at Torbrick's Tavern, near the center of town.

"Don't forgot to ask around about the Enchanted Mists," I reminded Vanessa and Jasmine as they headed down opposite paths. "And look for supplies too."

"We will," Jasmine assured me.

"Yes, yes, we know." Vanessa waved her hand. "This place is like your kingdom, isn't it? Go and enjoy yourself. We'll see you in a couple of hours."

"Are you going to be okay?" I glanced at Miles after the girls had left.

Miles nodded half-heartedly. "I do have Goon, so I won't be entirely alone," he said. "And if you need me, I'll be at Carmen's Toffee and Candy Floss. It's just down on Knocking Thrush Avenue."

"How do you know that?" I asked, raising an eyebrow.

Miles pulled a pamphlet from his pocket. "I took this from

Pavio's. The sign said, 'Free—take one,' so I did. It lists the top ten must-visit spots in all of Trouble's Landing. Did you know they have an aquarium here?"

"I don't remember seeing any free pamphlets," I said.

"They were right near the door," he explained. "I don't know what candy floss is, but it sounds yummy."

Gazing at the glossy pamphlet, I recognized a name of one of the shops halfway down the list, not too far from where we were standing, and decided to make my way toward it.

After we said our goodbyes, Miles shuffled away down a side road.

· ◆ ● ◆ ·

Wandering in and out of the shops looking for supplies wasn't proving too successful. I knew we needed food, but most of the places on the north end of the city sold only random items like boots or arrows or a dozen different sorts of telescopes.

At one of the shops, I did find a talking plant sitting behind the counter. There was nothing else for sale. No other customers or employees, just a massive Venus flytrap promising to pay me in sap if I fed it forty Liplop beetles. When I asked what a Liplop beetle was, the plant hissed at me until I left.

"I wouldn't buy that if I were you," I heard a voice say as I examined a fancy waterskin at an outdoor booth.

Glancing up, I noticed a teenage boy standing nearby eating an apple. Maybe a year older than I was, the boy could've easily passed as someone from my middle school.

"Most of those sprout horrible leaks," he said, pointing at the waterskin. "Before you know it, you'll be all wet and thirsty."

"Thanks for the tip," I said, placing the item back on the shelf.

"Are you hungry?" the boy asked, holding up a second apple. "It just so happens I have a spare."

Feeling a little wary of his offer, I shook my head, politely declining. I may have been hungry, but I wasn't about to accept food from some strange kid.

"You can have it if you want," he said. "What am I supposed to do with two apples?"

"Eat them both," I suggested, perhaps a little harshly.

Maybe he was just trying to be nice, but as I moved away from the booth, I picked up my pace. I didn't feel intimidated, at least not yet, but there didn't appear to be many people near the north end of town, and I didn't want to take any chances.

"I couldn't help but notice that peculiar-looking tool you have hanging on your belt," the boy said, hurrying to catch up. "That wouldn't by chance be a . . . Gadget, now would it?"

The question stopped me cold in my tracks, and I instinctively slipped my fingers around the handle of my Gadget. "Why?" I asked, eyes narrowing. "Who are you?"

The boy immediately retreated, holding out his palms as though surrendering. "No, sorry, I didn't mean any disrespect. I'm not looking for a fight, if that's what you think." After sticking the spare apple in his vest pocket, he wiped his hands across his chest. "My name's Fawson. Fawson Bendfollower, that is."

"Lucas," I replied.

My name seemed to momentarily register something in his eyes, but he shook it away. "Anyway, I'm a member of the Exploratory Guild of the Northern Reaches. Ever heard of us?"

Loosening my grip on my Gadget, I shook my head.

"Well, that's all right," Fawson said. "Can't expect everyone to know of us, can I? But we are a real guild and what we do is actually quite impressive. We make the maps here. All of them."

"So like Pavio?" I asked.

That prompted a loud snort. "Pavio? That stuffed shirt? Nah, he just copies the maps we make and then slings insults at anyone stopping by his Pavilion."

"No kidding," I said. "He's tons of fun."

"Oh, you've been there, then? He made you an etching, did he?"

"Two, actually," I admitted. Though one of them was now burned to ashes—for good reason.

After looking boggled, an expression of understanding appeared on Fawson's face. "My goodness." Covering his mouth, he lowered his voice to a whisper. "You're Lucas Silver, aren't you? Of the Wild Crows?"

I didn't know how to respond because this was the second time someone had recognized me. It was almost as if the members of my Band were legends, though we hadn't done anything legendary yet.

"Are you on a Quest right now?" Fawson asked.

"I mean, uh . . . sort of, I guess," I said with a shrug.

"Say no more, say no more. I am so sorry to have troubled you. You have a wonderful day." Shoulders drooping, Fawson walked away.

"Hey, wait up," I called after him. "What did you want to talk to me about?"

Kicking at the dirt with his heels, Fawson glanced back, looking embarrassed. "It's just . . . I'm a recruiter for the guild," he said. "You see? I've been tasked with finding some muscle to accompany our group on our next journey north."

"Muscle?" Scrunching my nose, I started to snicker. This

was a first. Lucas Silver, bodybuilder. Not a chance in the world that I'd have ever heard that comment back in Bentford.

"Perhaps they're well hidden, but yeah." Fawson chuckled as well. "You're a Champion, aren't you? And that's a real Gadget. Bet you've seen some things and fought some real nasty monsters along the way, haven't you?"

"Not exactly," I replied. "Nothing too dangerous. Just some goblins, dwarves, a few giant scorpions . . ."

"Scorpions?" Fawson's eyes nearly bugged out of their sockets. "You've fought scorpions? What are they like?"

"Mean and poisonous." I thought back to my unfortunate run-in with the scorpion nest and, more specifically, their stingers. "They're exactly like the tiny ones—except they're as big as a horse."

Fawson reared back in alarm. "*Tiny* ones?"

"Yeah, you know?" I held up my thumb and forefinger, and Fawson almost turned green.

"I didn't realize they came in miniature size," he gasped. "Again, I'm sorry for even asking you. You're obviously on an important Quest, which I'm sure makes my task seem like a waste of your time. Here I was offering you an apple when you've probably made enough gold to buy a whole apple orchard."

If only that had been the case. I had yet to see a single piece of gold on this adventure. My Band of Wild Crows barely had enough money to survive.

"However, if you do manage to finish your Quest soon, and if you're in need of some extra money," Fawson continued, "the Exploratory Guild of the Northern Reaches sets out from the Highwater Crossing at the end of the week. We have a big boat, plenty of room, and it would be an absolute honor to have you join us. Lucas Silver of the Wild Crows. Wow."

Without another word, Fawson hurried away.

Had I not been already committed to slaying some mythical beast named Foyos, I might have considered the offer. Fawson seemed like a nice kid, and traveling north with the Exploratory Guild as their hired muscle seemed like something right up my alley.

Blinking in shock, I caught myself and shook my head. Had I really just referred to Fawson as a kid? That boy was taller and thicker than I was and at least a year older, maybe even more. And yet, for reasons I couldn't understand, Fawson had actually been impressed by me.

I may not have been the most skilled warrior, but I was starting to figure out how to act like a Champion. Maybe I was cut out for this adventuring thing after all. Participating in role-playing games had allowed me to fight monsters—all on paper—but I knew about their strengths and weaknesses. I understood about guilds and side quests, and I could follow a map easily enough. It was difficult to explain, but Champion's Quest was starting to feel more and more familiar to me. That is, until I wandered out from the side road and stepped back onto the main strip and the night lit up with a blinding neon light.

CHAPTER 18

BARGAIN PRICES AT MADAME C.'S

An enormous pink sign flashed above the entryway of Madame C.'s Armory and Potion Parlor. Balloons, in all shapes and sizes—one as large as an elephant—bounced lazily around the building. On either side of the entryway, huge spotlights shot columns into the sky, illuminating the stars overhead, while choppy jazz music blasted out from inside the store.

Madame C.'s Armory and Potion Parlor may have been listed on Miles's pamphlet, but it looked like nothing I would have ever expected to find in Trouble's Landing—just when I thought things had become familiar in Champion's Quest.

"You've got to be kidding me," I muttered, screwing my face up in disbelief.

Where had this store come from? Most of the other shops, with the exception of the one with the giant Venus flytrap had been small, some no bigger than a cart, and if they had been decorated at all, it was with cast-iron horseshoes or smoldering candles.

An old-timey red-white-and-blue barber pole turned at the top of the marble staircase leading up to the entrance. As I walked up the steps, the doors opened automatically as though

I were about to enter a grocery store, and a familiar female voice called out as I stepped through the opening.

"Ah, Lucas. I wondered when you would be stopping by."

"Madge?" I asked, doing a double-take to make sure it wasn't my imagination. "What are you doing here?"

Madge Crockery hovered behind a long display counter, counting back change to a family of fauns. Curtseying, she pressed her hand against her heart. "Madame C. at your service," she said.

No longer in pixie form, Madge had grown significantly since last I saw her. She still had on her bulky winter coat, along with a pair of woolly mittens and earmuffs, but it was the bottom half of her body that shocked me the most. Smoke trailed down from her waist, coiling into a golden urn on the back counter.

"You're a genie?" I asked, after the fauns had completed their transaction and wandered away.

"No, my lad. Have you not been paying attention? I told you before, I'm one of a kind," Madge held up one mittened hand. "I am whatever I choose to be."

I blinked in surprise. Of all the creatures I had bumped into so far in the game, she had to be the most impressive.

"And you run this shop?" My eyes drifted around the store.

Madge shrugged. "Only on weekdays. I *do* have my own life." Shivering, she took a moment to blow into her cupped hands. "Pardon me. It's a bit colder here than I'm used to."

"So, are you like all-powerful? Do you grant wishes and stuff?" I asked, unable to keep my focus off the urn and Madge's trail of cosmic smoke funneling into it.

Guffawing like a donkey, Madge slapped the spot where her knee would have been had there been a pair of knees connected below her waist. "Wish granting? All-powerful? Your head's going to explode," she said in between boisterous fits of laughter. "Never mind me. How goes your Quest?"

"Okay, I guess," I grumbled.

Madge drifted away from the counter, and when she returned, she held a pewter mug filled to the brim with a fizzy caramel-colored drink. "You look like you could use that."

"What is it?" I asked, warily sniffing the foam. "It's not like . . . ale, is it?"

"Ale?" She snorted. "It's only root beer with a scoop of butterscotch ice cream. And it's on the house."

That was all I needed to hear. Tipping back the mug, I downed half the contents in one greedy gulp. It was the best root beer float I'd ever tasted.

"Why does your store look like it belongs in Las Vegas?" I asked, muffling a burp.

"I *love* Las Vegas," Madge admitted. "I go there whenever I'm able. Don't blame me for bringing a little piece of home along with me into the game."

"A little piece of home? Where are you from?"

"I call all places I love to visit home. Including Bentford," she said.

"You love Bentford?" I asked, shocked.

"Of course! You don't?"

For the next half hour, Madge and I shared a drink. I hardly knew her, but discovering her in this place felt like chatting with an old friend. From time to time, Madge would break away from the conversation to help a customer with a purchase and then return to listen. I filled her in on all we had been through so far on our Quest, and she gobbled up every juicy detail, filling the shop with laughter at our many mishaps.

"Didn't I say you'd figure it out eventually?" Madge asked after I'd finished telling her about our short trip down the Goblin Road.

"You're joking, right?" We'd been in the game for almost three days and barely made it to half the checkpoints on our Active Quest Log.

"These things take time," she said. "Besides, you've only had one toes-up so far. That's impressive."

"Toes-up?" I wiped the last of frothy ice cream from my upper lip.

"You know?" Madge clamped her eyes shut and stuck out her tongue. "Toes-up in the ground. Dead. Worm food. The grave robber's gravy. It all means the same thing."

"Yuck," I said, disgusted.

"The important thing is you've made it here and you've learned a ton. Now—can I give you some advice?"

I nodded eagerly. "Yeah, of course."

Snatching my empty mug away, Madge began wiping it out with a towel. "If you intend to win, you need to truly step into your role."

"What do you mean? I *have* finally figured out my Gadget. I think." I knew there was loads more to learn about my Hero's Device, but I felt as though I were stepping into my role.

"I'm not talking about that," she said. "You didn't *want* to take the Goblin Road, did you? You let the others convince you to do something you knew would end poorly, and you didn't put up much of a fuss." Bobbing over to the far end of the counter, her trail stretching away from the urn, Madge swept several empty glass bottles into a trash can. "That's not very Band Leader–like, now is it?"

"I'm trying," I said, her words stinging a bit. "But Vanessa's so . . . so . . ."

"Stubborn? Bullheaded? Determined to get you killed whether she intends to or not?"

"Yes. All of that." I brought my palm down on the counter.

"Doesn't mean she won't listen to you. They all will, but you need to stop being afraid of letting everyone down. Or of letting yourself down. You're *supposed* to make mistakes. Being a Band Leader isn't an easy task, but it's an important one—and you've been given this role for a reason."

"No I wasn't." I sighed in frustration. "It was just a coincidence."

"The sooner you realize your potential, the sooner you'll start seeing progress. Now, obviously you saw a need to stop by my store. What can Madame C. supply you with?"

Less than ten minutes later, I stepped back from the counter with a plastic shopping bag in each hand emblazoned with the Madame C. logo and overflowing with supplies.

"I can't afford all this," I said, seeing no point in checking my coin purse.

Madge gave me a baffled expression. "You mean to tell me you don't have a spare silver in your inventory? I could loan you one, I suppose. Put this on your tab . . ."

"One silver?"

She had to be pulling my leg. The ration packs alone were six silver each, and Madge had stuffed my shopping bags with at least two for each member of my Band. And a torch, a fancy compass, and a simplified version of the "Compendium of Monsters" from the Field Guide on a laminated, double-sided parchment. Miles was going to flip.

"I told you I had fair prices and wouldn't lead you astray. Of course, I do swing a deal for Champions on occasion—particularly those I like," Madge said with a wink. I paid her the one silver. What a bargain.

CHAPTER 19

NOT THE ONLY ONES IN THE GAME

A fight broke out across the room between three orcs, one of them missing an ear, as the four of us watched timidly from our booth. Wrestling and growling, the orcs smashed chairs over each other's thick skulls. Contrary to what Jugger had told us, Torbrick's Tavern seemed anything but a friendly spot.

At least a hundred arrows were stuck in the walls, and the floor was covered with a sticky residue that made a *thwopping* squelch when I peeled my boots off it. The menu had only three items: raw mutton, filthy water—probably from a mop bucket—and Torbrick's very own homemade mead. There was no telling what he used to make the drink, but the bottoms of all the tankards looked as though they had been warped by acid. Then there was Torbrick himself.

Before that night, I had never met a bugbear in any of my safe role-playing games. For starters, they weren't actually *bears* at all, but rather giant apelike creatures with bloodshot eyes, mouths filled with rows upon rows of fangs, and backs covered in coarse black hair that stood on end like porcupine quills.

"Four waters," Torbrick grunted, slamming the mugs of warm, stagnant liquid onto our table. The bartender had a steady stream of drool dripping from the corner of his mouth. "You best be leaving here soon."

"Why?" Jasmine asked. "We're paying customers."

Torbrick's eyes narrowed. "Water's cheap. And what is *that* you're eating?" He glared at Jasmine's package of wafers lying on the table, the ones I had purchased from Madge's shop.

"Just a snack," Jasmine replied.

"Either buy something worth my time or get moving." One of the orcs mistakenly shattered a chair leg against the bugbear's back, but Torbrick hardly flinched.

"A bugbear has twenty Strength, twelve Speed, nine Wisdom, and thirty-two Vitality," Miles whispered after Tolbrick had returned to the counter. "This is a scary place. Maybe we should leave and find someplace else."

"Are you memorizing the info from your monster compendium?" I asked.

"Yes," Miles said matter-of-factly, "just in case I lose it again. A bugbear's preferred weapon is a war hammer," he continued. "They're pretty nasty. I wouldn't want to make him mad."

"He's already mad," Jasmine said, keeping her voice low.

"Speaking of nasty, you haven't seen Jugger by chance, have you?" I asked, peering around the room. Other than the violent orcs and Torbrick, the tavern looked empty.

Jasmine and Vanessa both nodded grimly.

"He left just before you arrived. We followed him from a safe distance. Now he's down the road," Vanessa said, lowering her voice ominously, "branding salamanders."

"Branding salamanders? That's weird," I said. "What's he using? A paper clip?" I was trying to imagine Jugger wielding a red-hot poker against a tiny lizard.

Miles tapped the compendium, showing me an image of a

snakelike creature with a long tail, dangerous claws, and about the length of a school bus.

"They're not those kinds of salamanders." He gulped.

Maybe it was time we moved on from Torbrick's before Jugger dropped by for a post-branding mead. He'd specifically recommended this place to lay low, but I was starting to think he'd set us up.

"So, what did you all find out?" I asked.

I'd already told them about my conversation with Madge, and they'd been impressed with the supplies she'd given us. Even Vanessa seemed grateful.

"I didn't find out much," Jasmine admitted, hunching down next to me, her hood casting a shadow across her face. "No one would give me any information, and when I started asking about Faylinn, people got a little agitated."

"You got into a fight, didn't you?" Miles asked, looking slightly worried.

"I did, but it's not what you think." Jasmine pulled an item from her Dispenser and tossed it onto the table. Lying on its side, the small object looked like a spinning top. "It's called the Token of Necessity," she explained. "If ever we find ourselves in trouble, I can spin this token and help will come."

"When did you get this?" Miles asked, his forehead crinkling.

Jasmine raised her eyebrows. "Oh, just after I helped that poor lady get her chicken back from the thief."

More violence broke out from across the room between the party of orcs, but we barely noticed the distraction.

"Don't look at me like that," Jasmine said, blushing. "It's no big deal. I didn't even have to roll the Die of Opportunity. I only threatened the thief with my Spade, maybe roughed him up a little, and then he dropped the chicken and ran. I just felt bad for not helping her. This might be a game, but it doesn't hurt to be kind."

"Aw, look at you." Reaching over, Vanessa squeezed Jasmine's hand. "You're turning into a lovely young lady."

"Get off me," Jasmine said, jerking away. "Anyway, it turns out it was worth it. That lady gave me two gold pieces as payment—and this." She plucked the token from the table and put it back in her Dispenser.

"Oh, man." Miles tried smiling, but he ended up looking more gassy than anything else. "Lucas bought supplies. Jasmine saved a chicken. All I did was eat a lot of sweets. I wasn't going to, but candy floss is *delicious*. I was too busy eating to ask any important questions."

"It's okay, Miles," I said. "I kind of figured we wouldn't learn much about our Quest." Still, Jasmine's prize had definitely made splitting up worthwhile.

"You're not going to ask me what I discovered, are you?" Vanessa asked, her nostrils flaring. "Hmm. Doesn't surprise me, but I'll tell you anyway. For starters, there's a pathway through the Enchanted Mists, but the entry only appears at sunset. The mists go in for about a kilometer or so into the Hagwoods, and after that, the forest clears up enough to make our way through. However, if you wander off the path at any time while trying to pass through the mists, you'll end up going insane." She swirled the muddy contents of her tankard. "The undead horde isn't really made up of undead. It's just a bunch of poor heroes who got lost in the mists and fell under Faylinn's spell." When she finished talking, Vanessa gave a satisfied sigh and casually gazed at the wall.

"Who told you all that?" I asked, looking at the others in astonishment.

"Philip," Vanessa replied. "He was a ton of help."

When I frowned, Jasmine rolled her eyes. "He's some guy she met shopping earlier. I saw them talking to each other."

"He's not just *some guy*. Philip's a soldier, and he's cute. And he gave me these." Opening her hand, Vanessa revealed a trio of star-shaped beads resting on her palm.

"More jewelry?" I asked, squinting down at the unusual objects.

Vanessa sneered. "You're kidding, right? What would I even wear them with?" Picking up one of the beads, she rotated the object in the crackling torchlight. "This is called a Surge. And I have one for each of you."

"Uh, thanks?" I said, as she dropped the bead into my hand. "What are we supposed to do with it?"

"Stick it on your Medallion and it will add one extra Bloodstone to your Vitality Meter." Leaning back against the bench, Vanessa reveled in our bewildered expressions.

"Shut up," Jasmine said. "It can't do that."

Shrugging, Vanessa pulled out her own Advancement Medallion and showed us the row of red Bloodstones, which now numbered eleven.

"H—How?" I asked, baffled.

"Don't act so shocked," she said. "Just because I'm older, prettier, and *way* more popular than the three of you combined, it doesn't mean I can't contribute."

"Why would a complete stranger give us something so valuable? This feels like a scam," Jasmine said.

"Philip would never do that," Vanessa replied. "Believe me, we can trust him."

As we eagerly added the Surge to our Advancement Medallions, I couldn't help but notice how quiet the inside of the tavern had become. The unsettling silence filled the room until the front counter suddenly exploded. We immediately covered our heads and ducked, knocking our mugs of water across the table.

At first, I figured the orcs had steered their scuffle toward the bar, but then I caught sight of Torbrick wading through the demolished pieces of wood directly toward us, wielding his deadly war hammer.

"I told you *Champions* to leave," the bugbear snarled, his footsteps rattling the whole tavern. "You should have listened."

Taking a time out from strangling each other on the floor, the orcs sprang to their feet. They howled ravenously, grabbing their swords and scrambling over to join Torbrick. There may have only been three orcs and one bugbear, but we were clearly outmatched. I felt anxious and sick, and my stomach started turning in on itself. It seemed like we had giant targets on our backs because every creature in this crazy world was out to get us. Torbrick's heavy footfalls thundered against the floor as he lumbered right up, preparing to attack.

"Where is it?" Miles demanded. "Where's the Champion's Catch?"

I had been wondering the same thing and waiting for time to stand still to at least give us a chance. Something wasn't right because Torbrick wasn't stopping and neither were those orcs.

Feeling trapped beneath the table, I leapt up onto the bench. The others tried squeezing out, but none of them could unwedge themselves in time. It was just me against the four hulking monsters. Grabbing my Gadget, my pulse echoing in my eardrums, I was about to press the button when Torbrick shot out a claw and snagged hold of my cloak, pulling me right up to his snarling, horrid-smelling mouth.

"What's the meaning of this?" a voice demanded from the front of the tavern.

Helpless and trapped, I waited for Torbrick to chomp me to bits, but the bugbear paused for a moment, his eyes shifting to one side. "Mind your business," he growled, replying to the stranger. "Else I'll be sending *you* to an early grave too."

I heard the crisp twang of unsheathing steel, and I chanced a quick glance over the bugbear's shoulder at a woman, possibly in her early twenties, standing in the doorway. With her pale skin, long blonde hair braided over one shoulder, and a jeweled headband lighting up the poorly lit tavern, the woman looked like an elf.

"I don't appreciate vain threats," she said. With the clinking of heavy chain mail, the woman took a step into the tavern, a gleaming longsword in her outstretched hands. "So unless you intend to back up your claim, I suggest you step away from that table."

With his eyes still fixed on me, Torbrick screwed up his face in rage and wobbled around. "You picked the wrong time for a drink, stranger. Now you've made me—" He turned his head, and sputtering, unable to complete his sentence, the bugbear immediately dropped his war hammer and released his grip on my cloak. "Oh, Ms. Avery, I . . . I . . . didn't know it was you."

"And I didn't come alone," she replied as another figure stepped up behind her. With his dark skin and scraggly goatee, the man looked like a college student, but one wearing a horned helmet and covered in plate armor.

"Not Carl too." Torbrick's booming voice became a pathetic

whisper as he released his hold on my robe and dropped to his knees. The orcs behind him followed the bugbear's lead, until all four monsters knelt on the floor, begging for their lives.

Lowering my Gadget in confusion, I tried to figure out why Torbrick seemed so afraid. The strangers may have looked tough, but they weren't *that* tough. Even with his armor, I imagined Torbrick could have easily folded Carl in half.

"My . . . my deepest apologies, madame," Torbrick stammered, bowing his thick noggin and spreading his arms in surrender. "I would've never intentionally threatened you. I mistook you for someone—" He stopped short as Avery confidently strode forward, jabbing the pointy end of her longsword under the bugbear's chin.

"You will clean up this mess," she demanded as though scolding a young child. "You will get us fresh food and drink and not that garbage you normally feed your customers, and you will leave these people alone. Is that understood?"

"Yes, of course," Torbrick's jowls blubbered as he vigorously nodded his head. "That's what I was about to do. Only having a little fun. Never meant to take it too far."

"That's enough," Avery said. Torbrick clamped his mouth shut. She glared at the orcs. "You three look familiar. Don't I know you from somewhere?"

One of the creatures instinctively grabbed the spot where his ear had once been. Then, squealing like pigs, the orcs scrabbled on all fours over the top of each other and raced out of the tavern.

"That was fun," Carl said, folding his arms and leaning against the tavern wall. "You just scared away the entertainment."

"Cool it, Carl," Avery replied. "You really need to be more careful with who you show *that* to," she said, pointing at my

Advancement Medallion after Torbrick had retreated behind the bashed-in counter. "Someone should have warned you monsters in this part of the city will jump at the chance to slay a Champion." She slid her sword into the scabbard at her waist. "Those Medallions are a dead giveaway."

Too late, I remembered Jugger had warned us about that.

"Thanks for your help," Jasmine said. Scooching over on the bench, she made room for me, and I crawled back into my seat.

"Don't mention it. I'm always willing to lend a hand to fellow Champions."

Fellow Champions? I looked around at the others, not sure if I had understood the warrior woman.

"Thought you were the only ones?" Avery asked, her lips pulling into an affectionate smile. Tugging on the gold chain draped around her neck, she revealed the top edge of her own Advancement Medallion. "My name's Avery McDonald, and I'm the leader of our Band. We call ourselves the Orc Slayers. I can't tell you how delightful it is to meet new friends."

CHAPTER 20

QUARRELING
WIZARDS

"Will there be anything else, madame?" Keeping his eyes glued to the floor, Torbrick placed a humongous roasted turkey on our table. Juicy meat and cornbread stuffing spilled over the edges of the platter.

After dunking his head into a trough outside to remove the smell as per Avery's instruction, the bugbear had delivered us a buffet of delicious food. Mashed potatoes and gravy, pistachio cream-filled pastries, and steaming buttered rolls. Torbrick had to slide an extra table over next to ours just to hold it all.

"Yes, Torbrick. I would like a carafe of pomegranate juice, please, and some of Carmen's candy floss should do the trick," Avery replied. "Have you tried it yet?" She tilted her head toward me.

Miles nodded eagerly.

"Oh, and I'd like a spiced cider while you're out," Carl added.

"Uh . . . uh . . . pomegranate juice, candy floss, and a . . . a spiced cider." Torbrick scribbled the items on a crinkled piece of paper. "Very well, I shall be back in a jiffy," he announced, studying his list. "Though might I just say . . . it seems an odd request for pomegranate juice. I doubt any business sells it and certainly not at this hour."

"It's the Festival of Bonnie Barters, Torbrick. I'm sure you'll find a way," Avery said, leveling her eyes at the beast.

"Yes, well, I meant no business around *here*," he clarified, looking hopeful as he swirled his clawed finger in the air.

"Then I suppose you'll have to venture farther north in the city."

Torbrick paled. "North? What, with all that merriment and happiness going on all about? I don't really want to . . ."

Avery cleared her throat. "Should I give you a reminder of what happens to bugbears who defy me?"

Torbrick hastily shook his head.

"Then scoot," she demanded

Without another peep, Torbrick skulked out the door.

"This is amazing," Vanessa said, slicing into a piece of turkey oozing with juices. "You didn't have to do all this for us. I'm not complaining, of course."

"Yeah," Miles agreed, his cheeks crammed with at least three buttered rolls. "This has to be expensive."

"Oh, it definitely is," Avery replied. "But we won't be paying, and neither will you. Not after how cruelly he treated you."

"Okay, I just have to know. How did you do that?" I asked, swallowing a bite of turkey and wiping my mouth with the back of my hand. "Torbrick was terrified of you."

"It comes with the territory," Avery said, sharing a look with Carl. "Throughout our Quests, we've developed a reputation around these parts. Torbrick may be a slobbering idiot, but he's no fool."

For the next little while, we stuffed our faces with as much food as we could handle while Avery and Carl shared amazing tales from their adventures. They had seen it all, had been all over the map, and had slain many impressive monsters. Sea monsters, vampires, the Quavering Queen of the Wolves—that story had us all on the edge of our seats. Before they had been drawn to the tavern by all the commotion, Avery and Carl had been on their way to the stables near the east end of the city to meet the other members of their Band. They were on a Quest at that very moment, and, just like us, had been gathering supplies before setting out.

Eventually, Torbrick returned and began clearing the plates off our table. He lumbered around the tavern, dragging a broom and dustpan through the debris.

"Now, it's your turn to tell us your stories," Carl said.

"We don't have any stories," Vanessa replied. "This is our first Quest."

Avery's eyes narrowed. "Don't be modest. You've made it to Trouble's Landing. That's no easy feat. Surely, you've encountered something worthwhile."

Grudgingly, we shared our pathetic tale of running from dwarves and giant scorpions. We told them about our Quest and our struggles to travel to the Hagwoods. They acted interested, but they were both Emerald Champions—level six—which meant not only had they been playing Champion's Quest for months, maybe even more than a year, but they had enough experience to travel down the Goblin Road if they wanted to.

"But we would never take that road," Avery insisted. "The goblin horde is endless. It's the result of a wicked spell. Even if you had an army at your disposal, you could never vanquish them all."

"Good to know," I said, eyes flitting awkwardly to the others.

Opening up her Dispenser, Avery pulled out a strange bird-like device that she placed at the center of the table. Like a wooden toy with hinges and springs, the bird's head bobbed up and down like a seesaw.

"I hope you don't mind," she said. "I just don't want that scoundrel hearing any more of our conversation. Bugbears have a tendency to be nosy."

"What *is* that?" Jasmine leaned in close, studying Avery's device.

"It mutes our conversation from prying ears," she explained.

I then noticed how the grunts and swishing sounds of Torbrick's sweeping had suddenly grown distorted in the background. Avery's device had surrounded our table with a sort of invisible force field, preventing the monster from listening in.

"Did you win that from the Gifting Meadow?" I asked.

"I made this," she answered, chuckling.

"Made it?" I wondered aloud. "How?"

Avery fiddled with her braid. "That's what I do, Lucas. I'm an Artisan, just like you."

At that moment, I spotted the familiar Gadget attached to a loop on Avery's belt. She was an actual Artisan like me. No, not like me. We weren't similar in any way. Avery was braver, more experienced, and knew things about her Gadget I might never fully understand. Like Jasmine, Carl was the Orc Slayers' Harvester, though he had moved way beyond simply hurling dirt clods at opponents. Within a few minutes, Carl had taught Jasmine a trick with her Spade. He called it "mudding," and with just a flick of his wrist, he could turn a patch of solid ground into a swampy mush.

"Have you ever given much thought to who else might be playing this game? And I'm not talking about my Band of Orc Slayers either," Avery said, the seesawing bird continuing to peck at the table. "Where do you think the cards come from?"

"What cards?" Vanessa asked.

"Certainly you've noticed them by now," Carl said. "The cards that appear in the Champion's Catch after you roll the Die of Opportunity."

"I have," I replied. The cards had only lasted a few moments before dissolving, but they were impossible to forget.

"Those cards are just one way in which they manipulate the game. From what I've discovered, there are multiple decks in Champion's Quest from which they draw." Avery traced her finger along the rim of her goblet. "A Hero's Deck, consisting of weapons, armor, and attribute boosts. There's the Deck of Wonders representing the items claimed in the Gifting Meadow. But there's also the Characters' Deck. Many of the characters you encounter throughout your Quest have been placed in your path for a single purpose. Sometimes for good reasons, but often for bad."

"Like Torbrick?" I shot a glance at the bugbear. I had been suspicious of his sudden attack. Even for a monster as burly and aggressive as Torbrick, his behavior had definitely come from out of the blue.

Avery's head bobbed. "That's a decent comparison, only Torbrick has certainly not been drawn from the Characters' Deck."

"How can you tell?" Miles asked.

"Someone or something drawn from the deck will act differently. It takes time and experience to recognize it, but they'll be more persuasive," Avery said. "You see, they use these characters to steer you in a specific direction."

"Who's this 'they' you keep talking about?" Jasmine asked. "Are we supposed to know them?"

"You should." Avery drummed her fingers on the table. "After all, one of them is your Questmaster."

"Hob?" I asked, exchanging a look with the others. I had always suspected Hob had been more than just some strange guy interested in sending a bunch of kids on an adventure.

"Silly old Hob." Avery jabbed a sticky twirl of candy floss into her mouth.

"You said for bad reasons too," Miles muttered. "Why would *he* want bad things to happen to us?"

"Hob wouldn't," Carl said. "But your Questmaster's opponent would."

"Do you mean Bogie?" I asked.

Avery and Carl both nodded.

"Well, I've never met either one of them," Vanessa said, smacking her lips. "I was forced into playing Champion's Quest against my will."

Carl gave a sympathetic chuckle. "That happened to one of us too. Before Champion's Quest, I had never met Javier, our Luminary. The poor guy accidentally stopped by Hob and Bogie's shop to ask for directions, and the rest is history."

"What are Hob and Bogie? Are they like gods or something?" Jasmine asked.

"Not gods, but they are powerful," Avery replied matter-of-factly. "Hob and Bogie are wizards."

Miles tittered nervously. "Wizards aren't real."

After biting off another chunk of candy floss, Avery tossed the remaining bit onto the table. "From all you've witnessed so far, you can't honestly tell me you believe that anymore, can you?"

"Can they see us, right now?" Jasmine asked. "Like, are they watching?"

"There's a game board, and each of us has a mini figurine representing our character on our Quest," Avery explained. "They know our general location based on positions of the game pieces and have certain information on our statistics, but aside from that, they can't actually watch us from afar. Besides, we're not the only ones playing."

I flinched in surprise. "We're not?"

"Hardly," she said. "The shop is open six days a week. We're just their Thursday crew."

Nodding at Avery, Carl pushed his chair away from the table and stood up. "We should get going now."

"Champions need to look out for each other, wouldn't you agree?" Avery asked, returning the bird-shaped muting device to her Dispenser. "Not that you need our protection, but I can't promise Torbrick will honor you as his guests once we've moved on. You could accompany us out, if you'd like. Our journey takes us to the eastern gate."

"That's where we're going, isn't it?" Miles asked, double-checking the map. "We have to go to the Hagwoods to meet a witch."

"Good luck with that," Carl muttered.

While we'd been eating our meal inside the tavern, night had completely settled in. Trouble's Landing had become something more sinister than what it had been during the day. Having Avery and Carl as our bodyguards seemed like a no-brainer.

"What's that?" Miles asked, after we had walked some distance from the tavern.

A covered wagon with barred windows and four massive horses tied to the front was parked along the road. Perched on top and clutching the reins with long, bony fingers was an eerie hooded figure. The horses whickered as we hurried past, and the figure gazed down, his face nothing more than a black hole in his cloak.

"The rougher parts of any city always have a Reaper Cart on hand, especially after nightfall," Avery explained. "Though I'm not sure what it's doing here. That building hasn't been occupied for years."

As we approached the stables, I spotted one of Avery's companions carrying a saddle out of a stall. Though shorter than the others, she had a muscular build, curly red hair, and a wide-set jaw. Balancing on her shoulder, one clawed hand clinging to the woman's curls, was a creature I hadn't expected to see anytime soon.

"Sheba?" Miles asked, recognizing the sloth from the curiosity shop.

At the mention of her name, Sheba slowly rotated her head, her glassy eyes never blinking.

Carl smirked. "You know Sheba?"

"Sort of," I said. "We met her at the shop."

"Sheba is Susan's Familiar," Avery explained. "And don't let her fool you with her molasses-like behavior. She can be quite crafty."

"Sheba's your familiar? That would have been cool," Miles said, waving his fingers at the sloth. "Ouch! No, Goon, I didn't mean cooler than you." He squirmed as his armadillo clawed his skin beneath his cloak.

Though I couldn't quite put my finger on it, something seemed off about Sheba's appearance. "Out of curiosity," I said. "Who's *your* Questmaster?"

Avery exhaled softly. "That would be Bogie, of course."

Lowering her saddle, Susan took a step toward Avery and

Carl as Javier emerged from inside the stables, plucking out a tune on his own Spark.

"You never told us anything about your Quest," I said, suddenly feeling the need to squeeze my Gadget. "What are you supposed to do?"

Swallowing, Avery's eyes shifted between the other members of her Band. "Therein lies the problem, my friends." She lowered her voice. "We're on the same Quest as you."

Quickly covering her nose and mouth with a piece of cloth, Susan approached, squeezing a Viper Pod with her hands. I tried to make a run for it, but Avery seized me by the arms as the poisonous vapors sprayed directly into my face.

Then the lights went out for the second time.

CHAPTER 21

AN ALMOST UNANIMOUS VOTE

Ah, there you are, Lucas," I heard Avery's voice declare as I groggily opened my eyes. "You shouldn't oversleep too much."

Expecting to discover myself back at the shack, I jolted up. Oddly enough, we hadn't died—not yet, at least, but I wasn't able to move much. Blinking away the blurriness, I looked around at the others, realizing I had been the last one roused from our Viper Pod–induced sleep. Miles sat next to me on a bench with Jasmine and Vanessa across the way, our knees bumping together. We had been captured, our wrists and ankles clamped in heavy shackles and bolted both to the benches and the floor. I could wriggle my fingers and toes a bit, but that was the extent of it. We were in some sort of wagon but no longer inside the walled city of Trouble's Landing. I could hear the wet clop of hooves and whinnying horses as a cool breeze swished through the barred window.

"I hope you understand that we had no choice," Avery said, peering in through the bars while leading her horse next to the slow-moving wagon. "But in this game, there's no room for competition."

"Where are we?" I asked. "Where are you taking us?"

"It's the Reaper Cart," Miles answered, looking downcast. "The one we saw on the way to the stables."

An image of the hooded driver crouching like a vulture popped into my head as the cart rumbled forward.

"They're sending us to the mines," Jasmine said. "That's what Avery told us. It's a four-day journey through the mountains."

Four days in the opposite direction? My stomach lurched. At that rate, we'd never finish our Quest.

"Out of respect, we didn't kill you," Avery explained. "That's why we modified the Viper Pod's poison. Goodness knows there will be plenty of monsters willing to kill you, and I wouldn't stand for causing you any further frustration. We were all in your shoes once, perhaps not as young as you are now, but definitely inexperienced. And I meant what I said earlier. Champions should look out for each other. We should be friends, not enemies. Under different circumstances, I believe we would be. This was just the first we've ever encountered another Band on an identical Quest as ours. It's unfortunate, and I'm truly sorry, but I have given you a gift to blunt the blow."

"You've what?" I scowled at Avery.

"It's my muting device. You liked it, didn't you? The bird?" She pointed through the window at an iron chest lying on the floor between our feet. The bulky padlocked box rattled about with the bumping motion of the cart. "You'll find it in there, along with all your Heroes' Devices. We couldn't leave them on you, of course, but there *are* binding rules about stealing another Champion's Device. Anyway, I thought you would appreciate the gift, from one Artisan to another."

"How am I supposed to use it in prison?" I asked.

"You won't be there long," she insisted. "Once we've completed our Quest and slain Foyos, I promise we shall free your

Band from the mines. You will only have to endure a week or two at most, and then you'll be back on your way."

"Oh, that's not so bad," I muttered sarcastically. It would practically be a vacation now that I had Avery's bird-bobber to play with.

"I guess you'll go to the Hagwoods next, then?" Miles asked as the cart clumsily wobbled about and a chorus of chuckling broke out among the members of Avery's Band.

"We have no intention of going there," Avery said. "Through our travels, we have discovered an alternate way to access Foyos's lair. Trying to coerce Faylinn could take weeks, perhaps longer, and we don't want to waste our time doing that."

After another a mile of rolling, the cart veered to the right, and Avery's Band came to a halt at a fork in the road.

"Farewell, Wild Crows." Standing beside her horse, Avery held up a hand and waved goodbye. "We shall be seeing each other again, perhaps sooner than you think." Then the cart pulled wide down a windy road, and the Orc Slayers slipped from view.

"Well, this is stupid," Vanessa griped. "Nothing's ever easy here, is it? You know, I really want to blame this on somebody, and I think it might be you, Lucas."

"Me?" I gaped at her in shock. "What did I have to do with this?"

"I said I *think* it might be you," she said. "I'm still deciding whether it is or not. Don't push me."

"Whatever," I grumbled. I was in no mood for her attitude, especially while stuck together less than a foot apart.

I could feel my anxiety threatening to kick in, and I needed to concentrate to keep the panic at bay. During each terrifying situation I had been through so far in the game—attacked by monsters, poisoned by Viper Pods—the Creepers only appeared whenever I found myself backed into a corner with no hope of escape.

"Nobody's to blame," Miles said.

Goon climbed out from beneath Miles's cloak and dove down one of his shirtsleeves. The armadillo curiously sniffed at the manacle before climbing on top of the iron chest.

"I just can't figure out how they knew where we would be," Jasmine said, straining to slip her hand through the clamp. "It's like someone told them we would be in that tavern."

"Like a spy?" I asked.

"Maybe Madge is the spy," Vanessa suggested. "She seemed a little sketchy to me."

"I like Madge," Miles said. "She's nice."

"Yeah, well, I liked Avery and Carl too," she fired back. "And look where that got us."

Shaking my head, I dismissed the idea. "I don't think it's her. Madge has had a couple of chances to mess with us, and she's been a ton of help."

"Jugger, then?" Jasmine asked. "Maybe as payback for the Grains of Persuasion."

I half nodded, but that idea didn't stick either. Betraying us to another Band of Champions didn't seem like it fell within Jugger's guidelines as protector of the Entry Bridge.

"It was Torbrick," I concluded. I had sensed the bugbear's ulterior motives from the beginning, and now I felt certain of it.

"The bartender?" Vanessa scoffed. "Avery bullied him around and made him give us all that food."

"Or was it just an act?" I asked. "Remember when Torbrick attacked us and we were waiting for the Champion's Catch to appear, but nothing happened?" The three of them nodded. "I think that's because we weren't actually *under* attack, so there was no need to roll the dice. Torbrick was just pretending to come after us so that Avery could swoop in and save the day."

"Then we let our guard down," Miles agreed. "Oh, if I ever get back there, I'll—"

"You'll what?" A wry grin crinkled the corners of Jasmine's eyes.

Miles wilted back into his seat. "I'll probably just buy more candy floss and steer clear of Torbrick's altogether."

"Okay, fine," Vanessa huffed. "Now we know *how* we were tricked and *why* those punks did it. So what? I'm not interested in spending the next couple of weeks in some prison camp."

"That's why we have to escape," Jasmine said.

Vanessa sniffed. "Good idea. And then what?"

"We go to the Hagwoods," I said.

"Um, veto." Vanessa shook her head. "You heard Avery. They're not even taking a chance with this witch. Why would *we* go there?"

"Because we don't know any other way," I reasoned.

Groaning, Vanessa thumped her head against the wall. "Then I think we should just forget about it."

Miles blinked. "Forget about . . . our Quest?"

"Why not?" Vanessa asked, pulling back her hood. "If those guys are going to kill Foyos, what does it matter what we do?"

"Don't you want to go home?" I would have thought of all people, Vanessa would be the most interested in getting out of the game.

"More than anything," she said, her eyelids fluttering. "But wouldn't we get to go home if the Orc Slayers finish the Quest for us? This game may be dreadful, but forcing us to hang around for no good reason just seems cruel. I say we go to Trouble's Landing, find some sort of respectable hotel—definitely not one near Torbrick's—and spend the next week eating and relaxing. I could pretend this was just some weird road trip my parents forced me to go on with you three."

"But what if they fail?" Miles asked.

Vanessa squawked out a laugh. "Who? The Orc Slayers? Did you see them? They're awesome and confident and *way* more prepared than any of us. They're not going to fail. Not like we would."

As the rickety cart trundled along, hitching over rough patches of road and rebounding off rocks, we fell into a fidgety silence, thinking about Vanessa's proposition. We could just go back to the city, explore the rest of the shops, and let someone else go about handling the dirty work. Despite how easy that seemed, however, I couldn't help but feel sad about giving up. Were we actually as horrible as Vanessa had made us out to be?

"Um . . . I don't think we should do that," I mumbled.

Vanessa raised her eyebrows. "That's nice, Lucas. Unfortunately, it's not up to you."

"Actually, it is," I said, preparing myself for what I knew had the potential of becoming a full-blown argument. "I'm our Band Leader, and I say we finish this Quest."

After letting my words sink in, Vanessa snorted like a warthog. "Some Band Leader you turned out to be. You've already gotten us killed once and now duped by another group of Champions. And I don't care about the rules. I didn't have a say in who became our leader, so why don't we just put it up for a vote and see what the rest of the group wants to do?"

"I agree with Lucas," Jasmine said just as Vanessa finished talking. "I think we should go to the Hagwoods."

"Me too." Miles nodded his support.

"Besides, why do you hate Lucas so much?" Jasmine asked.

Vanessa recoiled in surprise. "Who says I hate him?"

"You treat him like garbage," Jasmine said. "And Miles too."

"Oh, it's okay," Miles muttered, staring at Jasmine awkwardly. "We don't need to talk about this right now."

"I don't *hate* them," Vanessa said, leveling her eyes on me. "I'm just *annoyed* by them."

"Why? Because we're orphans?" I asked.

"No, I don't care that you're both orphans." Pursing her lips, she offered me a scornful smile. "But you happen to be orphans in *my* house. My parents have been caretakers at Sunnyside since before I was born, and I've had to deal with other kids all my life. It's exhausting trying to get my parents' attention for just five minutes. I'm sick and tired of being responsible for other people. Especially ones who drive me crazy and suck me into board games with monsters trying to murder me."

"Well, I'm sorry. *I'm* not trying to drive you crazy." I had no idea that was the reason why Vanessa could be so difficult, but it wasn't our fault Miles and I had ended up being transferred to Sunnyside. "When we get home, I'll just leave, and you won't be bothered by me anymore."

Scoffing, Vanessa rolled her eyes. "Oh, right. You'll run away, is that it?" As I started to nod, she leaned toward me in an almost challenging sort of way. "Do you think you're the first foster kid to run away, Lucas? Give me a break. You'll never go through with it. And even if you do, you won't get far. Then it'll just make things worse for me because my parents will have to worry about you."

I felt my hands start to shake. Vanessa had no idea what I was capable of. Did she even know about my train ticket? And if I honestly drove her that crazy, maybe she should try helping me instead of putting up a fuss just because I'd wandered off from the pool.

Groaning, Vanessa slouched back on her bench. "You guys do what you want. I'll just go back to Trouble's Landing."

"Then you'll be all alone," Jasmine reasoned.

"And you're almost out of money," Miles added.

Vanessa hissed so loudly the anxious horses, probably mistaking the sound for a nearby snake, gave a collective jerk and the cart nearly tipped over.

"It doesn't matter anyway if we can't escape from these handcuffs," she growled.

Suddenly, the chest at our feet bounced sharply as the padlock dropped off. Goon released a shrill cry of excitement and then leapt back onto Miles's sleeve.

"Wow, Goon!" Miles exclaimed. "I'd been thinking it would be really neat if you could somehow pick locks, and then you go and do it?"

Jasmine laughed in surprise as I kicked the chest and the lid sprang open, revealing our Heroes' Devices inside.

"Do you think Goon could pick one of those up?" I asked.

Most of our items were too heavy for the tiny creature to heft around the cart, and Miles didn't think he could form his Tether into a whistle without using his hands. Vanessa's Spark lay at the bottom and was the heaviest. Figuring out how to finagle my Gadget with limited movement in my wrists seemed like an impossibility. After quite a bit of straining and grunting from the armadillo, Goon managed to drag Jasmine's Spade from the chest and into her fingers.

"What are you going to do with that?" Vanessa asked. "Grow a bunch of plants in here?"

"Nope." Jasmine gripped her Spade, and taking a great deal of effort, she began twisting her wrist. "If I can just"—she gritted her teeth—"move my thumb . . . up to the . . . blade . . ."

The cart started smacking up and down against the uneven road even more so than usual. The poor horses released a frightened fit of whinnying as I watched one of the wagon's spoked wheels rise up above the window. Jasmine was doing something with her Spade—turning the solid ground into mush. Screeching horribly, the wheel strained against its axle to the max, and then fell off with an earsplitting crash.

Then the ground rushed up to catch us, cradling the prison wagon in hot, steaming mud that immediately bubbled and belched and poured in through our window.

CHAPTER 22

A PURPLE SUNRISE OVER THE HAGWOODS

Instantly, the nails securing the iron shackles on my wrists and ankles pulled free from the rotted wooden bench. Then I was no longer sitting on my bench but falling and landing on something soft and covered in hair.

"Sorry," I apologized to Jasmine.

"It's okay," she replied, her dark eyes staring back at me through her tangled mess of bangs.

"That was absolutely brilliant," I said, trying to pull myself off her.

Jasmine looked like she had just won the lottery as sparks popped across the surface of her glowing Spade. "Carl had barely taught me how to do that mudding trick. I didn't expect it to actually work."

"Miles, are you going to move or what?" Vanessa demanded.

Since our side of the wagon had been the one tipping topsy-turvy, gravity had taken over from there, and Miles had dropped as well, plowing into Vanessa like a medicine ball.

"And would you get that thing off me?" she pleaded, her patience hanging by a thread.

Dangling from Miles's cloak, the armadillo had taken an interest in Vanessa and started chewing on clumps of her hair.

"I'm trying to break you out," he explained. "Except I don't think I know how."

Eyeing my Gadget curiously, I pressed the button and instead of a blade appearing, the curled metal hook of a crowbar emerged from the end of my Device.

"Aha!" I cheered. I may not have been much of a handyman, but my Gadget now had a tooth, and I shimmied that tooth right underneath one of Jasmine's manacles. Applying a little pressure with a nibble on the tip of my tongue for good measure, I got the manacle to pop free.

"Got it," I announced.

It took me the whole of five minutes to remove the rest. Then, feeling a thrilling surge of confidence, I pried the wrench through the barred window now on our ceiling and squeezed my body up to the outside. Courtesy of Jasmine's magical Spade, a section of the road about the size of the lap pool at Greenwillow had turned into a swamp of swirling mud beneath our overturned wagon. Crooked trees draped over the path like tangled umbrellas, and the aura of the Trouble's Landing torchlights twinkled maybe less than five miles behind us in the distance.

Stooping over, I helped Miles through the window. Jasmine followed next, and then I shot a wary eye over at the Reaper, lurking nearby on one side of the path. Watching me from beneath his hood, the ghostly figure had already unhitched the six cart horses, and now held them at bay, their leather reins looped around his skeletal fingers.

"Nice, Lucas," Vanessa griped, slapping the back of my heel. "Thanks for helping me out."

"I was going to help you," I insisted. I mean eventually I was going to help her.

"This must be the Merchant Road," Miles said, teetering on top of the wagon. "Or at least it runs into it back that way."

Checking my compass, I confirmed our easterly direction, zigzagging back to the fork where we had said our goodbyes to the Orc Slayers.

"What about him?" Jasmine nodded at the Reaper.

The statuesque cloaked creature had yet to make a move toward the wagon.

"Well, let me check." Humming softly to himself, Miles removed his "Compendium of Monsters" from his Dispenser. "Um . . . that's a wraith, actually. Looks like one, don't you think?" He showed me the monster, and I more or less agreed. "'Wraiths are fey spectral spirits,'" he read. "'Four Strength, five Speed, three Wisdom' . . . geez, he's kind of dumb, 'and four Vitality.'"

"He doesn't look like much of a threat," Jasmine said.

"The compendium says wraiths will never attack humans unless provoked." Miles shrugged and pocketed his cheat sheet. "So unless we have a good reason to provoke him, he'll probably just leave us alone."

"Oh, I don't know," I said, the inklings of an idea giving my nose a playful twitch. "I think those horses could come in handy."

"I have allergies, remember?" Vanessa said. "And do you even know how to ride a horse?"

I started to nod, but then I shook my head. Who was I kidding? I had never been on a horse before, and those ones didn't have saddles.

"How about it, Gamekeeper?" Jasmine asked, nudging Miles with her elbow. "Do you think you could help us out?"

"With my whistle?" Miles's eyes suddenly perked up as he brought his Tether up to his lips.

· ◆ ● ◆ ·

Let me just start off by saying that traveling by horse was *way* more convenient than hoofing it on foot to the Hagwoods. We didn't even have to fight for them either. By the time we had climbed down from the wagon, Miles had worked the horses into a frenzy with his Tether and they'd trampled that Reaper in a matter of seconds. Vanessa had sneezed violently for about five minutes straight, but then she got used to the horses, and as Miles's whistling soothed the powerful animals, the four of us easily mounted our horses and galloped east.

Eventually, I had to give Miles the map because no matter how hard I tried taking the lead, his horse always ended up several yards ahead. One of the many benefits of being a Gamekeeper, I supposed. The road split and forked, crossing over three different rivers—one without a bridge—and through a stretch of sketchy tunnels swarming with beetles. But with Pavio's etching as our guide and our awesome horses charging ahead, we didn't have to stop once. By the time we arrived at the end of the etching, morning was approaching and the sky had started turning from black to a dark purple. We set up camp a short distance away from the Hagwoods. Per Miles's command with his Tether whistle, the horses stayed close by, clustered beneath a small grove of trees and next to a burbling river flowing out from the forest.

Traveling through the night had turned our sleeping schedules upside down. Since we wouldn't be able to see the hidden path through the Enchanted Mists until the sun had set, we decided it would be a good idea to take a long nap. The day may have started off a bit rocky, but I could live with the ending. We were tired and stiff from riding so many miles, but I couldn't remember a time when I'd been in such a good mood.

After several miserable days, we had made it to the next checkpoint on our Quest. The Hagwoods were right there, just behind a layer of puffy clouds.

At some point after the fire fizzled to nothing more than ash, and while the dream I was having morphed into one involving a bandit dwarf and Torbrick's roasted turkey, something else decided to join our camp.

I smelled it first. A musty vegetable-y smell, like an old tossed salad baking on a hot sidewalk. Don't ask me how I know that smell. Peeling open my eyelids, I caught a glimpse of Vanessa on the opposite side of the fire, staring back at me and quivering with panic. Her lips were moving, trying to send me a message, just as I heard what sounded like hundreds of twigs snapping at once, followed by the groaning, twangy sound of an elastic band stretching to its limits. Then a splintery-fingered hand yanked me up from my wildflower bed and into the face of a nightmare.

Partway through my scream for help, the world around me froze. Unable to move and trapped in the monster's clutches, I discovered a new problem.

"What's this?" I mumbled, trying not to swallow the strange flavorless cube that had appeared inside my mouth. As it shifted temperatures, growing hot and then once again cold, I understood what it was. How in the world was I supposed to roll the Die of Fate with it stuck inside my mouth?

A desperate scrabbling of feet at least fifteen feet below me announced that the others had leapt up from their beds.

"What *is* that thing?" Vanessa demanded.

Squeezed inside the monster's prickly fingers and staring into its gaping jaws filled with vines and oozy sap, I hadn't the foggiest idea what we were up against.

"A Treant!" Miles shouted. I couldn't see him, but I knew he had grabbed the compendium. "A warrior of the wood. Oh, wow. Thirty Strength, seventeen Speed . . ."

"We just need to kill it, right?" Jasmine said, interrupting him. "Where's the Die of Fate?"

"Up here," I said carefully and not very plainly, the uncomfortable game piece clattering against my molars.

Craning my neck, I could see the Champion's Catch floating in the middle of the group down below. This was going to be tricky. Tilting my head back as far as I could, I spat the Die of Fate out of my mouth. Ricocheting off the Treant's bark-covered nose, it bounced against my forehead before dropping out of sight.

"Nice shot!" Miles cheered as the die toppled into the Champion's Catch, which had to have been more than luck. I wasn't *that* skilled of a spitter.

I could only guess what happened next as the series of events all took place beneath my line of sight. Someone earned their roll of the Die of Opportunity, followed by a bustle of excitement and confusion. Then time sped back up, and I continued on my horrifying journey into the Treant's mouth.

The monster screamed at me. It sounded like an avalanche of toasters smashing down the side of a mountain. I screamed back. What else could I do? Then a high-pitched whistling filled my ears. The Treant took notice as well and, instead of swallowing me, it snapped its attention elsewhere and began thrashing and staggering sideways. The world became a blurry swirl of nonsense as the monster began swinging me around like a club.

"I think I'm going to be sick," I groaned. It seemed to go on forever, with me never actually hitting anything but never stopping long enough to let my eyes catch up with the rest of my body.

Finally, after nearly throwing up at least half a dozen times, I dropped from the Treant's grasp and splashed into the river.

"How am I not dead?" I gasped, jumping up to join the others with two fewer Bloodstones on my Vitality Meter. Not that I was complaining. A little dip in health seemed worth it, considering I had been only seconds away from becoming tree food.

During the time I had been clutched in the Treant's claws, Jasmine had managed to dig a crater deep enough to hold a full-size car. A barrage of dirt was flung from the hole, showering the monster as she continued digging. Miles sprinted about furiously, blowing his Tether whistle while a family of pit bull–sized beavers went to work, gnawing on the Treant's wooden legs. They had already chipped away two-thirds of an ankle, and it wouldn't take much before they broke through.

"What's Jasmine doing?" I asked Miles.

"Don't know," he answered between puffs on his whistle. "She didn't tell me."

"What did we roll on the Die of Opportunity?"

Before he could answer, the Treant launched something from its chest. Arcing through the air, the twisted mass of thorns and sap smashed against the earth, shooting out debris. One of the pieces of shrapnel struck Miles in the back before he could dodge out of the way.

"Vanessa rolled a six, which gave that thing Thorn Bombs." Examining his Medallion, Miles showed me how four of his Bloodstones had gone out. "If it hits me again, I'm a goner."

"Gave *it* Thorn Bombs?" That made absolutely no sense.

"You rolled an X," Vanessa snarled, appearing at my side.

"I rolled an X?" I blinked at her in confusion.

"Yes, an X," Miles explained. "It's one of the options of the Die of Fate. It means no one gets to roll the Die of Opportunity for themselves or their Band."

"And, instead, I had to roll for *that*," Vanessa added. "You just keep spitting those things out, don't you?" she bellowed at the Treant.

The Treant released a fearsome roar as the beavers gnawed their way through its wooden leg, and I braced for the earthquake. Instead of falling to the ground, however, the monster brought its mangled leg straight down, righting itself before tipping over. Wobbling and unsteady, the Treant staggered back directly toward the terrified horses.

"Miles, get them out of there," I demanded.

With three quick breaths on his whistle, Miles sent the horses leaping to safety just as the Treant plowed through the small grove of trees. Once again, the monster's chest began to bulge, readying to launch, as a crazy light bulb went on in my head; one with definite potential of getting me killed.

While Vanessa and Miles gaped in shock, I raced straight for the monster. Pulling out my Device, I searched my mind for what could be the most useful tool in this situation, and then I activated the button. This time, the gleaming edge of an ax shot out from my Gadget, which was exactly what I needed. The Treant howled in anguish as I immediately started whacking. It tried smashing me with its claws, but with Jasmine showering dirt on top of both of us, it was too distracted to find me and I managed to leap out of the way. I chopped and chopped at its one good ankle. The beavers may have been way more efficient at biting through the monster's leg, but I still managed to cut through the last bit of its splintery flesh before it had a chance to form another thorn bomb. When I finally finished chopping, I was exhausted and dripping with sweat, but I could hear the sound of groaning wood, like a tree just about to topple to the earth. The monster struggled to keep its balance and I was afraid it might succeed as it had the first time. But then Jasmine scampered out of the massive crater she had finished digging with her Spade and called out to me.

"Great job!" she yelled. "Now, have that thing chase you this way."

I didn't even have to run far. As soon as I began hopping up and down, yelling at the top of my lungs, the Treant made a hungry swipe and took a step toward me.

"Timber!" I shouted as the monster, its legs now all but splinters below its shins, came crashing into the hole Jasmine had dug.

CHAPTER 23

OUT OF THE MISTS AND
INTO THE SMOKE

Once we had buried the Treant in the hole Jasmine had dug, we spent the rest of the day on edge, waiting for the next attack, which thankfully never happened. As the sun crept out of sight the following evening, a magical rip, like a snag in a wispy curtain, formed in the Enchanted Mists and an eerie, shimmering pathway into the Hagwoods appeared.

"Told you so," Vanessa muttered.

Vanessa seemed to have lost most of her Luminary skill. Earlier that day, she had tried baking us a cake, but each of our missing Bloodstones remained missing. I had my suspicions as to why it hadn't worked. It was one thing to accidentally figure things out even though you didn't care about playing the game, but it was something entirely different to feel like a complete loser, unable to help even when you were trying.

"I can't see anything," Miles whispered, running into me as we stepped into the Hagwoods and the Enchanted Mists closed in. "Does anybody have a flashlight or something?"

Remembering the torch Madge had stuffed in my shopping bag, I produced it from my Dispenser and struck my fingernail down the edge of my Gadget, sparking it to life. As the fire blazed, Vanessa sucked in a panicked breath. Abandoning what had to be rule number one of her personal code, she grabbed my arm.

"Look at how many there are," she gasped.

Dozens of shadowy figures had emerged from within the forest, shambling about next to the path and brushing up against the mists.

"Are they zombies?" Jasmine whispered.

The four of us had turned into an overstuffed sandwich, crammed tightly together, trying to avoid the mists, with me squished in the middle. Normally, I might have liked the extra attention, but feeling claustrophobic, I tried wriggling out.

"Not zombies," Vanessa said. "Just people who've wandered off the path."

"That's not a person." Squirming frantically, Miles pointed at a long-haired goblin walking at the edge of the mist. Noticing Miles's desperate squeals, the goblin's ears quivered, and its head snapped toward us. "Not more Barrys," Miles squeaked as the torchlight briefly illuminated its name badge before it eventually staggered away.

"I don't think they can get to us," I said, following a hunch and gazing at the endless rows of bobbing heads crowding the mists. "Just don't touch the mists."

As it turned out, staying on the path was no easy task. The mists never remained safely gathered in one spot. Sometimes they spilled onto the path and we had to hop over or crawl underneath them. At one point, the path became so narrow we had to pass through single file. Miles insisted we rock-paper-scissors to determine our marching order, and since I always picked scissors—which he must have figured out months ago—I ended up bringing up the rear.

That had been by far the worst. The farther along we

walked, the more aggressive the bewitched figures became, and, for some reason, they seemed most interested in me. Yes, they would snarl and howl at the others, but when it was my turn, they would run full-sprint toward me only to bounce off the misty barrier. I felt like a scared gerbil trapped in a cage.

"Where does the map say we go next?" Jasmine asked after the mists eventually receded and we stepped out into the clear woods.

"It doesn't," Miles said. "It only had directions to the Hagwoods. Not through them."

"Please don't tell me it's that creepy house over there." Vanessa nodded to a shadowy area a short distance away.

Squinting into the murky darkness, I spotted the small structure nestled between two enormous trees and camouflaged with an overgrowth of moss. I almost didn't believe it was a house until I spotted a trail of smoke coiling from its chimney. The wobbly rattle of laminated paper filled my ears as Miles anxiously scanned the "Compendium of Monsters."

"Faylinn," he announced, sighing with relief. Then he swallowed, his eyebrows crinkling. "She doesn't have any stats. No Strength, Wisdom, or Vitality."

"Faylinn's immortal, remember?" I said. "We don't need to fight her. We just have to convince her to help us."

"And how do you propose we do that?" Vanessa asked.

"You could try asking her," someone suggested.

"That's not a bad idea," Miles agreed. "Maybe she'll want to help us."

Halfway through nodding in agreement, I caught myself. "Wait. Who just said that?" I realized the scratchy-sounding voice hadn't come from any of us.

"I did," the voice replied, much louder than before.

Warm and soft, like a blanket fresh from the dryer, and carrying the faintest hint of toasted marshmallows, the chimney smoke had worked its way over from the moss-covered house and drifted down, surrounding us in a circle. I felt an instant icicle of panic, but then the dread vanished as a lasso made of vaporous tendrils looped around my waist and tugged me gently into the witch's lair.

CHAPTER 24

HOW TO DEAL
WITH A WITCH

"Whatever you do, don't eat the cookies," Miles whispered loudly.

The four of us sat in wicker chairs in front of the fireplace of a log cabin as an elderly woman hummed and bustled about in the nearby kitchen. Though I may have been lightheaded, I knew exactly how we had ended up inside. I could distinctly remember sensing the danger, but then the soothing, singed-sugar smell of the chimney smoke made it so I no longer cared.

Wrinkled and whiskery, with sunken eyes and wart-covered knuckles, Faylinn the witch hunched over a walking cane that clacked in rhythm with each step. She appeared to be baking and had cluttered her kitchen with a variety of mixing bowls and measuring spoons.

From my initial observation, the inside of Faylinn's cabin looked as though it had been decorated by an angry Torbrick, its furniture haphazardly scattered about and covered in thick dust. Tucked away in the far corner of the room, a chair rocked back and forth, a massive skull resting on the seat cushion. Two purplish orbs glowed inside the skull's eye sockets as it whistled a tune.

"What are you talking about?" I asked Miles, screwing up my face. "What cookies?"

"These will have to cool first," Faylinn announced, pulling a baking sheet from a brick oven and dropping it onto the kitchen table with a dull clang. Steam wafted off rows of ooey, gooey chocolate chip cookies.

Eyes widening, Miles jabbed his index finger at the "Compendium of Monsters." He then mumbled the words *cookies* and *magic spell* and something that might have to do with enchanted mists, but I didn't quite catch it all because, oh, my goodness, I needed one of those cookies.

"Ah, ah, Lucas." Clucking her tongue, the witch whacked the back of my hand with her spatula. "You'll have to wait."

"Yes, you'll have to wait," the gigantic skull repeated from its rocking chair in a sort of deep, bumbling voice.

"How did that happen?" Dreary and dazed, I wondered how I came to be standing in the kitchen hovering over the table, next to Jasmine and Vanessa.

Miles was still sitting in his wicker seat, looking beside himself with panic and violently shaking the compendium as though it had caught fire. Within seconds of his warning, I had almost snatched one of the bubbling cookies right off the baking sheet.

"What's going on?" Vanessa rubbed her temples. "Why does it feel like I'm dreaming?"

"Such a lovely thing to say, my child," Faylinn purred, linking arms with both Vanessa and Jasmine, her head barely cresting the top of their shoulders at full hunch.

"Why is that so lovely?" asked the skull, which I think may have once belonged to a giant troll. "It's not as though she gave you a compliment, as I always do."

"Quiet down over there, Scipio," the witch snapped, shooting a warning glare at the skull. Grinding his teeth together, Scipio made a blubbering sound and then went back to whistling.

"I'm the one who's dreaming," Faylinn said, pinching the girls' cheeks and leading them back to their chairs. "It's always so good to talk with people, don't you agree?" Crooking her finger, she lured me away from the table and then helped me into my seat before ambling back to the kitchen.

"Lucas, what are you doing?" Miles hissed. "I told you not to eat them."

"It's obviously some sort of spell," I said, smacking the side of my head. "Why aren't *you* affected by it?"

Miles shrugged. "Maybe because I'm allergic to chocolate, remember? I break out in itchy hives every time I eat any."

A loud clatter sounded in the kitchen as Faylinn abruptly smacked her spatula against the table. "Allergic?" she asked, glancing into the room. "That will not do."

"You have a recipe for oatmeal raisin, your loveliness," Scipio chimed in.

Cocking her head to one side, Faylinn gazed over at her cupboards. "I do, don't I, Scipio? What do you say, Miles? Shall I whip you up a batch?"

Miles nodded eagerly. "Oh, yes, that would be super-duper."

"I don't think it would, remember?" I asked, snapping my fingers to break his trance.

Miles groaned in frustration. "We have to get out of here."

"No, we have to talk to her," Jasmine insisted. "We need her help."

"Well, if you're so confident, go right ahead," Vanessa said.

Initially recoiling from the suggestion, Jasmine sniffed and dragged the back of her finger across her upper lip. "Fine, I will," she said. "Uh . . . Faylinn. That's your name, correct?"

"One of my names," the witch replied, whipping a wooden spoon through a new batch of cookie batter.

"She's also known as the Dame of Dismalness, the Waker of the Dead, the Ageless Angel of Darkness," Scipio suddenly blurted out. "Ofttimes she goes by Ushbarax, or the Princess of Pleading and Pain, or Marigold the Mushy—"

"That will be all from you." Faylinn flicked her chin, and the talkative skull suddenly floated up from the rocking chair. I heard Scipio finish with the words *Mushroom of Misery* before he shot up the chimney, his voice growing muffled and silent as he launched from the cabin.

"As I was saying," the witch continued, spooning dollops of cookie dough onto a fresh baking sheet. "Faylinn is one of my many names, and because I haven't had visitors in such a long time, I shall allow you to continue calling me that. How does that sound?"

"Terrific," Jasmine replied uneasily. "But why haven't you had visitors?"

"No one has traveled to my home since I enchanted the forest," she said. "It's that nasty Dabraxus. He's always turning them away."

Dabraxus? I looked over at Miles, but after checking both sides of the compendium, he just shook his head.

After sliding the pan into the oven to bake, Faylinn gathered up the cooled chocolate chip cookies and placed them in a cloth-lined basket. "I kept Dabraxus from attacking you at the edge of the mists," she said. "And now he's in such a foul mood."

"Why did you stop him?" I asked.

"I was curious about this rabble of overconfident Champions

and I simply had to discover what possibly could have possessed them to risk life and limb to brave the Hagwoods." Hobbling back into the room with her basket of dangerous cookies in tow, Faylinn took a seat in the empty rocking chair. "Now, who wants one?"

"I do!" Vanessa shot up from her seat, but Miles immediately tugged on her sleeve. "No, wait . . ." she said, staring uneasily down at Miles. "I'm . . . uh . . . actually on a diet right now."

Faylinn clacked a pair of tongs together above the basket. "Anyone else?"

More than anything in the world, I really wanted a cookie. "What happens if we eat one?" I asked.

"Nothing." Faylinn looked appalled. "They'll rot your teeth, as I'm sure you've heard yummy sweets tend to do."

"And your souls," Miles added, cupping his hand over his mouth to keep her from hearing, which never worked.

"Tell me, does your Gamekeeper always butt his nose into other people's business?" the witch asked, fixing Miles with her most withering of gazes.

"All the time," Jasmine admitted. "But we prefer it that way."

"You don't want a cookie? Fine," Faylinn huffed. "Why did you come here?"

"We need your magic," Jasmine said. "We need to get close enough to Foyos to kill him."

"Yeah, we know the spell he's under is wearing off," I added.

"Or so the story goes." Faylinn smiled cryptically. "And why should I help you? What's in it for me?"

"Won't he be coming for revenge against you?" I asked. "Technically, we'll be doing you a favor if we destroy him."

Faylinn shrugged. "Yes, technically that's true. But I am also old and ornery, and I'm not the least bit concerned with that foolish monster." Then her eyes narrowed. "And I don't do *anything* for free."

"What if we made a trade?" Miles suggested. "Maybe there's something we have that you want?"

Placing the basket on the floor, Faylinn began rocking back and forth in her chair. "Will you then agree to enter into a deal with me?"

Before Miles could answer, I asked, "Would it be all right if we discussed this together for a moment?"

Twirling her cane, the witch relaxed. "Oh, I don't see why not. If you'd like, I'll even plug my ears."

"That would be great," I said, not believing her for a second.

After the four of us had scooted in our chairs and ducked our heads into a circle, I tried sounding as serious as possible.

"A deal with a witch?" I asked. "Do you even know what that means?"

"Do you?" Jasmine narrowed her eyes at me.

"Well, no," I admitted. "But it can't be good." The kinds of deals witches made in scary books and movies never turned out well for the other people involved.

"We need to leave," Vanessa said. "We should go back through the Enchanted Mists and head for Trouble's Landing— like I suggested we do in the first place. I've never wanted a cookie so bad in my life."

"I agree," Miles added, grimacing in fear. "Once those oatmeal raisins are done baking, I'm done for."

Jasmine leaned in closer. "This is part of our Quest, so if striking a deal with Faylinn is what we have to do, I say we give it our best shot, right?"

"I guess there's no harm in asking," I said. "We might not even have what she wants."

"I'm afraid that's not how it works, pumpkin," Faylinn replied, having listened in all along. "When you enter Foyos's lair, the magical talisman around his neck will immediately drain all your energy. The spell powering the talisman may be old and fading, as you say, but it still packs a punch. However, I will agree to cast my Ward against Withering spell upon each of your Medallions. That will provide you with the protection you need so you don't rot away into nothing. Then you may face off with the mighty Foyos and achieve glorious victory. All this I shall do for you if you agree to a blind trade with me. And yes, sweet children, you *all* have something I want."

A blind trade? I had an icky feeling about that.

"If you're not going to tell us, then we're not going to deal," I said.

"Then you shall eat a cookie, and I shall take what I want regardless," Faylinn purred.

A bell chimed in the kitchen as the oatmeal raisin cookies finished baking, and Miles released a sniveling moan. The sumptuous scents of deliciousness poured out once more from the basket, and I felt my stomach gurgle with hunger.

"All right, we agree to deal," I announced, snapping Vanessa from her bleary-eyed stagger before she covered half the distance to the witch.

"Perfect." Faylinn clapped her hands, and the cookies, basket, and mouthwatering smells of chocolate instantly dissolved.

The walls of the hut began trembling, trickles of dirt cascading down from the ceiling. Springing up from my seat, I reached for my Gadget as Faylinn stood as well, her old bones creaking almost as loud as the rocking chair. Then she wiggled her fingers, and I felt a buzzing vibration against my chest.

"There, I've kept my end of the bargain," she said as I snatched my Advancement Medallion and noticed my Bloodstones had turned from red to a smoky gray. "Now, it's time you keep yours."

"What is it you want?" I asked, my voice now the only sound in the quiet room.

The rumbling of the floor had stopped, the streams of floating dust no longer dribbling. Miles, Jasmine, and Vanessa sat frozen in their seats, Faylinn and I the only two able to move.

"Fear not, Lucas," Faylinn said, noticing my look of panic. "It is only a spell that will last as long as I need it to. But you are the Band Leader, therefore I think it best *you* decide."

"Decide what? We told you we would make the deal."

"Oh, the deal has been struck. That much has been settled," she said, her voice sounding more threatening than before. "You must now make the decision on my payment and choose your sacrifice."

"What are we supposed to sacrifice?" Why hadn't I just eaten a dumb cookie and been done with it?

Faylinn's eyes seemed to sink farther into her wrinkled skull, turning the color of fiery brimstone. "A single member of your Band must race against my Dabraxus through the Labyrinth of Bones, and you must decide which of you to send."

Looking down at the others still frozen in their seats, I wondered if they had heard the witch's proposition. Who was I supposed to pick?

Faylinn's lips drooped in a sad frown. "I sense your resistance, your refusal to choose. If you don't, none of you shall ever leave my mists. You shall never complete your Quest, nor shall you ever go home," she said. "Do you believe I have power to carry out that claim, Lucas Silver? Or have you already forgotten who imprisoned the mighty Foyos for centuries within his tomb with nothing more than a flick of a finger and a few words uttered across a talisman?"

"Let me get this straight," I said. "We just have to beat Dabraxus to the end?"

The witch's head bobbled. "More or less. You need only cross through the archway at the end of the labyrinth, but my Dabraxus won't necessarily be trying to reach the finish line first—if you know what I mean."

Not a race but a chase. And one of us would be running from a monster inside a twisting maze, all alone.

"Why don't you just challenge us yourself?" I asked. "Is it because you don't think you could beat the four of us in a fight?"

Faylinn made a croaky gargling sound in the back of her throat. "Nice try, but I am not easily lured into that sort of nonsense. But I do enjoy a good show, and my poor Dabraxus is so grumpy. He needs to stretch his legs. No, I'm afraid even with your best taunting, you won't change my mind."

"Can I talk with the others first?"

"You could . . ." She tapped her wrinkled lips with her wrinkled finger. "But I thought you were their *leader*. Can you not make up your mind? Or would you rather squabble and debate and leave it up to a match of rock-paper-scissors to decide?"

It wasn't that I couldn't make up my mind, I just didn't want to make the wrong decision. I knew I should be the one to go, but how could I do it alone? I could just see myself passing out from a panic attack and getting gobbled up by some awful monster. Vanessa would never volunteer, and I wouldn't want to send Miles, even with Goon as his companion. Jasmine may have been our best fighter, but she didn't always think before rushing in, and I knew she wouldn't allow anyone else to take her place.

"And you'll let the rest of us go once I make my choice?" I asked.

Faylinn offered me a near toothless grin. "I'll even grant you safe passage through my Hagwoods all the way to the northern edge, right up to the border of Mount Restless."

Fearing I was about to make the biggest mistake of my life, I took a deep breath, and nodded. "Then I'll do it," I said. "I'll race Dabraxus."

Gleefully throwing her head back, Faylinn screeched with laughter as the fire in the fireplace snuffed out with a whooping pop. The rumbling walls returned as did the dirt dribbling from the ceiling. When I looked around at the others to tell them about the mess I had gotten myself into, I saw that they were no longer sitting in their seats.

"Hey, I thought we had a . . ." I started to shout as the wind snatched the last of my sentence from my mouth and left it hanging in the air. The floor beneath me gave way, and I tumbled into a cavern of endless darkness.

CHAPTER 25

THE LABYRINTH OF BONES

W ell, this was a bad idea," I grumbled, pulling myself up from the cold, stony ground. "You could have at least warned me about falling!" I shouted into the darkness, hoping to elicit a response from Faylinn. I knew she could hear me from somewhere up above. She was probably watching my every move and wearing a smug grin.

The cavern remained in darkness for several moments, making it impossible to see even a foot past my nose. I stumbled about, nearly tripping over what felt like rocks and branches covering the floor. Then several pinpricks of light blinked on a short distance away, appearing like tiny purple fireflies. I heard the sound of something toppling, like a pile of blocks tipping over, as the pinpricks rose up from the floor and hovered in the air a few feet off the ground. Hushed voices began to murmur, sounding as if they came from the direction of the lights.

"Hello?" I called out warily, reaching for my Gadget. I gripped the handle and rested my thumb on the button. Now would be the perfect time to bring out my blade. "Who's there?"

The voices grew louder, but they weren't making any sense, just chattering nonsense, when fire suddenly ignited all around the corridor. Torches ensconced along the cavern blazed with orange flames, and I realized what I thought had been rocks and branches covering the floor were actually piles and piles of bones. The walls and ceiling were also completely plastered with thousands of bones. Some of them were absolutely massive. What were they? Dinosaur bones? Where did they all come from?

The light had appeared so abruptly and was so bright I shielded my eyes, but not before spotting the source of the strange garbled voices. Three skeletal imp-like creatures stood clustered together less than twenty feet away, next to a massive mound of bones easily the size of a small house. Beyond the mound, three tunnels emptied into the wall, heading in different directions.

The imps had long triangular skulls, beak-like noses, and hollow eye sockets from which purple pinpricks of light glowed and quivered. The anxious creatures seemed to be studying me from across the way. They couldn't have been more than four feet tall, and each imp wore a pair of raggedy toga-like robes that hung loosely about their thin, fleshless frames.

"Uh . . . hi there, fellas," I said, swallowing.

I knew it was pointless to hope these creatures were friendly, especially since they were the first to greet me in Faylinn's labyrinth. But despite their gnarly appearance, I didn't feel particularly threatened. From what I could tell, they carried no weapons, and they almost appeared to be cowering away from me in the corner next to the towering pile of bones.

Holding out my hand in what I thought was a non-threatening manner, I took a step to my right, planning to work my way around the creatures toward one of the tunnels. I figured the sooner I made it out of the labyrinth, the better, but the imp in the middle of the group immediately began chanting louder, its voice hissing and squealing like some sort of agitated gopher.

"I don't want any trouble," I said. "I'm not here to attack . . ."

But before I could finish the sentence, the two imps on either side shot away from the center, their eyes trained on me, their clawed fingers extending like weapons. And then the Die of Opportunity appeared in my hand and magical dust swirled beneath the Champion's Catch, freezing the skeletal monsters in their tracks.

"Oh, thank goodness," I gasped. I knew those monsters were up to no good. At least now I had a moment to assess the situation.

Three monsters. Three tunnels. Loads of bones. I figured the little imps might have been Faylinn's Dabraxus, though they seemed a little on the wimpy side. Maybe this challenge wouldn't be as hard as I thought after all.

Growing anxious, I stepped up to the Catch and took my roll. The hissing die rattled around, landing on the number three, and I hurriedly snatched up the playing card.

THE ROD OF WHISPERS

When cornered by danger or fleeing from death,
Deception is key and can come in one breath.
Throwing your voice is an excellent fraud;
Escape might depend on this magical rod.

I had expected to have my Gadget float out of my hand and morph into something useful, but as the card dissolved, I was surprised to see my Hero's Device remained intact. Instead, a stick no bigger than a pencil formed in my free fingers, quivering with a tingly chime as if a microscopic bell were trapped inside.

The Rod of Whispers? I wondered to myself, frowning down at the lightweight stick and eyeing my Gadget suspiciously. "What do you do?"

"*What do you do? What do you do? What do you do?*" a hushed whisper echoed out, mimicking both my words and my voice.

"Okay?" I muttered with a smirk. The Rod of Whispers echoed that as well.

What kind of weapon was this? And how was I supposed to use it to find my way through a labyrinth?

As the voice from the Champion's Catch announced the battle's inevitable start, I felt my frustrations began to grow, and I readied myself to bolt. Then time sped back up, and two of the bony imps attacked.

With a flick of my wrist, I brought up my Gadget and instantly thumbed the button. The blade shot out with a whistle and connected with the nearest imp just as it ran in to grab me. The tiny creature screeched, staggering backward and vanishing into the massive pile of bones. Whirling around, I caught a second imp right in the shoulder with my dagger. That one crumpled with a wail, its beak still jabbering nonsense as my Gadget turned the creature into a pathetic heap of flying debris. The third imp, the one that had been standing in the middle and chanting the loudest, made no sudden movements, but its purple eyes had definitely narrowed.

"You want some of this too?" I asked the creature, shaking my Gadget threateningly toward it. The Rod of Whispers called out from my other hand, startling me, as I heard it repeat my voice.

In response, the imp grew silent, its chanting coming to a close. It looked at me and then at my hand and the Rod of

Whispers in confusion. Then it leapt into the air, tucked its legs up to its chin, and dove into the mound.

"Huh," I huffed. "That was easy."

Once again, my gift from my roll of the Die of Opportunity called out at my side. I was about to cram it into my Dispenser when the bones began to move. Not all of them, mind you, just the pile. The whole pile. An avalanche of ribs, claws, and skulls cascaded down, shattering against the cavern floor as something buried underneath began to shimmy out.

Eyes widening, I caught a glimpse of a tail, followed by two enormous hind legs. Like the imps, this creature was a skeleton—but not *just* any ol' skeleton.

Towering almost to the ceiling, its head the size of a boulder, this dragon skeleton unfurled its spiny wings like the framework of an ancient airplane. Two purple orbs spotlighted from the creature's eye sockets as they darted about the room, homing in on the corridor and, of course, me. With a deafening *kerchunk,* the dragon chomped its fangs together and roared.

Then I ran, slipping and tripping and righting myself before tripping again over the mess of bone-covered floor, right through the room with the creature rising from its scrap heap, and into the first cave on the right. I didn't know where it would lead me, but I heard the dragon roar again, followed by an even more chilling sound—his colossal footsteps barreling down after me. I now knew what a Dabraxus was. Not a trio of insignificant imps but a massive, horrifying monster. And for a skeleton, Dabraxus could really move. Within a few moments, the clop, clop, cloppity sound of his claws scrabbling across the floor rang out from right behind me. Gasping for every breath and using the Rod of Whispers as a flashlight, I blindly picked another path as the corridor split into several more tunnels.

"Where am I supposed to go?" I shouted when I slid up to a wall without a way through. The Rod of Whispers immediately called out as well, and Dabraxus bellowed with rage.

Doubling back, I weaved my way through the tunnel until I arrived back at the fork and came face-to-face with the dragon. The monster's emotionless eyes glowed in their sockets. I heard the familiar sound of high-pitched voices squealing in their unrecognizable language. Clinging to the inside of the monster's rib cage were the three skeletal imps leaping up and down, chattering nonsense, and pointing at me eagerly. I couldn't understand what they were saying, but I knew what it meant. I had messed up big-time trying to fight them, and Dabraxus was on their side to make sure I learned my lesson.

With a sudden bolt of speed, Dabraxus sprang forward, his mouth opened wide. I almost succeeded in leaping out of the way, but the top of the dragon's rock-hard snout tagged me on my hip as he dove past. I barrel rolled through a smaller pile of bones and felt my Medallion buzz as I lost another Bloodstone.

"Why don't you just go back to sleep, you big, skinless pterodactyl!" I shouted, and the Rod of Whispers joined right along with me.

Dabraxus reared back, staring around in confusion as my voice echoed off the walls. Taking advantage of the distraction, I climbed back to my feet and dashed down another tunnel. I began wondering if Faylinn had dropped me into a never-ending labyrinth because every tunnel gave birth to more, and on and on it went.

At the next fork, I chose an opening on the left and skidded to a halt. I crammed the Rod of Whispers under my cloak to extinguish its light just as Dabraxus charged into the room and thundered to a stop. The dragon's skull glowed orange in the torchlight, tilting to one side as he listened through his ear hole. The impish creatures enclosed within his hollowed-out skeleton lowered their voices as well, their gibberish becoming whispers as they appeared to debate which path to take. After a few moments of hesitation, Dabraxus made his choice and, fortunately, tromped down a different tunnel, his stuttering footsteps growing muffled in the distance.

My feet began to throb from endless walking. My sides felt as though they were being ripped apart. I began to notice a light growing brighter up ahead, pouring out from a small crack in the wall. I approached the crack, realizing I could see into the middle tunnel. Water dripped from at least a dozen jagged stalactites jutting down from the ceiling, and bright-green moss carpeted the floor. But where were all the bones? It looked like a normal cave. More exciting than that, I could see an archway at the far end bathed in light, with stars blinking beyond it. I just had to run back to the beginning of this tunnel and skip over to the middle. If I picked up my pace, I could be . . .

An earsplitting roar drove my train of thought right off the tracks. Looking back through the crack, I spotted Dabraxus prowling back and forth in front of the archway.

"No!" I hissed, and I didn't even care about the Rod of Whispers echoing my negativity.

With the dragon barricading my escape, I would never make it out of this horrible labyrinth. I might as well have shouted at the top of my lungs and let the rod give away my position. For a brief moment, I felt the Creepers approaching. I shook my head and willed them away.

"Hold up a second," I whispered, staring down at the rod. What if I gave away my position? What had the clue on the card said again? Something about how throwing my voice was an excellent fraud.

Testing out my theory, I tossed the Rod of Whispers down the corridor. It bounced and flipped and rolled beneath an oblong skull with three eye sockets lying on its side.

"Hey, there," I said.

Bluish light glowed from beneath the skull as my voice called out, clear as a bell. I wasn't out of trouble just yet because I didn't know if I could trust that Dabraxus could be so easily tricked. I needed something to make sure my plan was foolproof, and I remembered just the thing to do it.

Had I not absolutely hated Avery, I might have enjoyed her gift. Instead, I smashed her wooden muting device against a pile of bones, gears and wire and tiny gimbals spilling out. Grabbing my Gadget, I concentrated on the button and pressed it down, hoping for something useful. With a whoosh of clanging metal, a new tool appeared at the end of my Device. This time it was a wrench.

Taking a deep breath, I cleared my mind. Now it was time for me to discover what it really meant to be an Artisan.

Several minutes later, I held up my modified contraption. It still somewhat resembled Avery's, except the bird no longer bobbed, I had added wheels, and I'd reversed the muting effect—now it amplified sound.. Twisting the new windup key in the device's side and placing it gently on the ground at my feet, the bird began hastily puttering forward. Hopping and clicking as the key slowly unwound, it continued on until it bumped against the cavern wall and tipped over.

Not bad, I thought, smiling at my creation. I might just have a chance.

Now to lure the beast.

CHAPTER 26

NOT AT ALL
AS I HAD PLANNED

I backtracked to where the middle tunnel began, and, moving along cautiously, I continued until the cave widened, and I saw Dabraxus sprawled out in front of the finish line, his jaw resting on his massive claws. The endless trees of the Hagwoods rose up behind him through the glowing archway. I could still hear the imps chattering inside the dragon's belly, could see their eyes flitting back and forth.

What I was about to do was either incredibly stupid or totally brilliant. It was going to work—or I was going to be joining those imps inside Dabraxus's stomach. Either way, there was no turning back now.

Cupping my hands around my mouth, I started running, shouting, "Hey, there, Dabraxus! I've got your dinner right here!"

The dragon instantly exploded from the ground, the imps squealing with delight. With the monster in hot pursuit, I raced through the tunnel until the stone walls turned back into bones, the path spilling out into the exterior room. I dashed down the far-left corridor and applied the brakes, heels skating across the floor as the dragon barreled out of the tunnel a few cave-rattling moments later. Just as he had done before,

Dabraxus slowed to a stalking prowl, cocking his skull to one side and listening for my footsteps.

"I'm over here," I cried out through my cupped hands.

The imps started gibbering nonsense as the dragon snarled and began walking toward me. As I braced to run, to my relief, the Rod of Whispers called out from the far-right passageway where I had attached it to Avery's bird-bobber, set it down, wound up its key, and turned it loose. The dragon paused. I could sense its confusion, and though my invention had seemed to work, the voice hadn't carried quite as loud as I had hoped. I might not have snuck far enough down the corridor to throw the monster off my trail. Sure enough, just as I had feared, Dabraxus ignored the Rod of Whispers. It unleashed a blood-curdling roar and began advancing toward my tunnel.

Voice trembling in desperation, I tried one more time. "You'll never catch me going that way!"

As the rod again echoed—only this time from farther down the corridor as my little bird contraption continued hopping along—Dabraxus finally took the bait.

I waited a solid minute before creeping out to confirm the beast was really gone. Then, weaving my way back through the tunnel to the main cavern, the dragon pounding away in the opposite direction, I crossed onto the wet, mossy floor. With the archway up ahead—more importantly my freedom just beyond it—I could have done a backflip in celebration. Or at least a cartwheel.

But then the crack in the far wall burst with an explosion of showering rocks and Dabraxus smashed through. Running as though something had given him a boost, the dragon covered the distance within seconds, making a beeline straight for the archway. There was no way I would make it to the finish line before he cut me off, but I couldn't just give up. Even if I did double back and hid somewhere else in the tunnels, Dabraxus wouldn't fall for the same trick twice.

It was now or never.

And it was almost never.

As I raced to the finish line, pumping my fists as hard as I could, I tried propelling my body through the glowing archway as Dabraxus collided with me like a freight train. We became all knotted up together, rolling across the floor. I felt my chest buzz at least three more times as, one by one, my Bloodstones blinked out. Best-case scenario—I would wake up all alone back at the shack. Worst case, I wouldn't wake up at all, transformed instead into one of Faylinn's mindless wandering souls.

But I wasn't dead. Not yet at least.

Had the dragon been whole and not just bones, I had no doubt in my mind I would have been "toes up." Instead, I had somehow survived the crash. The collision with Dabraxus had wedged my leg in between his rib cage, and one of the imps, trying to sneak a Lucas snack, started gnawing on my ankle as the other two celebrated behind it. I gave the creature a sharp kick, and it hissed, its eyes quivering with rage. Then, with the dragon trying clumsily to pick its massive body up off the cavern floor, I pulled my leg free and limped across the finish line. The archway lit up with a brilliant flash of amber light, and Dabraxus unleashed a mournful howl. Then I heard the distinct sound of clapping hands coming from off to one side in the forest.

Standing beneath a row of gnarled trees, with a basket hooked on her elbow, Faylinn happily nibbled on one of her magical cookies.

"What a delightful show," she said, all smiles. "Good thing

I'm not a betting witch, or I would have definitely lost a decent chunk of silver on you."

"Did I win?" I asked, looking over my shoulder, preparing for a sneak attack.

"You won," Faylinn replied.

"Then, where are my friends?"

Pointing with her half-eaten cookie, Faylinn nodded up ahead. "Waiting for you," she said. "I keep my promises, Lucas Silver. I brought your horses as well. Those poor spooked animals proved to be a little tricky coaxing through the mists, but they calmed down eventually, and I even fitted them with saddles. Couldn't imagine how uncomfortable that must have been riding bareback to the forest. It was the least I could do, you being such a good sport and all."

"And we can just go now?" It sounded too good to be true.

"Yes, and do you see that craggy peak rising up over there, a few miles away?" I followed her finger to where a snow-covered mountain loomed above the forest, wreathed in storm clouds. "That's where you need to go in order to finish your Quest. That's where you'll find Foyos, up near the top, withering in his cave. Though he might not still be withering once you get there. It all depends on when my spell wears off, of course."

Just like that, Faylinn had transported our Band all the way through the Hagwoods. We could make it to the mountain in a couple of hours, maybe even before Avery's Band had a chance to catch up.

"Would you care for a snack before you go?" The witch's eyes gleamed as she held up her basket, giving the cookies an enticing shake. "They're still warm."

I suspected this was Faylinn's way of teasing me, but I wasn't about to take the bait. Besides, at that moment, I didn't think I could have stomached a cookie, let alone an enchanted one.

"Thanks, but I think I'll pass for now," I said.

"Suit yourself." She dipped her chin in a slight bow. "Good luck with your Quest. All the better if you defeat Foyos, and I do hope you come back to see me sometime soon."

Then Faylinn, the immortal witch, hobbled away, back through the forest.

The others stood at the edge of the forest, the horses nibbling buds off a nearby bush, as I jogged up to them.

"Did you guys see what happened?" My hands were shaking from exhaustion, but I had just defeated a dragon, albeit a skeleton one, and I couldn't wait to talk about it.

"We saw it," Jasmine replied, her tone harsher than I would have expected.

"Yeah, great job, Lucas." Folding her arms, Vanessa glared at me with a look of disdain.

Uh, what was with the ice-cold reception? Maybe I had gotten my hopes up, but shouldn't they have been dancing around and hoisting me up on their shoulders right about now?

A miserable sniffling spluttered from Miles as he kicked at a rock with his boot.

"What happened to you?" I asked. By the look of his tear-streaked face, Miles had been crying for quite some time.

"It's Goon," his voice hitched as he tried to stifle a sob.

"What about him?"

"He's . . . he's gone." Whimpering, Miles finally looked up, his eyes bloodshot.

I flinched in confusion. "Gone?"

"Yes," Jasmine said, stepping toward me with her fists clenched. "And so is his Tether and *her* Spark." She nodded at

Vanessa. "And my Spade. They're all gone. Faylinn took them from us."

Dropping my eyes in panic, I searched for my Gadget but discovered it back inside my Dispenser. Right where I had put it after exiting the labyrinth. The witch hadn't taken my Hero's Device. Why had she stolen theirs?

"She can't take them," I said, almost beginning to laugh despite the gurgling sensation in my stomach. "Madge told me our Devices would always come back. That's part of the rules."

"No, Lucas." Jasmine shook her head. "She said they would *almost* always come back. But because of the deal you made with Faylinn, that rule no longer applies."

Could that really be true? Could we actually lose our Heroes' Devices? Forfeit them because of a bargain I made with a witch?

"Then let's go get them back," I said. It had to be a mistake. I was determined to trudge back through the forest to the witch's lair.

"We *can't* get them back. That was part of the negotiations." The corners of Vanessa's eyes crinkled as she glared at me. "Don't act clueless, Lucas. We all heard you agree to surrender our weapons to Faylinn. This may be just some game, but you're not the only one playing it, and you took it too far this time."

My palms turned clammy, and my throat constricted as a feeling of sickening despair weaseled its way through my veins and a stinging needle of guilt set my stomach ablaze.

"That's not what happened," I insisted. "I had to choose someone to sacrifice. To race against Dabraxus through his labyrinth, and if I won, which I did, she would let us all go free. I didn't want anyone else to have to do it, so I picked myself."

"And you sacrificed all of us." Jasmine's eyes formed into slits, and I started to worry she might strangle me. "That's what Faylinn said when you agreed to her terms."

I shook my head, my heart beginning to throb. "That's just what you heard. She never told me that would happen. She tricked us all!"

Faylinn's deal had never been just about me beating her dragon. She had wanted something else all along. But why? Why their Devices? Did she need them for some other sinister plot, or had she only wanted to cause misery to me? If that was the case, her plan had worked to perfection.

"It doesn't matter," Vanessa said. "You didn't ask anyone else for their opinion. You didn't consult with your Band. You let being our so-called leader go right to your head, and you made the decision all on your own. And just like always, you made the wrong one."

"We could have challenged her to a fight," Jasmine added. Her voice had softened a bit, and she no longer appeared on the verge of throttling me. Instead, she just looked betrayed—which hurt way, way worse. "Powerful witch or not, we could have tried to beat her together."

How could this be happening? We should have been one step closer to the end of our Quest, but now they had all turned against me.

"I was just trying to help." My voice cracked as tears suddenly erupted, streaming down my cheeks. It felt as though my lungs would explode at any moment. "This isn't my fault."

"It's *all* your fault," Vanessa fired back. "You tried running away from Sunnyside, and you dragged Miles into that shop. That's how this all started. You don't listen to anyone because all you care about is yourself."

I had been able to hold them off for as long as I could, but the Creepers had finally arrived. Screaming at the top of my lungs, I sobbed uncontrollably. I didn't even care that Jasmine could see me like this, or Vanessa. They could think whatever they wanted. Feeling my cheeks flush and wanting nothing more than to punch myself over and over in the face, I turned and stomped over to my horse.

"That's right, go ahead." Vanessa laughed scornfully as I climbed into the saddle. "Run away like a sad little orphan. If only you had succeeded in doing that in the first place, none of this would have ever happened."

"Stop it, Vanessa," Jasmine demanded. "Leave him alone. She doesn't know what she's talking about, Lucas. She's just upset. None of us feel that way about you."

"Yeah, don't go," Miles called after me. "I know Goon isn't really dead. It's only a game, and we need you."

But I wasn't listening anymore. With each breath shuddering out and setting my lungs on fire, I snapped the reins with a furious crack, hoping my horse would respond. Miles had commanded our animals to obey us, but that had been earlier, when he still had his Tether. Fortunately, my horse remained obedient and didn't buck me off into the mud. I wasn't even sure which way to go, but anywhere was better than the forest and being surrounded by my disappointed friends.

Refusing to look back, I spurred my horse into a gallop, and we burst through the edge of the forest, racing away from Mount Restless, leaving the others behind.

CHAPTER 27

MUSCLE FOR HIRE

Maybe Vanessa had been right all along. Maybe I did only care about myself, but only because I had never mattered to anyone else. A flurry of angry, hateful thoughts filled my mind as I galloped away.

The others didn't need me.

No one needed me.

Not my dead parents. Not all the other caretakers who had put up with me for as long as they could before having me shipped off to the next foster home.

Jasmine could be the new leader in my absence. She should have been it in the first place.

They could still finish the Quest without me.

I had always been better off on my own.

After almost an hour of stewing and feeling sorry for myself, the Creepers slipped back into hiding, and my horse slowed as we approached the river.

Fence posts trailed along the rim of the river, ending at a large gate. Beyond the gate, a massive boat with a steel tube rising up from the center had been anchored to a wooden platform on the river's glossy surface. Dripping with water and festooned with seaweed, the top half of an immense steel paddle rose up at the rear of the boat, the bottom half disappearing underneath the river.

"Lucas Silver?" a voice snapped my attention away from admiring the boat. "It is you, isn't it?"

On the nearby riverbank, Fawson Bendfollower, the teenage boy I had met in Trouble's Landing, sat at a table next to an elderly woman. Both he and the woman held feather quills and had apparently been in the process of scribbling in some sort of journal. An enormous, hulking creature with crumbly brown skin, perhaps a foot or two taller than Jugger, loomed behind them.

"Uh, hi, Fawson," I said, warily watching the creature remove an armful of suitcases from a tower of luggage. It then lumbered off toward the boat, through a crowd of waiting passengers, and carried at least a dozen suitcases up the gangplank. "What's going on here?"

"Oh, we're just loading up," Fawson replied. "The steamship *Stettler* is set to shove off, and me and my gram were unfortunately pegged with ledger duty. So we get the boring job of double-checking the ledger for passengers—and a lot of other pointless tasks, if you ask me." Fawson's gram glanced up from her feather-quilling long enough to smile politely from behind a pair of thin-rimmed spectacles.

Moving out from behind the table, Fawson took my horse's muzzle in his hand and began gently stroking her chin. "I'm afraid the *Stettler*'s no place for a pony, but there's a stable nearby, and I can have Prunessa take her there if you'd like. The owner's son is a chum of mine, and we'll cover the cost of boarding your horse until you return."

"Return?" I asked, feeling slightly puzzled.

Snickering, Fawson playfully nudged the older lady with his

elbow. "Didn't I say he'd show? That's why I didn't even bother looking for another."

"You still want me to come with you?" I honestly had never expected to see Fawson again.

The boy's snickering petered out. "Yeah—of course we do. The unexplored spaces of the map are definitely not for the faint of heart, but with an Artisan on board, we wouldn't sweat it. That's why you came here, right?"

"I don't even know where *here* is," I said, pawing at my eyes. The tears had all dried up, the puffiness had gone down, and hopefully it was too dark for Fawson to notice I had been crying.

"Well, this is the Highwater Crossing of the Frostbound River, though, due to a dry winter, she ain't so high and proud as of late. It's the very last spot to put into the river before she turns all bubbly and swarming with monsters all the way to the Northern Sea." Digging a fist into his hip, Fawson cast a wistful glance at the river, as if taking it all in for the first time. "Don't you worry, though. The *Stettler*'s too bottom-heavy to be capsized by some hungry leviathan, so the chances of us ending up in the river are slim to none."

The sound of heavy footsteps approached as the suitcase-carrying creature returned from the boat. Carrying the musty scent of wet mud, the muscular figure once again stepped up to the teetering tower of luggage for a second load.

"That's a golem, isn't it?" I asked.

"Who, Prunessa?" Fawson replied with a sigh. "Well, technically, yes. But she's not much more than a grunt, if you ask me. Mostly just clay and ox manure, but she's all right, I suppose. Had we been smarter with our silver, we could have paid that sketchy sorcerer a bit more to carve us up an actual stone golem. Then we wouldn't need to hire a Champion like yourself to join us. Just an added precaution, of course. I can't promise you it will be a vacation, but I can promise an adventure. If you've ever wanted to get away and leave everything else behind, your timing is perfect."

Stretching out a hand, Prunessa began gathering more suitcases but paused abruptly when Fawson made a shrill whistle with his fingers.

"Oi, you big ball of dung! Stop what you're doing, will you? Take Master Silver's horse down the road to the stables. As long as it's still okay by you, that is?" he asked, his eyes drifting up to mine.

Fleeing on horseback had been the extent of my planning. Beyond that, I hadn't given much thought to where I would go next. Back in Bentford, I honestly had been ready to ride the Carrington Express all the way to New York City and disappear forever. Climbing onboard the steamship *Stettler*, as intriguing as it may have sounded, would mean a lot more than simply taking a break for a side quest. What about Foyos? What about going home? Could I really abandon the Wild Crows?

The memory of my Creeper attack no more than an hour ago came rushing back, and my face flushed again.

No, I couldn't return to the others, and it wasn't like I had a home to go back to in Bentford anyway. If running away was my only option, no matter where I was, even if it was just a game, I could be somebody else. Somebody important.

"Actually, that sounds good to me," I said, swinging my legs over the side of my saddle and climbing down. "That's why I came here in the first place."

My days as a member of the Wild Crows had come to an end.

CHAPTER 28

SOMETHING WORTH LIVING FOR

A rickety *boing* shrieked as I plopped down on my cot. Wet and possibly squirming with mice, the mattress drooped and sagged in the middle, as though I were jelly spread over an enormous slice of bread. I was too tired to care, especially after traveling cross-country and tossing and turning on the hard ground, barely sleeping a wink.

Kicking off my boots, I punched the down-filled pillow for good measure. It felt soft and warm, and I imagined how jealous the others would be if they could see me now. Then I shoved the thought as far away as possible, no longer wanting to think about Miles, Jasmine, and Vanessa.

Through my bedroom's rusty porthole with chipped glass I watched passengers dressed somewhat like Fawson scaling the gangplank and climbing aboard. Prunessa the clay golem worked tirelessly, sending the platform swaying beneath her heavy footsteps, and beyond her, the glimmering moonlight reflected across the mirrorlike surface of the river.

According to Fawson, I needed to be present for a meeting on deck just before the steamship *Stettler* shoved off. After that, I would no longer be Lucas Silver, Champion Artisan on a

221

dangerous Quest. Instead, I would be Lucas Silver, hired muscle. Like a mercenary or a bodyguard.

"What's so funny?" someone right next to me on the bed asked, interrupting my chuckling.

Screaming in terror, I catapulted backward into the wall.

Madge Crockery, human-sized but with legs this time instead of smoke, sat at the end of my mattress. In one hand she held a wrinkly, black leather bag by its handles and a Popsicle in the other.

"Madge?" I clutched my chest in shock, my heart thumping my rib cage like a xylophone. "What are *you* doing here?"

"Was going to ask you the same question," she replied, sticking the berry Popsicle into her mouth. Removing the frozen treat, Madge licked the drippy syrup from her lips. "What *am* I doing here?"

"Giving me a heart attack, I think." Peeling myself off the wall, I sunk back into the mattress.

"I can see that." Cracking a smile, Madge nodded, but then her expression turned quizzical. "Are you taking a boat to Mount Restless? Seems a smidge out of the way, if you ask me."

"I'm not going to Mount Restless."

Biting a huge hunk off her Popsicle, Madge chomped for a moment but then squinted in pain from an apparent brain freeze. "Why do I always do that?" she groaned.

"You haven't answered my question yet," I said, crossing my arms.

"And you haven't answered mine."

"I don't know why you're here. I didn't call for you."

"Well, somebody did," she said. "The other members of your Band aren't passengers with you on this boat, are they?"

I didn't answer her.

"Mm-hm. And you've left them to finish the Quest without you," she continued, a definite hint of disappointment in her tone. "You've thrown in the towel, haven't you?"

"It's not like that," I said, even though it was exactly like that. "I had no choice but to quit. The others don't want me in the Band anymore—"

"Oh, pish-posh-pooh." Madge jabbed her half-eaten Popsicle at me. "I don't believe that for one second."

"I messed up. Big-time." My voice almost cracked, but I held it together as best I could. I was all cried out.

Madge's eyes turned serious as she listened. I didn't tell her everything that had happened since last we spoke, but I told her enough. And when I finished sharing about my meltdown following the horrible decision of trusting a witch, she didn't offer an immediate reply. Instead, she just sat there staring at the floor, nose twitching back and forth in thought for more than a minute.

"Well, I suppose you're right about one thing," she said, forcing a blubbering sigh. "That definitely falls under the category of messing up big-time. You let your friends down, no doubt about it, and you may have thrown any hopes they had of finishing this Quest right out the window."

"I know," I agreed. "I ruined everything."

Madge's head bobbled. "But you still have a chance of fixing it."

"How?"

"For starters, climbing off this death trap of a boat. What did they use to build it? Cardboard?" She stomped a boot against the floor, and the board nearly cracked.

"I can't go back," I said. "Didn't you hear what I said?"

"Yes, indeedy. And the way I see it, the Band Leader of the

Wild Crows is the only one fit to repair the damage. A true leader isn't a perfect one. Far from it. But he is someone who doesn't run from his problems. A true leader owns up to his mistakes, as painful as they may be, and does whatever he can to make them right."

"I'm not a leader, okay?" I could hear voices out in the hallway as more passengers made it to their rooms. I didn't want to cause another scene, but Madge was wrong about me, and she had been wrong since the beginning.

"I tried to tell you this before," I said. "You don't know anything about me. Neither does Jasmine or Vanessa. Not even Miles. I should never have been the one in charge. This was all just a big mistake."

"It's no mistake—"

"Yes, it is." I stopped her before she could say anything else. "Hob was looking for anyone, but he should have waited for the next random kid to wander into his shop. Don't you get it? I only stopped to check out the store for a moment, and then I was running away."

"On a train to New York City," Madge said, nodding. "And that wasn't the first time you had tried it either. When your parents died when you were eight, you were left without any family willing to take you in, and you spent the next four and a half years devising elaborate plans of escape from almost a dozen different foster homes. But this last one might have worked. No one at Sunnyside would have ever suspected you would travel by train, though Miles would have eventually spilled the beans. He's too faithful of a friend not to."

Hiding the look of surprise on my face would have been almost impossible. "How do you know that about me?"

"The question should be 'How *long* have I known that

about you?'" she replied with a giggle. "Now, don't panic. I haven't been watching you since birth, but a few months ago, Hob came to me with a request. He had begun fearing his current Band of Champions was falling under par, and he had grown desperate for some new recruits. So I went directly to the orphanages and the foster homes all over town."

"Why?" I asked, interrupting her story. "Why orphanages?"

"Because that's where you find some of the bravest heroes. Those are the ones who've experienced some of the greatest disappointments—and who know how to survive. And that's when I stumbled upon you. I did my research, of course, found out what I could about this troubled boy with his collection of dice and about his roommate, Miles, a fitting companion for any hero on a journey. When Jasmine came into the picture shortly after, all filled with fire and rage, Hob had himself the pieces of a worthy Band."

Outside, the massive paddle had begun churning ever so slowly as the steamship *Stettler* entered its final stages before departure. I was supposed to be headed up top for the meeting, but for some reason, my legs had lost all feeling. Hob had sent Madge out to find someone, and out of all the kids in Bentford, she had chosen me. Was this all a trick? Just Madge's clever way of changing my mind? Instead of a wobbly, tickling-my-stomach-with-pins-and-needles type of feeling, however, this felt like an eerie, puckering-my-forearms-with-goose-bumps type of feeling.

"What about Vanessa?" I asked. Could she have been part of Madge's recruitment process?

Madge sucked back on her teeth. "No Band would be complete without a little conflict thrown into the mix. The grit on the sharpening stone, if you will. And while she acts the part of someone loathing every minute of her time, Vanessa needs this game in her life. *And* she needs you."

"Yeah, right," I scoffed.

"Think what you want, but it's true."

"So, you're saying Hob planned everything out," I said. "That he knew we would all come together that day in his shop." It seemed too outrageous to believe.

"He's a wizard, Lucas," Madge replied. "It's what they do. Look, I won't bore you again, but I think you're starting to understand where you fit into my little boulder-rippling pond spiel on randomness—and why you abandoning your Quest is the worst thing you can possibly do."

I tried nodding in agreement, but I couldn't bring myself to do it. "It doesn't matter anymore. I wanted to run away before all this happened, so why should I stop now? My life is my adventure," I said. "And there's no one else who can help me on my way."

"Oh, brother, what is that you're barking on about now?" Madge demanded.

"It was just some quote written on my train ticket back home."

"Well, it's a load of hogwash," she said with a scowl. "*My life is my adventure*. Absolute garbage."

"It's not garbage." I had always liked that quote from the Carrington Express.

Madge clucked her tongue. "Life isn't an adventure, Lucas. Life's just life. And no matter how hard it may be for some people, everyone has to live it no matter what. Friendship, on the other hand, now that's the real adventure. Friendship's something that makes life worth living for. And that's why you can't just leave your friends, Lucas. Not in the moment when they need you the most."

From out of nowhere, Madge's words hit me right between the eyes, and a painful lump formed in my throat. "But I'll just mess everything up again," I muttered, trying to swallow. "I can't help them win."

"Someone seems to think you can," she said, glancing around my room. "And he sent a whole guild across your path to try to separate you from your Band just to stop the Wild Crows and Hob. Who do you think really wanted you to climb aboard this abysmal boat and drift away?"

"Um . . . Bogie?" I asked, not sure I followed her.

Madge's eyes twinkled mysteriously. "If that doesn't boost your confidence, nothing will."

"Wait, does that mean Fawson and his whole Exploratory Guild are really evil?"

Madge crowed loud enough to rattle the porthole window. "Of course not! They're just doing their job, heading north, I suppose. But Bogie's the one who drew their card and put them into play."

My head started to spin. Meeting Fawson in Trouble's Landing and then bumping into him once again at the Highwater Crossing had not been purely by accident. Bogie had played a card in the game against me, and it had almost worked.

"I can't be on here," I gasped, springing up from the mattress.

"First intelligent thing you've said all night," Madge said. "Now, stop moping around and put on those boots."

I nearly split the leather bindings trying to squeeze my feet into my boots, but I couldn't put them on fast enough.

"Wait a minute." I looked at Madge with one heel halfway down my boot. "You were sent here, weren't you?"

"I was," she admitted, looking sheepish.

"By Hob?" That had to be the only explanation.

Shaking her head, Madge nodded at the door. "No, I was sent by *them*."

Immediately, the door swung open and a swarm of frighteningly gigantic insects rushed in. I cried out in alarm as the insects attacked, buzzing around me and fluttering right up into my face. Madge, finding the whole scene hilarious, nearly buckled over with laughter.

"Help me!" I demanded, covering my eyes as I fell back onto the bed. There was nothing funny about massive hornets stinging me to death.

"Sorry, I didn't know the hummingbirds would burst into the room first," Madge said, still laughing hysterically.

"Hummingbirds?" I risked peering through my fingers at the swarm.

Instead of giant wasps or murderous mosquitoes, a flock of hummingbirds hovered in the room. And they weren't trying to peck my eyes out either. Wings blurring, the birds only circled and chirped excitedly around my head.

"Hey, you three can't just come aboard!" I heard a man shouting outside, followed by a flurry of pounding footsteps racing overhead. The footsteps descended the stairs and seconds later, Miles burst into the room with Jasmine and Vanessa right behind.

"Nice job, guys," Miles cheered. "You found him." The hummingbirds let out a chorus of chirping before breaking from their orbit around me and returning to Miles. "Now, go and uh . . . be free," he instructed, puffing a few sharp notes on his whistle. Before I could blink, the birds promptly obeyed and zipped from the room.

"Miles, where did you get that?" I asked. I may have been amazed to see them on the boat, but the reappearance of Miles's Tether surprised me the most.

"Madge got them back for us," he said breathlessly, nodding at Jasmine and Vanessa. Jasmine held up her Spade while Vanessa lingered in the doorway, her Spark once again strapped to her back.

"And check this out." Miles tugged on his shirt, and a familiar snout appeared, Goon poking up above his collar.

"But how?" I gaped over at Madge.

She grunted with annoyance. "Faylinn and I go way back. She still owed me for doing something for her almost a century ago—which I'd rather not talk about."

"She gave you back their Devices, just like that?" After what that witch had put us through, I found it almost impossible to believe.

"Not just like that," Madge grumbled. "I had to strike a deal with her, which I'm sure may come back to bite me—and you, for that matter—down the road. And they're just on loan for the duration of your Quest. Faylinn is now the sole possessor of your Heroes' Devices. Yours too, Lucas, I'm afraid. Except for Goon, of course. He should have never been a part of the bargain to begin with."

"What does that mean, on loan?" I asked.

"Don't know yet," she said. "But we'll sort it out eventually. And I didn't do it for free. I'm no pushover, mind you."

"We paid her," Miles said.

"Paid her?" I frowned. "With what?"

"Did you know these diamonds have come all the way from the Ice Caverns?" Madge fluffed her hair back, revealing a pair of sparkling earrings. They were the same earrings Vanessa had purchased from the street vendor back in Trouble's Landing.

"I don't know what to say, Madge." I shook my head, baffled by what had happened. Without Madge, where would we be? I would have been down the river and out of the Wild Crows forever. "Thank you."

"You're welcome," she replied, shrugging. "But you need to be smarter now. All of you. The Fate of your Quest hangs by a piece of cobweb no bigger than my pinkie finger. And if you want to take control of your Destiny, you're going to have to be as clever and crafty as that witch, if you know what I mean. Right, Miles?"

Miles's eyes shot up from staring at the floor. "That's right," he said. "I mean . . . um . . . what are you talking about?"

"Your Destiny," she replied with a wink. "It's in your very capable hands. So don't botch it, all right?"

"We'll do our best," I said.

"That's all a Crockery can ask. Now, if you don't mind, I do believe I've more than delivered on your requirements of the Token of Necessity, have I not?" Madge asked.

Jasmine nodded. "Yes, you have."

"In that case, I'll head back." Smoothing out the wrinkles in her brightly colored pants, Madge stood from the bed. "So long, my good friends. Until we meet again, yada, yada, yada, and all that jazz—" Then, without fanfare, swirling pixie dust, or any other fantastic puff of smoke, Madge vanished.

"You used your Token of Necessity to get your Heroes' Devices back," I said. "That was pretty smart."

"No, we used it to get *you* back," Jasmine explained. "Getting those was just a bonus."

"And it was all Vanessa's idea," Miles chimed in. "We weren't even sure what to do after you left, but then she remembered Jasmine's Token."

Blinking in surprise, I glanced over at Vanessa. "Seriously?"

"Don't make this more awkward than it already is," Vanessa said. "It's not like I don't think you're still a dork or anything like that. I just want to be done with this stupid game."

"That's not what she said back in the Hagwoods." Miles giggled. "You should have seen her crying and talking about how horrible she felt about the way she treated you—"

"Shut up, Miles!" Vanessa took a threatening step toward him. "Those Hagwoods irritated my allergies, that's all."

Hunching his shoulders, Miles cowered from her wrath, but flashed a quick wink when she looked away.

"Look, Lucas, I didn't mean what I said back there," Vanessa muttered. "You know that, right? I don't hate you, and I definitely don't think you're a sad little orphan. I should have never said any of that. It was wrong, and I feel really bad, because I don't blame you for what happened."

"None of us do," Jasmine added. "If you hadn't been the one to volunteer, someone else would have had to."

"And we wouldn't have been able to beat Dabraxus like you did," Miles said. "That was amazing."

Though it did feel awesome hearing that, especially coming from Vanessa, I still felt embarrassed about the way I'd acted. I guess my face must have shown it.

"No one cares about your meltdown," Vanessa said. "It's in the past, and we need you back as our leader."

"What do you say, Lucas?" Jasmine asked.

With both feet firmly snug within my boots, I held out a hand, and Miles helped me up from the bed. "I say it's about time we made our way off this boat."

CHAPTER 29

THE ONE WITH THE
MOST TO LOSE

Almost a full week had passed since the beginning of summer vacation and that fateful afternoon when Miles and I first snuck into Hob & Bogie's Curiosity Shoppe. Back then—which felt like a lifetime ago—I barely knew Jasmine Bautista, and I had almost considered Vanessa my archenemy. Now, here we were, the four of us sitting together eating while the ominous Mount Restless, lair of the dreaded Foyos, towered overhead like a massive granite fang.

"Do we have any idea what kind of powers this creature has?" Vanessa asked, grabbing a handful of crackers as I passed the half-eaten container to her.

By the way we had spread our rations out on the ground, it almost felt like we were having a nice picnic instead of planning our strategy to slay Foyos. Along with the food, we had emptied our Dispensers as well. We didn't have much, just the two remaining gifts from Gilner's Gifting Meadow—my Zabor's Coin of Interrogation, which would allow me to ask two questions to any character in the game, and Miles's Revolutionary Die of Change, which would allow him to reroll any of his dice rolls. Not exactly a full arsenal of weapons. The monster may have been weakened and languishing due to Faylinn's magic, but that magic was wearing off and we were going to have our hands full with Foyos. Fortunately, the sun was shining brightly overhead, there didn't seem to be any other creatures lurking around nearby, and the extra rest had already helped recover more than half our Vitality Meters.

"The Quest Log just says Foyos terrorized the countryside, taking whatever he wanted and destroying anyone who attempted to stop him," Miles read from the scroll.

"But he's not our only problem right now," Vanessa added. "What are we going to do if we run into the Orc Slayers?"

Vanessa had a point. The Orc Slayers could be anywhere close by and posed a serious threat.

"Maybe we should use this." I picked up Zabor's Coin of Interrogation from the pile.

"How does that work?" Jasmine asked.

"Gilner just said I needed to drop it into water and then call out the name of the character I wanted to talk to," I explained, recalling the Gilded Gargoyle's instructions. "Then I can ask two questions, which they have to answer truthfully."

"Who should we ask?" Miles nibbled on a cracker, his eyes flitting around the group. "Who would know the most?"

"Madge would," Jasmine said.

Miles's eyes widened with excitement. "Yeah, she knows just about everything there is to know about Champion's Quest."

We had just spoken with Madge, and calling her back would be easy enough to do. But while she had been helpful, even encouraging us as though she was really rooting for us to win, I worried she would be limited in what she could tell us about our Quest.

"What about my friend Philip?" Vanessa suggested. "You know? The boy I met in Trouble's Landing. He knows a lot, too, and he *did* help us find the secret way through the Enchanted Mists. And no, I'm just not trying to see him again, though it would be nice."

Jasmine rolled her eyes. "I don't think that's a good idea. Philip would want to help you even without using the coin."

"Right," I agreed. "Which makes me think we should be asking someone who *wouldn't* want to help us. Someone with more to lose."

Jasmine frowned. "Are you suggesting Jugger?"

"I think he means Faylinn," Vanessa said. "She defeated Foyos once before."

That witch had been the cause of so much trouble, but if there was any character in the game who knew of a way to defeat Foyos, it was Faylinn. Yet asking her would only solve half our problems. Would she even know how to beat the Orc Slayers?

"What if we picked Bogie?" I asked, palming the coin as an uncomfortable hush settled over our picnic lunch. It was definitely a stretch, but I wondered if it might work.

"Pick Bogie?" Jasmine's eyebrows crinkled as she started grinning mischievously.

"Could we do that?" Miles whispered.

"I don't know," I admitted. "I think it might be worth a shot, right?"

"Maybe," Vanessa muttered, looking confused. "Except what if it doesn't work and we throw away our only chance?"

"It's certainly risky," Jasmine said. "But Bogie *would* have all the answers, *and* he's definitely the one with the most to lose."

"What do you think, Miles?" I asked.

Miles chewed his last bite of cracker and forced it down his throat. "Uh . . . I'll go along with whatever you decide."

"Forget it," I said. "Remember what happened the last time I made a decision? I'm not doing that again."

"Yes, you are," Jasmine insisted. "You have to. You're our leader."

"And we trust you," Vanessa added. "No matter what."

"Are you guys sure about this?" The uneasy feeling of reliving the whole Hagwoods ordeal all over again grumbled in my gut.

Vanessa placed her Spark flat on the ground. Using her waterskin, she squirted about an inch of water into the circular pan. Then I dropped in Zabor's Coin of Interrogation, and a plume of pink vapor rose up.

"Okay," I said, shooting a quick glance around at the others, making sure they were still on board with my decision. "I wish to speak with Bogie."

Rising out from Vanessa's Spark, the smoke widened into a pinkish square window, opening directly into a living room. It seemed as though we were staring at a projection screen, watching some sort of odd movie, only I knew this wasn't any movie. Bookshelves lined the walls, and I could see two closed doors near the back of the room on either side of a small stove and a refrigerator covered in colorful magnets. Centered on the floor and squeezed in between a pair of empty animal cages on pedestals was an ancient tattered sofa.

"What *is* this place?" Miles whispered.

Perched upon Miles's shoulder, Goon started chirping and eagerly stretching out his nose as if trying to get closer to the room.

"I think that's his home," I said, realizing what had sparked the armadillo's excitement. "It's the back of the curiosity shop."

Then Bogie suddenly bounded into the room, confirming

my suspicions. Dressed exactly how he had been when we last saw him—the same burgundy button-down shirt and leather pants jangling with chains—the long-haired man spooned cereal from a bowl, spilling it everywhere.

"But where did you see it last?" Bogie called out over his shoulder, dribbling milk down his whiskered chin. "Honestly, you search for things like a child."

An almost inaudible voice, possibly coming from Hob, answered Bogie from the other room, but was too muffled to understand.

"What did you say?" Bogie demanded, his eyes darting angrily toward us for just a second as he whirled around. "Speak up, old man. Don't mumble. Where do you think you—" Voice trailing off, Bogie's eyes drifted back, contorting with a mixture of curiosity and annoyance. "Hob, what did you do to the television? It's acting all wonky again, and . . . oh, good grief. What is *this* supposed to be?" Still holding his cereal, a trickle of milk now steadily streaming over the brim, Bogie lowered himself onto the couch. "Hello there, children," he said, squinting. "What brings you to my living room today?"

After several seconds of hesitation, Vanessa nudged me with her elbow.

"Uh . . . we . . . you see?" I stammered before clearing my throat. "What I mean is, we used Zabor's Coin of Interrogation."

Chewing on his lower lip, Bogie released an agitated sigh. "I assumed that was the case, but why on earth would use that coin with *me*?"

"We have questions," Jasmine said. "And you have to answer them."

"Do I?" Bogie leaned forward. For a moment, Bogie acted as though he were about to spring up from the couch and escape through the exit. But after struggling against some invisible bond, he forced a smile and, putting his cereal bowl down, reclined once again on his couch.

"I suppose I do have to answer," he replied, crossing one leg over the other and interlocking his fingers around his knee.

"I must warn you, however, whatever it is you feel you must ask—I don't believe you'll enjoy the answers."

"We'll see about that." Vanessa gave me an encouraging nod. "Go on, Lucas."

We hadn't been given any time to discuss what we would ask Bogie before Zabor's Coin had gone to work, but I felt confident in my first question.

"How do we stop the Orc Slayers?" I asked.

Bogie responded by holding up a long finger. "Technically, in order to evoke a question with Zabor's Coin, one must begin with a certain phrase. The gargoyle should have informed you of this. It's protocol, I'm afraid."

"Oh, yeah," I groaned, remembering the bejeweled monster mentioning something about needing to say specific words, but I had forgotten which ones.

Bogie waved dismissively. "However, seeing how I have no desire to sit here and wait for you to drum up a memory, I shall answer this question for free. You cannot stop the Orc Slayers. It is impossible."

"Impossible?" Jasmine asked.

He nodded, a wickedly joyful smile bending his lips. "That's right. Ooh, that stings doesn't it? I think I'm going to rather enjoy this little detour."

"He's lying to us," Miles muttered.

"I cannot lie to you," Bogie replied with a harsh laugh. "Zabor, the High Elf of the Murky Meadow Wood, forbids it. And you know what? I'll even tell you why it's impossible, no further question needed. The Orc Slayers have achieved Emerald Level status. They have advanced weaponry and armor. And this is your first Quest, which means you aren't fit to even carry their Dispensers," he said, enunciating every word with glee. "But that's not all, ye Wild Crows. You cannot beat them because the game will not allow it. A Champion may not slay another Champion, for such is forbidden. Page thirty-seven of the Field Guide, paragraph six."

"Is that true?" I asked Miles.

Miles didn't know the answer. Perhaps that rule had been contained within the Champion's Quest Field Guide, but we no longer had that as a reference.

"But Avery said she didn't kill us out of respect," Jasmine said.

"Well, of course. She lied to you," Bogie replied. "Don't you remember what happened when you first breathed gas from a Viper Pod? You died. And yet, when the Orc Slayers used the very same pod against you again, you somehow survived. Peculiar, don't you think? And why on earth would they leave your Heroes' Devices simply locked in a box at your feet? Do you think they could be that imbecilic? Your Devices are off-limits to them as well. They almost always return to their Hero. Unless, of course, you foolishly swing a deal with a powerful witch." He snickered, and I once more felt the pang of guilt.

"The Orc Slayers weren't trying to do you any favors," Bogie continued. "They were simply bound by the law. Ergo, you cannot kill them. Unless you have the power to change a Destiny, you've already lost."

"Change a Destiny?" I exhaled loudly in frustration. "Fine.

Then how do we kill Foyos?" Bogie's answer may not have been what we wanted, but our hopes hadn't been utterly dashed to pieces just yet.

"Again, you did not ask correctly," Bogie muttered. "And to answer that, I'm afraid I shall have to request the opening phrase. I'm willing to wait for it, and I have all the time in the world. Which is something I can't say about the four of you."

Gilner had only told me those words in passing several days ago. How was I supposed to remember that?

"I, Vanessa Crowe, of the Wild Crow Band, wish to ask you my second question," Vanessa suddenly announced. "How do we kill Foyos?"

Bogie's somewhat cheery expression immediately turned furious as his eyes shot up from staring at his fingernails and he and I both gawked at Vanessa in amazement.

"What?" she asked. "I was listening."

Frighteningly calm, Bogie's wispy mustache caught the tail end of a breeze swishing through the back room of the curiosity shop. "The many faces of Foyos certainly pose a difficult challenge for level one Champions, but he's not an impossible opponent. Not in the least. This is an accomplishable Quest for even the least accomplished, such as yourselves." Reclining on his couch, Bogie steepled his fingers beneath his chin.

"That's it?" Vanessa threw up her hands. "That has to be the worst explanation I've ever heard. If you're supposed to tell us the truth, it only counts if we can understand it."

"I was getting to it, young lady," Bogie snapped. "I was working up to the answer. In order to slay an unpredictable monster, one must become unpredictable themselves. You will have multiple chances to try, and you mustn't get discouraged when your first or second attempts fail."

"What does that mean?" I asked.

Bogie rolled his eyes. "Look, I've given you a textbook answer. One that can be found in the manual. As far as I'm concerned, that's all I'm required to do based on the rules of Zabor's Coin. Besides, it really doesn't matter what advice I give you now, be it vague or meticulously thorough. You are going to have a difficult time killing Foyos if you're too late to even try."

"Too late?" I asked, the inside of my mouth beginning to feel like sandpaper.

"Who do you think is on their way to Mount Restless as we sit here chitchatting?" Bogie made a tsking sound with his teeth. "The Orc Slayers have already moved ahead. You, my friends, are . . . what's that old saying again? Oh, yes—a day late and a dollar short."

Jasmine suddenly kicked the Spark, sending the window of steam jolting about as she leapt up from the ground.

"What are you doing?" I demanded, trying to keep Bogie's image from wavering. "We're not finished here."

"Yes, we are," Jasmine said. "We can't sit around here and wait any longer."

"But he hasn't really answered our questions," I reasoned. "He's just stalling."

"And while he stalls, the Orc Slayers get closer to the finish line." Jasmine stuck out her jaw. "I'm not wasting any more time. We have to go now!"

"Yes, go," Bogie said, shooing us away with his fingers. "Try your best. Give it your all. Be the Champions you're meant to be while I go pour myself another bowl of Cinnamon Burst cereal and take a front-row seat to your miserable end."

CHAPTER 30

THE ORC SLAYERS' ROLL

J asmine extended her lead, racing up the path. Even Miles's horse, which had always been the fastest, couldn't keep up with her.

"She needs to slow down," Vanessa said in between sneezing as she galloped beside me. "What's she going to do when she catches up with them?"

Though I agreed, how was I supposed to stop Jasmine? From the moment Bogie had sprung the bad news, a strange look had formed in her eyes. It was a scary look; the same one she had worn when she first burst into the curiosity shop on the hunt for Tugg Roberts. The kind of look that could give even an ogre the heebie-jeebies.

As the ground sloped upward, the trees giving way to jagged rocks and patches of snow, a flurry of buzzing feathers darted out from the woods, circling Miles's head. Three hummingbirds, the same ones I assumed had located me on the boat, hovered in the air next to Miles's ear.

"What do they say, Miles?" I asked as he nodded, dismissing his obedient birds back to the woods. They chirped, fluttered, and, like colorful bursts of lightning, vanished from the path.

"They're up there," Miles answered. "The Orc Slayers.

Maybe a mile up the path. They haven't reached the entry to Foyos's lair, and they're not really in a hurry."

"Why would they be?" Vanessa asked. "Avery's not worried about us, that's for sure."

"That's good," I said. "We can still pull this off." Though *how* was still a big mystery. Trying to outsmart a monster was one thing. But Avery and the Orc Slayers weren't monsters. They were players in the game. And they had loads of practice.

When Jasmine showed no signs of letting up, I knew we had to do something to grab her attention.

"Miles, can you try to stop her?" I asked.

Miles looked uneasily down at his Tether. "I suppose I could. As long as she doesn't take it out on me."

"Just do it already," Vanessa insisted.

Looping his Tether into a tube, Miles blew a single note on his whistle, and our three horses released a startled whinny at the sound. Jasmine's horse stopped abruptly and rose up on its hind legs, kicking the air. Jasmine reared back and struggled to hang on.

"Oh, dear." Miles gaped at me in horror as Jasmine's horse nearly bucked her off before dropping back down on all fours.

"That had *better* have been an accident," Jasmine seethed, glowering at Miles, her horse circling back to us. "Are you trying to get me trampled?"

Miles meeped guiltily and pointed a blaming finger at me.

"It was my idea," I told her. "We need to talk."

"What's there to talk about?" she asked, sounding almost as out of breath as her panting horse. "I'm not going to give up."

"No one's giving up," I said. "Miles just sent his humming-birds as scouts up ahead, and we know where the Orc Slayers are. We still have a chance to beat them to the top. But if we don't come up with a strategy together, we're as good as dead."

"Then what's our strategy?" Jasmine raised her eyebrows. "We can't kill them, and they can't kill us, so all that matters is that we get to Foyos first. They can chase *us* for all I care."

"Hold up a second," Vanessa said, swinging her Spark off her back. "There's no point in straining our brains when I have power to add a little inspiration."

Jasmine anxiously tugged on the reins. "This is not going to help."

Pausing briefly to shush Jasmine with her finger, Vanessa began plucking a tune on the strings. "At least wait for the best part," she whispered. Closing her eyes, Vanessa's melody became a mixture of twangy strums and deep, resonating chords that sent a barrage of vibrations through my chest.

Miles suddenly straightened in his saddle. "It's possible they don't know we escaped the Reaper's Cart, right? Couldn't we try to capture them instead, just like they did with us?"

"Like set a trap?" I asked, the blueprints of an idea popping into my head. "I think I could figure out how to make some sort of handcuffs." I saw no reason why I couldn't use my Gadget to fashion something from the leather saddles.

"Then Jasmine could do that mud-melting trick again with her Spade," Miles added. "They would never expect that."

"And while they're sinking in the ground, we'll jump out and tie them up." Now we were getting somewhere. I knew our plan could backfire horribly, but as Vanessa continued playing her mystifying song, my confidence grew. Once our Quest was finally over, she really needed to buy herself a guitar.

"I suppose I could." Jasmine said, dragging her fingernails through her horse's mane and untangling the knots, the fury in her eyes dying away. "But I would need to get close to them in order for it to work."

"You'll need a distraction," Miles agreed. "I'll take care of that. I'm sure there are animals nearby. I'll just call them with my whistle. Just like those beavers when we fought the Treant."

Jasmine smirked. "You make it sound so simple. Like this plan won't blow up in our faces."

"It probably will," I admitted. So far, not one of our cooked-up schemes had gone without a hiccup. "But it's better than nothing."

We still had the element of surprise on our side. If we were smart and extremely lucky, we might be able to spring our trap before any Orc Slayer knew what hit them.

"You're right," Jasmine said, scratching the corner of her nose. "It is worth a shot."

Beaming in satisfaction, Vanessa wiggled her fingers across the taut strings of her Spark. "I told you that was the best part. Never had a lesson in my life, but I think I'm ready to go on tour."

· ◆ ● ◆ ·

With the details of our plan finalized, we caught up with the Orc Slayers as they rounded a corner of the twisting path. Hanging back to stay hidden, we climbed down from our horses, and Miles sent them away. I hated saying goodbye to them, but we couldn't risk accidentally alerting our enemy.

Avery walked at the rear of her Band, casually leading her horse along, her golden hair shining in the midmorning sun. We could hear Javier and Carl arguing at the front about which fast-food restaurant made the best french fries back home. Susan gathered wild berries into a basket just off the path.

None of them appeared to be in any sort of hurry as Foyos's cave, a gaping mouth awaiting to swallow its next meal, loomed ahead.

Slinking in between the rocks, Jasmine split off from our group. We watched her silently creep into position alongside the Orc Slayers, ready to spring her part of the trap.

"This is perfect," I said, ducking down behind a craggy boulder. "They don't have a clue we're here."

I handed Vanessa and Miles each a set of the handcuffs I had crafted from my saddle. For the straps to work, all they needed to do was slap the leather loop down across the wrists of an opponent. The handcuffs would take care of the rest, instantly cinching tight. Pretty amazing, if I do say so myself, and I had whipped them up in a matter of minutes, all while riding on horseback.

"Look at how bored they look," Vanessa said, scrunching her nose with disgust at the meandering group of Orc Slayers. "It's like fighting Foyos is nothing more than another chore for them. It's so annoying. Shouldn't they be facing off with something way more difficult instead of doing the same Quest as us? You would think that would be against the rules of Champion's Quest."

Miles started to agree with her but then stopped. "What if it *is* against the rules?" he asked, looking troubled. "What if we aren't supposed to be on the same Quest as them?"

"What do you mean?" I looked over at him. "I rolled the Die of Destiny." Everyone had been there, well, everyone except Vanessa, but the rest of us had watched the Die randomly pick our Quest.

"But when you rolled the Die of Destiny, I remember Bogie

saying Hob had cheated. Do you think Hob may have changed our roll?" Miles asked.

"Why would he do that?" Vanessa asked. "If he wanted us to win, I don't think he would have sent us against the Orc Slayers on purpose."

"Unless we needed to *stop* them from winning," Miles suggested.

"I guess it's possible," I said, beginning to buy into Miles's idea. "But how could he change our Destiny?"

Miles wiped his nose on his sleeve. "He's a wizard. I bet he knows a spell or two."

"So, Hob changed our Destiny," I said.

Miles gave a nervous titter of laughter. "He must really believe in us."

Or he's ultracompetitive and will do anything to defeat Bogie, including sacrificing us.

Peering over our boulder, I saw a glowing triangle rise up from behind a row of rocks as Jasmine raised her Spade into the air. "That's the signal."

Miles ducked away from the rock, scurried off the path, and a few moments later, the piercing call of his whistle rang out from behind a thorn bush several yards away. Avery stopped marching at once, her head flicking to the side and her hand closing around the handle of her deadly longsword. Bristling as well, Susan dropped her basket of berries, the end of her Tether lashing out from around her wrist. Oblivious to the whistling, Javier and Carl continued jabbering on until their horses jerked free and bolted down the path toward us, ending their heated french-fry discussion.

"Oh, good grief," Miles yelped, his Tether nearly dropping

from his lips as an enormous blur of white fur and crooked horns exploded onto the path from out of nowhere. "It's a ram!"

Not just a ram—an entire family of mountain goats barreled toward the middle of the Orc Slayers like possessed bowling balls. Avery leapt back, narrowly avoiding a collision, and with a screech of steel, a long metal pole shot from the end of her Gadget. Blindingly fast, the skilled Artisan struck as one of the rams charged past, stabbing the pole in between the creature's knobby legs. The mountain goat tumbled and somersaulted into a dense tree trunk, popping with a firework of green sparkles. Carl and Javier, however, weren't as fortunate. The two Champions took the full-on brunt of a ram to their stomachs and tumbled backward, buried beneath an angry mound of woolly horns.

Whirling around, Avery pointed directly at Miles's bush, but as she took a step toward him, the ground began to shake. Rocky and solid at first, the path immediately turned into a steaming pool of roiling mud. Avery tried finding her footing in the sloppy mess, while the much shorter Susan sank down to her waist.

"Now!" I shouted, springing from our hiding place with Vanessa at my side.

Miles stopped whistling as the thorn bush he had been hiding behind started swaying back and forth. Then he toppled out with Sheba the sloth clinging to his back, her long arms gripping his neck tightly. Goon had fallen from underneath Miles's shirt and was nipping at the sloth's back, but Sheba paid him no attention. Struggling for breath, Miles desperately pawed at the ground, his Tether just out of reach.

"That meddling mutant squirrel," Vanessa growled.

Gripping her Spark like a hammer, she strode forward as

I spotted the trap, a second too late. There was a gusting *fff-foooom*, followed by a disheartening *thrrrroing*, as Vanessa's ankle snagged a trip wire stretched across the path. An almost invisible net rose up from the ground, gobbling both Vanessa and me like a pair of unsuspecting fish.

"You are full of surprises, aren't you?" Avery announced, using her Gadget pole like an oar to wade through the mud.

Behind her, Susan had managed to climb out and had already calmed down the skittish mountain goats with her own Tether. Despite Jasmine's struggling, Javier and Carl easily took her out of the equation, wrestling her arms behind her back and relieving her of her Spade.

"Call off your beast, Susan," Avery commanded.

With a snap of the redheaded Gamekeeper's fingers, Sheba instantly released her chokehold on Miles. Goon continued to nip and bite, but with a deceptively quick backhand, the sloth sent the pestering armadillo rolling away.

"Who told you we were coming?" I demanded, humiliated for having fallen into their trap.

"No one told us," Avery replied, shaking her head sympathetically. She pressed the button on her Gadget, and the pole retracted, vanishing into the cylinder.

"Then what's with the tripwire?" Jasmine asked, trying to weasel free from Javier's viselike grip.

"I lay traps wherever I go," Avery said. "It's a smart practice we Artisans do."

Leaning forward, Avery reached through the net and tugged my Advancement Medallion above my collar. Eyes brightening, she took in a soft gasp of surprise. "And you somehow succeeded in acquiring a Ward against Withering spell too."

"Don't touch me," I hissed, snatching back my Medallion.

"How did you do it?" Carl asked. "How did you convince Faylinn to help you?"

"Oh, it was nothing," Vanessa answered, leering through the net. "Lucas just beat Dabraxus in a race. Obviously, something you weren't brave enough to do."

Pursing her lips, Avery looked skeptical. "But that means you would have had to surrender your Hero's Devices, and I can clearly see you haven't."

"I guess we have a few more tricks up our sleeve," Jasmine said.

"Indeed. Unfortunately, you're still no match for the Orc Slayers. Get them up," Avery issued the order, and the others forced us to our feet. "Now, what to do with these bothersome little crows?"

"Why don't you kill us?" I asked, maybe a teensy bit worried Bogie had fibbed about that rule. "That would be the easiest thing to do."

"That *would* be the easiest," Avery agreed. "But something tells me you've learned that we can't kill you even if we wanted to."

"Fight us, then," Jasmine said, clenching her jaw defiantly. "Let us go free and challenge us head to head to see who's the best."

"Didn't we just do that?" Javier raised one quizzical eyebrow and elbowed Carl in the ribs.

"How about you let us help you?" Miles suggested. "Eight heads are better than four. We could work together to kill Foyos."

Pressing her hand against her heart, Susan squealed with delight. "Isn't he the cutest little thing?" she asked in a strong Southern accent. "We *could* use their help, couldn't we?"

"Yeah." Miles nodded enthusiastically. "We could finish this Quest together."

"Why, I think we could tie them up all nice and tight and toss the four of them into the cave," Susan continued, fluttering her eyelashes. "We could use them as bait. And then"—reaching over, she pinched Miles's cheek—"when we've lured out the beast, Foyos could chomp them down like a plate of hushpuppies. No need for us to trouble over the rules anymore. Let the monster take care of this nasty business for us."

"Er . . . Or you could let us go," Miles added hastily. "And then we'll just leave."

"I don't believe that for one second." Avery glanced at the cave up ahead. "Why do you keep putting me in this position? I like you guys. I really do. You're playing the game with such passion and zeal, but you keep getting in the way."

"Well, you're in *our* way," I said.

"And we always will be," Javier said. "At least for this Quest. Let's just hurry up and figure out a way to put an end to their troublemaking."

Avery glanced at Javier, her eyes gleaming sympathetically. "But they're trying so hard," she said, almost laughing. "It doesn't feel right to just squash them like bugs and contribute to their deaths."

"Oh, come on, Aves," Carl groaned. "Isn't it time we moved past this? Because of these nuisances, our Quest has already taken longer than any of the rest. And I'm kind of eager to get home and go get some french fries."

"From Fry Days," Javier insisted.

"No, from Greasy Tots," Carl fired back. "Fry Days doesn't even use real potatoes."

French fries? A moment earlier, they had been determining

how to dispose of us, even going so far as to suggest feeding us to Foyos as a snack, and now they were back to fighting about fast food?

"We're not going to kill them *or* use them as bait." Avery cast a sidelong glance at Susan, who sighed in disappointment. "But we will have to take them out of commission. Perhaps another Viper Pod, but a stronger dose this time to knock them out for several hours. You have one, don't you?"

"Always," Susan replied.

"Wait," Vanessa pleaded. "Think about this for just a second. You don't have to—"

"We already have," Avery cut her off. "And our minds are made up. You made a valiant effort, you truly are worthy to bear the Champion name, but it's not our Destiny to battle another band. Honestly, I don't even know how or why you're on the same quest we are. Either way, our Destiny is to finish this Quest. And that's what we're going to do."

As Susan opened her Dispenser and the ugly, veiny bulb appeared in her hand, already leaking toxic fumes, something dropped on the stone ground beneath Miles's feet. Rattling, the object tumbled over into the steaming pool of mud.

"A Die of Change?" Javier stooped over and picked up the final item claimed from the Gifting Meadow. "Is this yours?"

Pursing his lips, nostrils flaring, Miles nodded slowly.

"Do you want it back?" Javier asked, holding out the six-sided cube.

"I rolled it," Miles said. "I thought I would have to toss it into the Champion's Catch, but I guess I didn't."

Avery chuckled. "Defiant to the end, aren't you? But re-rolling for a new weapon will make no difference to this outcome. Artifacts and items can carry over to your next Quests. You should have saved that one for another day."

"I didn't roll for a new weapon." Miles's eyes focused in on the Die of Change resting in Javier's palm.

Perhaps Miles was stalling to buy us a little more time to break free, but I couldn't figure out his strategy.

"Sweetie, if not for a new weapon, what did you roll for?" Susan asked in her singsong drawl.

"A new Destiny," Miles replied.

Avery's forehead crinkled. "Interesting strategy. That would certainly save us the trouble of dealing with you. And I don't think it would count as giving up. Changing your Destiny is, in fact, a noble idea."

"You're right," Miles said, glancing up at her. "And the Gilded Gargoyle told me it would work for any Champion in the game. So I didn't roll it for *us*."

Avery's skin turned the palest shade I had ever seen as she released a deflated sigh. Then, with a gust of wind and a detonation of glittering sparkles, the Orc Slayer Band vanished from the mountain.

CHAPTER 31

THE MANY FACES OF FOYOS

J asmine's feet hardly touched the ground as she sprang over and tackled Miles, the two of them rolling together and laughing hysterically. Vanessa screamed, her eyes filling with tears, and I just stared at the spot where Avery once stood, too dumbfounded to even open my mouth. Miles had just pulled off the most epic magic trick of all time.

"How did you know that would work?" Jasmine asked, squeezing the smaller eleven-year-old.

"I didn't," Miles wheezed, struggling to catch his breath amid Jasmine's bear hug. "I just remembered something Madge said back on the boat."

"Madge?" I glanced at Miles.

"Don't you remember? She said something about holding our Destiny in our hands. And then she winked. It was kind of suspicious."

Now that he mentioned it, I did remember hearing Madge say that. Had she really been trying to give Miles a clue? Whatever the case, I was so happy Miles had paid attention.

"So, where are the Orc Slayers now?" Pressing her hands against her cheeks, Vanessa couldn't wipe the look of astonishment from her face, even if she tried.

"At the beginning of another Quest, I guess," Miles said.

They were gone. Actually gone. Avery, Carl, Javier, Susan, and even Sheba had been whisked away by a clever reroll of the Die of Change. Whether they had returned to the old, rickety shack beyond the Entry Bridge or to some other starting point on the map, it no longer mattered. Even if they could somehow make it back to Mount Restless in time to finish off Foyos, it wouldn't count as their victory. Thanks to Miles, the Orc Slayer Band had been given a brand-new Destiny.

"Sorry I let that sloth slap you like that." Miles coaxed Goon out from under the thorn bush and put him back under his cloak. The armadillo's jaw almost came unhinged from his worn-out yawn. "Sheba isn't very nice, is she?"

"Not to dampen the mood," I said, nodding at the cave, "but we still have one more challenge to deal with."

"But after we fight Foyos, we go home, right?" Vanessa asked.

I nodded. "If we beat Foyos, we go home." At least I hoped we would. If we lost, though, all bets were off. We would remain in the Lower Etchlands. Forced to try to defeat Foyos again, only by then the magic of Faylinn's talisman would no doubt be completely worn off and Foyos would have gained all his power back. "It won't be easy, though," I said.

"I don't care," Vanessa's voice rose with excitement. "We've gone through so much, and here we are together."

"Yeah, a week ago, I would have never imagined we would make it this far without killing each other," I said.

"We almost did," Jasmine admitted. "Several times."

"Does this mean we're friends, now?" Miles opened his ration of beef jerky from his Dispenser and began passing around the package.

Nibbling on a piece of the dried meat, Jasmine shrugged and nodded. "You guys are my friends."

"Mine too," I agreed.

It felt weird saying that. In fact, this may have been the first time in my life I had ever been able to call not just one individual but a whole group *friends*.

Chomping noisily, Vanessa wouldn't make eye contact with anyone.

"Hello?" Cracking a smile, Jasmine raised her eyebrows expectantly at Vanessa.

"Oh, fine," Vanessa conceded. "This doesn't mean we're forming a club after this is all over, but I definitely don't *hate* you guys anymore."

I knew we were only buzzing with excitement from eliminating the Orc Slayers, but the real challenge still remained. We had no idea what to expect from Foyos. Would he still be withering and weak from Faylinn's magic? Or would he have already returned to full strength and be nearly impossible to defeat? There was no other way for us to know. We just had to step into his lair.

"Do you think we're ready?" Jasmine asked, twirling her Spade with her fingers.

"We're ready," I replied, and the four of us faced the cave.

· ◆ ● ◆ ·

Fair warning to all foolish enough to approach the lair of Foyos. You may enter here if you wish, but only through death shall you leave. Either by your death or by the monster's, it matters not. For this cave is cursed and I am she who cursed it.

—*Faylinn Resbollah, the Immortal Witch of the Hagwoods*

The message had been carved into a stone pedestal right in front of the cave.

"That doesn't exactly fill me with warm fuzzies," Vanessa said.

"You don't think it means we can't run away if we get into trouble, do you?" Miles asked.

"I think that's precisely what it means, Miles," I said.

Judging from our previous experience with Faylinn, I didn't doubt her power for one second. Once we entered that cave, there would be no turning back. Not until we finished the job or died trying.

"Is it me, or is it, like, deathly quiet in there?" Jasmine asked, straining to listen.

There didn't seem to be any sounds coming from inside. Sticking out my hand, I wiggled my fingers into the opening, just past the pedestal. I felt no change in temperature, not even a gentle breeze. The air inside felt empty, as though it had been sucked dry.

"Maybe Foyos is farther in," I suggested.

Miles nodded his head rapidly. "It could be a giant cave with tunnels. The monster could be anywhere."

I forced a smile. "Like another labyrinth?" I asked. "That would be swell." I had already played that round before. Wandering lost in some winding tunnels was the last thing we needed right now.

The moment we crossed over the threshold into the sound-less cave, a wall of stone dropped from the ceiling, blocking our escape. The sheer force shoved us farther into the now pitch-black room, and my eardrums popped. I had to pinch my nose closed and swallow several times just to relieve the pressure. Unless one of us rolled for a stick of dynamite from the Champion's Catch, we wouldn't be exiting the way we entered.

The cave suddenly filled with a haunting, fluorescent-blue glow. Had we not been currently standing inside a mountain in a mythical world, I would have sworn somebody had just flipped a light switch. And then all the sounds we had been missing just outside the cave came whooshing in like a tidal wave as a dozen blackened cauldrons crackling with electricity suddenly ignited, encircling an expansive area across the room where a terrifying creature lay asleep on the floor. Filling in every possible inch of space between the cauldrons, the monster's chest shuddered with each breath, sounding like an airplane shooting down a runway.

"Is it a lion?" Jasmine took a cautious step away from the circle.

The upper half of the creature's torso and his two front claws certainly resembled that of a lion, as did one of his heads, covered with a mane of crimson hair. The rest of Foyos, however, made no sense whatsoever. Sprouting from between his muscular shoulders, Foyos's second head was some sort of goat and was snoring loudly. A pair of sharp horns jutted out from the goat's forehead, and a slobbery tongue dangled from his mouth like an octopus's tentacle. Coiling past the creature's cloven-hooved hind legs, a scaly tail lay curled up on the floor, ending in the head of a snake.

Tugging on my sleeve, Miles showed me an entry on his "Compendium of Monsters" and the tiny picture of a mythical, three-headed beast.

"A *chimera?*" I asked.

Not once in any of my other role-playing adventures had

I fought one of those, but I had learned enough to know how dangerous they could be.

"The most difficult challenge of facing a chimera is knowing how to prepare for its cunning, mischievous nature." Glancing up from reading, Miles paused long enough to give me a woozy stare before continuing. "Fifty Strength, thirty Speed, forty Wisdom, and sixty Vitality. Good grief."

I may not have been a pro at Champion's Quest, but an unconscious chimera had to be easier to fight than one that was awake. Gripping my Gadget, thumb poised ready to press the button, I took a step toward the circle but was immediately repelled back as a bolt of electricity shot out from one of the nearby cauldrons, zapping the floor at my feet. The sound startled Foyos, and the goat head suddenly yawned. Straightening his neck, the creature blinked lazily before glaring at me with his glassy eyes.

"Why did you do that?" the goat head asked, his voice nasal and pinched, as though recovering from a recent cold. "Why did you attempt to step past the barrier?"

Swallowing, I warily glanced around at the others. "We've come to—"

"We know why you're here," the goat chimed in, cutting me off. Squinting, he studied me momentarily, and I couldn't help but notice the mystical talisman around the goat's neck. Another bolt of electricity crackled, leaping from one cauldron to the next, filling the air with the smell of charred ozone. "You're Champions on a Quest to destroy us," the goat said, releasing a high-pitched snicker. Tilting his head, he pointed his beard at the talisman around his neck. "I see you've noticed we've been adorned with a dangerous, aging talisman. The witch, Faylinn, cursed us with this trinket. Causing us to—"

This time it was Jasmine who interrupted the monster. "We know about Faylinn and what her talisman does," she said.

The monster's eyes narrowed menacingly. "Oh, you know, do you? Then perhaps you already know that the magic of the talisman is wearing off and that our power is being restored. We grow stronger daily, and soon we shall once again be free to finish what we started long ago."

"And what would that be?" I asked.

"For starters, we will destroy the Hagwoods and that miserable crone of a witch, Faylinn. And then we'll lay waste to this garbage heap of a countryside and every soul living in it." Lashing out his tentacle-like tongue, the goat licked his lips. "Beyond that, maybe we'll find a nice, quiet castle, devour king and court, and settle down. Now, I have a question for you," the goat head continued. "What is the name of your Band of Champions? What do other peasants call you?"

"We're the Wild Crows," I replied.

"We've never eaten crow. Not yet," the goat said, the corners of its mouth turning up in a wicked grin. "My name is Capritrix. The lion head is Leoraptum." He bowed his head toward the lion's skull, but the massive creature never stirred. "And the snake is Conda." He jabbed his horns toward the rear. "Foyos is what we're called when we're all awake, which has not happened for centuries. As you saw for yourself, Faylinn convinced a powerful Artisan to help create this electrical prison. The cauldrons keep us trapped. Even so, the witch feared we might find a way out of this tomb together. Thus this talisman around our neck. Under the talisman's curse, we are each unable to stay awake at the same time. Clever ole gal, isn't she? Except the spell doesn't last forever," he said. "The magic has already begun seeping out. It won't be long until all three of our heads are awake and Foyos will rise again. But, alas, I see you're rather impatient."

Flicking his chin, Capritrix nodded across the room to where a lever was attached to the far wall. "To accomplish your quest of killing us, you'll first need to extinguish the cauldrons."

I turned toward the others. "What do you guys think?"

"What if it's a trap?" Vanessa asked. "What if he's just saying that so we'll pull the lever?"

"If we want to defeat Foyos," I said, "we're going to have to pull it eventually. Fighting one head is better than three."

With hardly any effort, I reached up and pulled the lever down. The crackling cauldrons were no longer hindered by bolts of electricity. The three-headed beast began rising from the floor. Capritrix's eyes gleamed like mirrors, but the other heads of Leoraptum and Conda drooped lazily, still deep asleep. Before it stood to its full height, the monster froze in place.

Just as I had expected, the Champion's Catch appeared, hovering in the air between us.

Miles gave a nervous little squeak. "Technically, this could be our last roll," he said. "Unless we all get killed."

I squeezed the Die of Fate tightly in my fist. "We're not going to get killed," I said. "We can beat this thing."

Jasmine gave me a supportive nod, and Vanessa smiled, her lips stretched into a thin line. Then I rolled the die. It took several seconds to complete its topsy-turvy course around the bowl of the Champion's Catch before finally coming to rest on the number four.

Miles gasped. "Me again? I was afraid of that," he said, shoulders slumping.

"Now you get to roll the Die of Opportunity. Don't you want an upgrade?" Jasmine asked.

"Not really," Miles replied. "I mean, it's a lot of pressure, and I think it would be better if one of you three had the advantage. You're all older and bigger and—"

"That doesn't matter, Miles," I said. "Age. Size. Who cares? We've all contributed to our success. You especially. And we all work together."

"And if one of us gets an opportunity, we're that much better because of it," Jasmine said. "Technically, it's all our advantage."

"Besides, we could have rolled an X," Vanessa added. "Which would have given that *thing*," she flicked her chin at the frozen Capritrix, "the opportunity. Can you even imagine?"

"You're right," Miles said. "I just don't want to mess everything up."

"You won't," I assured him.

With his confidence boosted, Miles rolled the Die of Opportunity, and the four of us peered into the Catch to read the card:

THE GLADIUS OF GALLANTRY

This magical sword is rare but well-known,
With a blade so sharp it can slice through stone.

Before the card vanished, Miles's Tether was replaced by a heavy-looking sword with a narrow handle and a gleaming blade. The weapon looked wholly out of place in Miles's hand.

"I think I miss my normal Tether," Miles said, his voice trembling.

"Look, the words on the card are changing," Vanessa said.

The Gladius is best, remember, Crows,
When fighting against a *trio* of foes.

"Wow, it's like this game knows exactly what we need," Miles gasped.

Once again, the words shifted a final time with a new message:

> Recklessly swinging might feel irresistible,
> But better to try something unpredictable.

As quickly as it appeared, the Catch and card vanished.

Miles tried swinging the sword.

"Careful with that." Vanessa reared back as Miles nearly dropped it.

"Are you strong enough to wield it?" Jasmine asked.

Miles didn't reply but lowered the sword to his side, his eyes nervously settling on the monster.

"Miles, since you have the weapon, you're going to have to be the one to take out Foyos," I said. "Which means you have to get close to him."

Upon hearing this, Miles's eyes darted back to mine. "How close?"

"Like *right* next to him," Jasmine said. "We'll distract him for you. We don't have a ton of room in here, but we'll spread out the best we can."

"On second thought . . ." Miles extended the sword to me.

I almost took it from him but then shook my head. "The Die of Fate chose you, Miles. And you rolled the Die of Opportunity."

"Maybe I can help," Vanessa said, testing the tautness of the strings on her Spark. A single rhythmic note twanged across the instrument. "It's just an idea, really, but I think I can direct my music in a way that can be of use."

"In what way?" I asked.

"Well." Vanessa cocked her head to one side, gnawing on her lip as she studied the Spark. "I'm going to try to make you unnoticeable."

"Really?" Miles said hopefully.

"You can do that?" Jasmine raised her eyebrows.

Vanessa replied with a confident nod. "I'm not sure how I know, but I think I can."

She strummed a full chord on her Spark.

Almost instantly, I felt a rush of courage coursing through my veins. Even Miles no longer looked on the verge of passing out.

"Okay, I can do this," Miles said. His entire countenance had changed. "But if something happens to me, I hereby bestow this sword upon one of you to defeat Foyos."

As the three-headed monster began to emerge from the circle, each massive paw padding heavily against the floor, Jasmine and I fanned out, trying to draw the monster's attention. Miles may have been small compared to Foyos to begin with, but with Vanessa playing her Spark, he almost vanished. Crouched low, his footsteps completely silent, Miles scurried across the floor, his tiny body blending in with the backdrop of stone walls and moldering cauldrons. In a matter of seconds, he easily slipped from view, ducking down beneath Capritrix's line of sight.

"Hold still, you squirmy little worms," the goat seethed, head bobbing back and forth, oblivious to the eleven-year-old beneath him.

Jasmine's Spade glowed as she jabbed it into the floor, chiseling up chunks of stone and hurling them at the beast with deadeye aim. A rock bounced off one of Capritrix's horns, catching his attention. Enraged, the monster bounded toward her, a flurry of rocks pelting his goat skull as his claws sparked against the floor. For dragging around the weight of two extra heads, both still fast asleep, Foyos moved dangerously fast.

Before Jasmine had time to slip out of the way, Capritrix cut off her escape. Pinned against the wall, the monster closing in, Jasmine shot a panicked look in my direction.

Picking up a rock, I flung it at Capritrix, but I didn't come close. I had always been a horrible shot. I scanned the ground, searching for Miles, and spotted him quivering just below the monster's stomach.

"Miles, what are you waiting for?" I shouted. "Do it now!"

Though hesitant at first, upon hearing my command, Miles screwed up his face with determination and leapt out from under the monster. With his sword gleaming, he swung at the beast's exposed belly and would have succeeded had the monster not pulled back at the last second.

"Ah, there you are." Dropping down, Capritrix trained his eyes on Miles.

Jasmine flung another barrage of rocks with her Spade at the monster's back, but they bounced harmlessly away as Capritrix's long neck lowered, drawing right up next to Miles.

I felt helpless from across the room. Even Vanessa had abruptly stopped strumming. Standing by the lever, she just watched, wearing a horrified expression.

"You're the youngest one, aren't you?" Capritrix asked. "I can fix that."

With a rapid dip of his chin, the goat's tongue snatched the chain of Miles's Advancement Medallion, dragging it out from under his robe. Instantly jerking in surprise, Miles released his grip on the Gladius of Gallantry, and it clattered to the floor. Goon clung to the Medallion, but his insignificant claws were no match for the giant monster's strength. Capritrix pulled the Medallion from around Miles's neck and tossed it aside. No longer protected by Faylinn's Ward against Withering spell, Miles's skin began to shrivel. Wrinkles appeared on his face, and his short black hair turned gray and then white. Knees buckling beneath him, the small, aged boy collapsed on the ground.

While the goat howled with laughter, Jasmine and I raced toward the circle. Miles was still alive and breathing, but he looked old and had curled into a crooked little ball. Diving across his body to shield him, I dragged Miles away just as Jasmine grabbed the Gladius of Gallantry from the ground and slashed with all her might, right through the monster's neck. Still cackling, Capritrix's hideous head instantly exploded with a shower of turquoise sparkles. Staggering back into the middle of the cauldrons, the now two-headed creature collapsed to the floor with a concussive boom.

Vanessa moved the lever back up, and the ring of cauldrons lit up once more with electric fire.

"Is he all right?" Jasmine demanded, joining us at the wall of the cave.

"Um . . . yeah?" Vanessa replied. "Sort of."

"I'm fine," Miles snapped. His voice had turned gruff and wheezy.

"How do you feel, Miles?" I asked, placing a hand on his shoulder. He looked like he'd been soaking in a bathtub for years.

"Old," he replied. "I feel like every muscle in my body needs to take a nap."

"Just rest," I said, hoping we could find his Advancement Medallion. Although I wasn't sure if returning the Medallion around his neck would remove the curse.

Goon peeked out from Miles's robe and sniffed his face.

"Hey, Goon, remember me?" Miles said, his breathing labored.

"Why are we still here?" Jasmine said. "We killed Foyos. We finished our quest."

"The mighty Foyos lives on!" Capritrix's voice called out, laughing from inside the circle.

As we slowly turned around, our spirits plummeted. The goat head of Capritrix rose up once again from atop the monster's back, grinning mischievously.

CHAPTER 32

DOUBLE TROUBLE

Didn't he explode?" I asked, helping Miles to his feet. "I could have sworn he did."

Jasmine had lopped off one of Foyos's heads. What good was striking something with the Gladius of Gallantry if the monster only stayed dead temporarily?

Smiling down from inside the circle, Capritrix's slotted eyes narrowed. "I can sense your fear, especially now that you have one less champion to help you and one more head to contend with."

A hissing sound like the air being let out of a tire filled me with dread as another of the monster's three heads suddenly stirred to life.

"Morning, Conda," Capritrix said as the chimera's tail unraveled and a black, scaly snakehead emerged.

"Why are we both awake?" the snake asked in a scratchy female voice, her forked tongue flickering. Her eyes were two glowing orbs shimmering in the light of the cauldrons.

Capritrix's ears waggled as he nodded at the talisman. "The witch's spell is almost gone. Soon we shall overpower these confines. And the little mice that entered our cave will be a tasty snack." Puckering his lips, he pointed at the four of us, and the snake's undulating neck whipped around.

"Ooh, what are *they*?" Conda asked, her golden eyes narrowing.

"A Band of Champions come to destroy us," Capritrix announced.

"Well, they'd better hurry," Conda hissed, "before we are three."

"They're all starting to wake up," Jasmine said. "If we're going to defeat this monster, we need to hurry. It's just going to get harder."

"But how?" I asked. "You cut his head off. That should have killed him."

"So, what do we do?" Vanessa asked. "Do we lift the lever or just sit here and wait for the lion to pop up?"

Even though my confidence was almost gone, I nodded at Vanessa. "Go ahead. Lift the lever."

As soon as the quivering flames in the cauldrons fizzled out, Conda struck without warning, her head cracking out like a whip. Even with the full mass of Foyos standing inside the circle, the snake easily reached us. Jasmine and I barely managed to duck. Lucky for Miles, his short stature saved him from disaster as the giant reptile shot overhead. But Vanessa wasn't so lucky. The full brunt of the snake's fangs clanged against her Spark, throwing her back into the stone wall. I heard Vanessa scream out and saw the lights of her Advancement Medallion winking as her health instantly drained.

Without hesitation, Jasmine sunk the pointed end of her Spade right into Conda's coiling neck. The snake hissed and snarled and attempted to lash around her, but Jasmine was too quick and dove beneath the monster's tail. Then she bolted away, drawing Conda out after her.

"How much health do you have left?" I asked Vanessa, surprised to see that she was still able to stand.

"I don't want to look," she said. "My Medallion keeps flashing. That means something terrible, right?"

Helping her to her feet, I shot a glance over my shoulder, watching as the snake darted around, trying to pinpoint Jasmine's location.

"Three hundred years ago, that would've been a killing blow," Capritrix tutted as the snake lunged at Jasmine but narrowly missed.

"I wasn't trying to *bite*," Conda said, withdrawing into the circle, and gazing disinterestedly in my direction. "Not yet. I was only fishing. I had to test the waters to see which Champion was the most fearless of the group, and now I know."

"Ah, I see." Capritrix nodded. "If you strike the heart of the Champion—"

"You have killed the soul," Conda finished, slithering away from the circle, going after Jasmine again.

Jasmine's Spade suddenly began to glow as she twisted her wrist. Despite being made of solid stone, the floor began to buckle and crack from Jasmine's Harvester powers.

"What is this? An eruption?" Capritrix demanded, his claws wobbling uneasily as a wave of stone rolled across the ground.

Conda had to maneuver to avoid catching a mouthful of jagged rocks, but the wave of stone still struck the slumbering lion square in the jaw. Leoraptum remained asleep, but Capritrix yowled in agony.

"Awesome!" I cheered. But my celebration was suddenly cut short.

"Lucas!" Vanessa called out. "The snake's got Jasmine!"

With all our attention focused on the rest of Foyos's body, Conda's head had circled around and plunged back down, striking Jasmine. She lay on her back, not moving. Lifeless.

Anger surged through me. Without thinking, I silently grabbed the Gladius of Gallantry and raced over to the snake. Wrapping both hands around the handle, I brought down the sword and cleaved straight through the monster's scaly neck. Streaks of green, blue, and golden light exploded.

I heard a snarl of annoyance and turned just in time to see Capritrix, yellow slotted eyes blazing with fury, as he barreled toward me, goat horns pointing right at my chest.

With no way to avoid a collision, I clamped my eyes shut, awaiting the blow, but it never happened. Instead, a crackle of electricity filled the cave, followed by the smell of burnt hair. When I opened my eyes again, Capritrix had slumped into a heap on the ground. Smoke sizzled from his fur, drifting toward the ceiling, and his tongue dangled limply from his mouth.

"What? But how?" I whirled around and saw that Vanessa had reignited the cauldrons. The magical force field must have fried the goat to a crisp, thrusting it back into the circle.

"Is she dead?" Vanessa asked, rushing over and stooping down next to me as I examined Jasmine.

I shook my head grimly. "I don't think so. She's still breathing, just not conscious."

Vanessa shook Jasmine's shoulders. Only a single Bloodstone remained on her Medallion, and it flickered sporadically, as though threatening to go dark at any moment.

"She should be dead," I said. "She wasn't at full health to begin with, and then to take a bite from that snake—"

"I think it's the Surge," Vanessa explained.

"The Surge?" I asked, not following.

Vanessa showed me her Medallion, and I could instantly see she wasn't fairing much better than the others. She pointed to the star-shaped bead she had attached to her medallion. She had given one to each of us back at Torbrick's Tavern. "It must be giving us a bonus hit point."

If it hadn't been for the Surge, both Miles and Jasmine would certainly be dead, forced to return to the shack and wait for us.

"Good thing I flirted with Philip, huh?" Vanessa asked.

I nodded. "I would say so. And thank you for saving my life back there."

"You *better* thank me," she said, grinning, though she looked exhausted.

"Why haven't we gone home?" Miles rasped once Vanessa and I had dragged Jasmine back over. We laid her on the ground next to him, hoping she would show some sign of recovery, but she remained unconscious.

Miles had a good point. Why hadn't we gone home yet? Our Quest should have been finished by now. We had killed the monster, twice. But even before I looked up at Vanessa and saw the defeated glint in her eyes as she gazed over my shoulder, I knew we weren't finished yet.

"You are never going home," Capritrix threatened from inside the circle.

Conda shuddered as she once again rose up from the rear of the monster.

"Ooh," she said, shivering with annoyance. "That blade tingled a bit, little mouse. You should be more careful with sharp things." Her fangs gleamed in the electrical glimmer of the cauldrons.

"Nothing's working," Vanessa said.

"I know," I whispered, not wanting Foyos to hear. "But he has to be beatable, right? There has to be a way to win."

"Probably," Vanessa said, raising an eyebrow. "But this is really hard for me. I don't know if you've figured this out yet or not, but I'm not the go-on-an-adventure-and-kill-a-three-headed-monster type of person."

"Well, neither am I."

"Oh, yes, you are, Lucas. Without you, we would have never made it this far. You're the smartest, bravest, sneakiest"—Vanessa rolled her eyes and groaned—"and I know I'm going to regret saying this, but the coolest little brother a sister could ask for. I'm just sorry it took facing down a three-headed monster for me to figure it out. If you can't do it, no one can."

"Did you just call me your little brother?" I said with a nervous laugh, starting to choke up.

"Yeah, I did, okay? I said it." Vanessa's eyes were glossy. "You and Miles are more than just foster kids to me. I've told my parents they should adopt you both."

"You have?" I could hardly believe what I was hearing. We may have been beyond hope, but my chest still swelled nearly to the point of bursting.

"I apologize for not being that helpful," Miles said, dropping a wrinkled hand on my shoulder. "Getting old stinks. The next time I see an old person, I'm going to give them a hug."

"It's okay, Miles," I said.

"I know the Gladius of Gallantry card said that our blade is the best," Miles said weakly, "but I'm starting to have doubts."

"Me too," Vanessa huffed. "We been fighting this three-headed monster and killed it twice but—"

"Wait, that's it," I said, thinking about the clues from the card. *"The Gladius is best, remember, Crows, when fighting against a trio of foes. We've never fought Foyos when all three heads have been awake."*

"True," Vanessa said, "but even fighting two heads cost us Miles and Jasmine."

Still lying on the ground, Jasmine began to stir. Clamping a hand to her temple, she slowly sat up and groaned.

"Ugh, did someone say my name?" Jasmine squinted up at me groggily.

I was so grateful to see her moving again.

"We thought we had lost you," Miles said.

"Yeah," I said. "Good to have you back."

For a moment, Jasmine stared at Miles in confusion, but then she nodded. "That's right. You're still old, aren't you?"

Miles grinned sheepishly.

"Maybe this will help." She reached into her pocket and pulled out Miles's Advancement Medallion. "I found it when I was running and dodging that snake head."

Vanessa helped Miles put it over his head. When it rested against his chest, he immediately grew younger until he was back to his former young self.

"Wow, I feel amazing!" Miles exclaimed. "No more wrinkles. Thank you, Jasmine."

Jasmine nodded. "I'm just glad we're all still here. Have you figured out how to beat this thing yet?"

Each of our Vitality Meters were barely blinking. Jasmine was our best fighter, and she was too weak to help. We had Miles back, but he was so small and thin and—

"Hey, I think I have an idea."

Everyone looked at me with tired expressions, except for

Miles who looked remarkably refreshed even if his life was hanging by a blinking light.

"Remember Bogie's advice," I said, "about how to win the game? He said in order to slay an unpredictable monster, one must become unpredictable themselves."

"That's sort of like what the Gladius of Gallantry card said," Miles added. "About the blade. *Recklessly swinging might feel irresistible, but better to try something unpredictable.*"

"Exactly," I said, keeping my voice soft enough so that Foyos couldn't hear.

"So my little brother has a plan that Foyos won't predict?" Vanessa asked, giving me a half smile.

I was really liking the way she called me her little brother. "Yeah, I do. It's a long shot, but I don't think Foyos will expect it."

Just then, the massive mouth of Leoraptum stretched wide, heaving a colossal yawn I felt rattle down to my toes. All three heads of Foyos were finally awake.

CHAPTER 33

AN UNPREDICTABLE FOE

S haking his mane, Leoraptum sent up a cloud of dust and fur, his black lips pulling back above yellowed fangs. They looked like sharpened rolling pins jutting out from either side of his massive mouth.

"Oh, it feels good to stretch again." Leoraptum's voice boomed, sounding all at once like a mix between a tuba and a hurricane and instantly turning my knees to jelly. While the lion may have been terrifying asleep, I didn't have the right word to describe him awake. Terrifying times one thousand.

Vanessa squeezed my arm, digging her fingernails straight through my cloak and into my skin, but I didn't react. I couldn't move out of fear. Miles grabbed my other arm, not as tightly as Vanessa, but I could feel him trembling with fright.

Licking his chops, Leoraptum gazed over at the snake. "We are all awake?"

"Yes, sire," Conda replied, moving around to the front and bowing respectfully. "The witch's curse has ended. It's been three centuries, I believe."

"Yes, the magic spell has worn off," Capritrix added.

The lion's voice turned sinister. "Finally, Foyos has returned." His laugh sent chills up and down my spine. "We will hunt down the witch and cause her pain and suffering and death."

"Yes, yes, of course." Capritrix bowed.

"Indeed," Conda agreed. "But I do feel hungry. Famished, actually. It's a good thing we have a meal waiting for us." She flicked her tongue toward our group.

Head dipping, Leoraptum turned his focus away from the discussion and stared at us for the first time, his eyes gleaming. "What do we have here?" he asked. Then, almost immediately, he frowned with disappointment. "They look sickly and small. Waifish. Are they dead?"

"Not yet. These Champions have tried to kill us but have failed miserably," Capritrix said. "They call themselves the Wild Crows."

This brought on another eruption as Leoraptum laughed once more. "Crows? Birds, is it? More like chickens, I'd say. Mmm . . . a roasted goose does sound delightful. I could eat a whole flock. I hope they weren't expecting mercy. Leoraptum shows no mercy."

Flexing his muscular front legs, the monster took a stride toward us but reared back as streaks of lightning ignited from the cauldrons. Leoraptum's frown of disappointment turned into one of disgust.

"The witch's sorcery still imprisons us," Capritrix reminded.

Eyes narrowing, Leoraptum studied the barricade. "Maybe for a defeated creature, but not for the full strength of Foyos. With the three of us working together, we will smash these puny cauldrons to smithereens." The beast lurched for one of the cauldrons, and the cave lit up with a crackle of immense power. Each attempt sent a concussion of splintering light showering out from the circle.

All eyes once again turned to me.

"I doubt that magical barrier is going to hold much longer," Vanessa said. "We'd better be ready. What's the plan?"

Keeping my eyes glued on Foyos, I picked up the Gladius of Gallantry. "We need to try something we haven't tried before," I said. "And I think it will take all of us to beat Foyos."

"Jasmine is too weak to fight," Vanessa said.

"But I can use my Spade to do the fighting," Jasmine said, slowly getting to her feet. "I want revenge on that snake."

I turned to Miles. "You're the Gamekeeper, right? Animals are your specialty. Any ideas?"

"What about music?" Miles said.

I wasn't the only one confused by his suggestion.

He continued. "It's scientifically proven that music can sometimes relax animals. Maybe Vanessa could play something soothing from her Spark that could lull Foyos to sleep."

"This isn't a three-headed dog named Fluffy," Jasmine said. "We're not inside a fantasy book. I don't think that will work."

"It's worth a try," Vanessa said. "I'll see what I can do."

"And the *best* weapon to defeat Foyos is this." I handed Miles the gleaming sword. "The Gladius is yours. You're the one who rolled for it, and you have to be the one to use it." Both Jasmine and I had used the Gladius of Gallantry on Foyos, and both times it hadn't worked. Maybe the weapon had to be wielded by the Gamekeeper to make the death blow. It was his Opportunity, after all.

Miles shook his head rapidly. "I already tried that."

"I know, but you never hit Foyos," I said.

"Right, but even if you had hit him before all three heads were awake, I doubt it would've worked," Vanessa added.

"If you guys think I can do it," Miles muttered. "I'll try again."

This was our last hope of defeating Foyos. If we failed now and the monster escaped his mountain prison, we might never get to go home again.

"Okay, Lucas, we're with you on this," Jasmine said. "What are you going to do?"

"What I do best," I replied, glancing at Vanessa and smiling awkwardly. "I'll be the bait."

Roaring with rage, the three-headed Foyos continued battering the cauldrons.

The first part of my plan was to do something Leoraptum wouldn't expect. We had to be unpredictable. "Jasmine, you go to the far left. Vanessa, you stay to the far right. Miles, you stick with me." As everyone took their places, I stepped up to the wall and activated the lever. With a gusting draft of scorched air, each of the fiery cauldrons went out.

Then the roaring stopped.

Leoraptum stared at the cauldrons, blinking in confusion.

"Look! The Champions let us out before we destroyed the cauldrons," Capritrix explained. "They willingly freed us."

"Did they now?" Leoraptum asked.

"Foolish little mice," Conda hissed as the monster moved out of the circle.

"We're not scared of you," I announced, sounding much braver than I truly felt. "We're going to destroy you once and for all."

I knew how silly my words must have sounded, especially in my trembling voice.

"Is this some sort of trick?" Leoraptum asked Capritrix. "That is your talent, is it not? Your wit. Your quick thinking. Your ability to spot a trap?"

"Your Majesty," Capritrix said, "I assure you this is no trap.

They are out of options. They know the only way to defeat us is to fight us."

"Use your fire, Your Majesty," Conda said, chuckling wickedly. "The one in the center is their leader. Blast him with your searing breath and turn him to ash."

"Miles, get behind me." I brought out my Gadget and took a shaky step toward the monster. I definitely remembered reading in some gaming manual a long time ago that one of the heads of a chimera could breathe fire like a dragon.

Leoraptum's grin suddenly widened, and then without any warning, he unleashed a spouting column of boiling flames.

With not a second to spare, I pressed the button on my Gadget. The sound of gears whirring rapidly rose from the cylinder as a spiral of steel plates emerged from the opening, connecting to form a full-sized shield large enough to block the oncoming blast. The flames splashed against the steel circle, pushing me back. I could feel the heat threatening to scorch me to ash, but I held strong and dug my heels into the ground. I gasped, totally shocked that Miles and I hadn't been burned to a crisp. "I love this thing!"

"You're only delaying the inevitable," Leoraptum seethed.

As the lion's fire fizzled and a plume of black smoke billowed up, he inhaled once more, rearing back on his hind legs for a second burst. Then Jasmine's Spade started to glow as she plowed it into the ground.

"Not that again," Capritrix whined as the stone floor began rolling beneath the monster.

Struggling to find his footing, Leoraptum clamped his jaws shut, stifling his second attempt to consume me in flames.

"Deal with her, Conda," the lion commanded. "Make it quick."

"Gladly, my king," Conda replied.

Neck unfurling, the snake stretched toward Jasmine.

Turning her eyes away, Jasmine crouched low to the ground.

"Frightened?" Conda asked, drawing right up next to the girl. "Shall I show you true fear?"

The rolling of the floor came to an abrupt stop, but the Spade still glowed.

"Please, don't come any closer. I'm scared," Jasmine said, her voice quaking.

"Don't play with your food, Conda," Leoraptum said. "Be done with her."

Conda moved even closer to Jasmine until the snake's head was inches from her back. "As you command, sire."

Jasmine squeezed her Spade tighter, and a boulder-sized stone fist burst from the ground, an upper cut right to the snake's jaw.

"Didn't see that coming, did you?" Jasmine sneered.

The snake bellowed in pain, its head and neck reverberating.

The distraction was perfect timing, making the other Wild Crows barely noticeable as we positioned ourselves closer to Foyos.

Conda shook off the brutal punch. Fury blazed in the snake's eyes. Fangs glistening with poison, Conda lunged at Jasmine but froze inches away from her throat. The snake was clearly muddled and disoriented as music wafted throughout the cave.

Vanessa's fingers slowly plucked each string, sending Conda into a bobbing rhythm. The music sounded soft and tinkling, almost like a harp. The melody reminded me a little of "Twinkle, Twinkle Little Star," probably the only song Vanessa knew.

Both Capritrix and Leoraptum wore similar expressions of bewilderment.

Conda drifted away from Jasmine as all three heads followed the music and spotted Vanessa standing on the opposite side of the cave.

I could hardly believe the music was working. Foyos was clearly mesmerized.

This was our chance.

As I started creeping forward, out of the corner of my eye, I saw Jasmine already halfway to the monster, her Spade clutched in her grip, eyeing her target.

Leoraptum flared his nostrils and then roared with a sound powerful enough to break boulders free from the ceiling and send them crashing to the ground, snapping both Capritrix and Conda from their trances. I almost dropped my shield in surprise, and Vanessa stopped playing.

Conda wasted no time. Striking with blinding speed, the snake sunk her teeth into Vanessa's shoulder.

"No!" I shouted as Vanessa winced, met my eyes from across the cave, and then disappeared.

"She's gone," Miles gasped.

At that exact moment, Jasmine rushed forward. Attempting to plunge her Spade into the monster's side, her attack was cut short when Capritrix's head bounded down from the monster's shoulders, driving his horns into her chest.

Just like Vanessa had done moments before, Jasmine vanished as well.

"That's more like it," Leoraptum said.

"Not again," I heard Miles's voice whimper. "We can't start all over again."

"Stay behind me and stay close," I instructed, fighting back tears.

They weren't really dead. As devastating as it seemed, Jasmine and Vanessa had only been sent back to the beginning. This wasn't permanent. I knew that, but I felt the emptiness of not having them fighting alongside me. But I wasn't willing to accept our defeat. Not yet.

With a burst of speed, I raced straight for the monster as Leoraptum's second blast of fire collided with my shield. It felt like being cooked inside the world's hottest oven. I knew that at any moment, I would black out when the Surge, my last hit point, finally faded, but I didn't stop running. Just a few more steps. Almost there. And then I was lifted off my feet. Captured in Foyos's two enormous claws.

"This one has heart," Leoraptum growled, staring down at me with a head the size of a minivan. "I hate heart. It makes the meat stringy."

The wind squeezed from my lungs, and my head grew fuzzy.

"I intend to eat you slowly," Leoraptum said. "Bite by bite. Piece by piece, so that you may know with each nibble how miserably you've failed."

My hand still clung tightly to the shield, and I could feel the Gadget's button. My finger was literally the only thing I could move. Pressing the button, the shield transformed into the long knife. From this close to the monster, the blade looked more like a letter opener than an actual dangerous weapon. But the smaller knife gave me just enough room to stab the monster's claw. Leoraptum didn't even flinch, the pointed blade hardly penetrating his thick skin.

Dark blips began bursting all around my eyes as the monster squeezed me tighter.

"Your strategy didn't work," I heard Capritrix say with a gleeful giggle from somewhere up above me. "You were outmatched in every way. Charging a chimera. What were you thinking?"

"I wasn't thinking," I croaked out a strangled whisper as the monster lifted me up and Leoraptum's jaws opened wide. "I was just the bait."

All three of Foyos's heads looked down in confusion. Miles had gone unnoticed this whole time and was small enough to slip away when the claw of Foyos snatched me up. Miles didn't hesitate this time. With both hands clasping the Gladius of Gallantry, he plunged the sword straight into the monster's heart.

Leoraptum reared back, snapping his fangs together and bellowing in agony.

Capritrix squealed and screamed.

Conda released a swooshing gasp.

My Advancement Medallion dimmed to nothingness as my bonus Surge finally kicked the bucket.

I fell backward, free from Foyos, dropping like a rag doll onto the hard stone floor with a thump. The cave began to quake. I could feel it rumbling as the floor splintered into a thousand fissures beneath me and the massive Foyos suddenly exploded. Rainbow-colored sparkles showered down like a fountain, and then the monster was gone—its three-headed form fading into oblivion.

I cheered louder than I had ever cheered. Shooting up from the ground, I whirled around, pumping my fists in the air. "Holy smokes! Miles, I can't believe you did it."

Miles still stood with his arm outstretched, the Gladius of Gallantry extended above his head like a torch, a wild look in his eyes. It was a combination of terror and shock and something that might have been exhilaration all wrapped into one.

"I did it?" Miles asked, keeping hold of the weapon as he lowered it to his side. "Is it really over?"

I faced the ring of cauldrons. The circle remained dark and empty of any light, and I waited for the monster to reappear, but after almost a minute of silence, I knew Foyos was really gone. We had finally finished our Quest.

More screaming erupted from the cave, some of it came from Miles, some of it from me—and some from Vanessa and Jasmine, who had suddenly reappeared. Flailing their arms about like crazy, they raced over, and we grabbed each other into a massive hug. We weren't supposed to be celebrating. We were supposed to be dead, but somehow, miraculously, we had defeated Foyos.

"That was the most amazing ending ever," Jasmine said, almost completely out of breath.

"You saw it?" Miles asked, screwing his face up in disbelief. "You saw what happened?"

Jasmine nodded. "The whole thing. It was like I was still in the room but with one foot stepping into the shack. I saw you kill the monster, Miles!"

"So did I!" Vanessa chimed in, her voice choking with tears. "I thought for sure you were a goner when the lion grabbed you, Lucas, but then Miles came out of nowhere."

Glancing sidelong at me, Miles sighed and smiled. "Not out of nowhere. Lucas planned it all out."

As my cheeks began to burn, I shrugged innocently. "Well, maybe not all of it. But it was crazy."

"Crazy and unpredictable." Vanessa wrapped her arm around my shoulders. "And it worked!"

"Only because of Miles," I said.

Miles rolled his eyes. "I just got lucky. All I had to do was wait around for Lucas to get chomped."

"But *you* stabbed the chimera," Jasmine said. "*You* defeated a three-headed monster."

Covering his mouth with his hands, Miles suddenly laughed. "Yeah, I guess I did. I can't believe I did that."

"I can," we all said in unison.

"But where do we go now?" Vanessa asked. "I want a shower."

From overhead, the all-too-familiar disembodied voice announced: "Well done, Champions. You have completed this game of Champion's Quest. Farewell. I shall be eagerly awaiting the next time you take your Destiny into your hands."

The cave walls melted away like hot wax. Dripping and puddling, they sloshed around until the stone floor melted as well.

We stood in absolute darkness for about ten seconds before a few lights began twinkling all around. At first, I thought they were fireflies hovering in the air, but they weren't moving, and as my eyes began to focus, I realized they were actually candles attached to the columns of Hob and Bogie's Curiosity Shoppe.

CHAPTER 34

BRONZE-LEVEL
CHAMPIONS

I recognized the bookshelves, Sheba's scratching post, and the glass counter of mini figurines, followed by the circular table with a game board and stacks of playing cards scattered about.

Behind the table, sitting in his chair stroking his beard with one bony hand was Hob, beaming up at us, overjoyed with excitement.

"Well done, my friends." Crossing his arms, Hob sat back in his seat. "That was some impressive adventuring. I must say I was pleasantly surprised, though I never doubted you for a second."

I looked down to see I was no longer dressed in my cloak and muddy leather pants. I wore my shorts and sneakers. In fact, we were all wearing the same clothing we'd been wearing on the day of our departure, as though we had just come back from the aquatic center. But that had been almost a week ago.

"Oh, thank goodness." Gasping in relief, Vanessa pulled her cell phone from her pocket. Holding her phone to her lips, she kissed the screen.

"What day is it? How long have we been gone?" I asked, gaping around the room, my eyes struggling to adjust.

Hob smiled awkwardly. "It is eight o'clock in the evening on June 7, the same day you left. You have been in the game for six hours of our time, though your avatars experienced several days playing the game. Time moves in a complicated manner in the Lower Etchlands, as I'm certain you've discovered by now, but for Jasmine, it was even a tinge more complicated. You see, the Quest clock of the game doesn't officially begin until all members of the Band join together. And since that didn't happen in the traditional manner, poor Jasmine had to endure a bit more, I'm afraid."

"Ya think?" Jasmine blurted. "I had to wait two days for these clowns to show up."

Sniffing indignantly, Hob waggled his finger. "Yes, well, I did try to explain that to you, but you didn't give me a chance. Now, my dear, before you rush out that door in a fury as you did earlier, please allow me to bring the four of you up to speed on what's been going on while you've been away." He extended his palm toward the chairs seated around the table. "Perhaps you could humor an old man for, say, five minutes more? And then you are free to leave."

We looked at each other for a moment, and then, without another word, we all took a seat.

"My Lola is going to murder me," Jasmine groaned. "What am I supposed to tell her now? She was waiting for me out on the road like six hours ago."

"There's nothing for you to tell her. It's all been taken care of," Hob replied.

"It has?" Jasmine asked. "How?"

"I called your spirited Lola and informed her you were conducting community service at the aquatic center for that little skirmish you and that Tugg Roberts boy were engaged in earlier," he explained. "Your grandmother is expecting you home within the hour."

Jasmine blinked for a moment and then laughed. "And she believed you? Not in a million years. My Lola's not an idiot. She would have called the aquatic center to verify everything you told her."

"I know," Hob said, raising his eyebrows and heaving a dramatic sigh. "Persistent, that one. But I also intercepted her phone calls, and I feel semiconfident she took the bait. Now, I did my best to smooth things over with her on the phone, and I assured her the incident was not your fault and that Tugg was the one who actually provoked you. And your grandmother seemed placated for the most part. You may still endure a bit of punishment once you get home, but at least now you shan't be *murdered*."

"What about Mr. and Mrs. Crowe?" Miles asked, looking worriedly at Vanessa, who was still scrolling through her texts. "Do you think they've called the police?"

Vanessa shook her head. "They're not even finished with their meetings yet," she said, holding up her phone and showing us the recent message from her parents. "It's crazy, but they're still there. I don't think they have a clue we're even missing."

"Right, the meetings." Hob gave a nervous cough. "I also had to pull a few strings there. I do hope I didn't inconvenience them too much."

"What kind of strings did you pull?" I asked, staring at the old man in disbelief.

"Oodles of them. And I believe I tied a few knots as well, but I did what I had to do in order to ensure the safe and somewhat peaceful return of my Champions. Which reminds me—I do have a little matter to settle with you, Lucas, before you go, so don't let me forget."

"Okay," I said warily.

Miles reached across the game board to pick up one of the dozens of playing cards lying overturned, prompting Hob to intervene, tapping on his hand.

"Best not to disturb the board, Master Maldonado," Hob warned. "Wouldn't want to bring any accidental trouble your way, now would you?"

Hob grabbed the card and flipped it over, but not before I caught a peek of the other side. The card had an image of a young man dressed in armor and holding out his palm with several star-shaped objects resting upon it. Printed across the top of the card was the name Philip Cottlesby.

Philip? I wondered. Was that Vanessa's Philip?

"Okay, seriously, who are you guys?" Jasmine demanded.

"Who?" Hob asked.

"You and Bogie," she said.

He swatted a hand dismissively. "We're just a couple of old fools."

"Or wizards," I muttered.

Hob's eyes twinkled. "Who on earth told you that?"

"Avery," Jasmine said. "Just before she poisoned us with a Viper Pod."

"Oh. Yes, I remember now. Quite suspenseful. Well, Avery's partially correct. In our world, Bogie and I were from separate wizarding orders, and we fought, frequently and destructively. But here, I suppose we're just gifted conjurers pitted against each other in a battle of Champion's Quest."

"So, are you like . . . bitter enemies or something?" Miles asked.

Hob chuckled. "Bogie may be a little bitter. It's a thorny matter and would take more than a few minutes to explain. Perhaps we should save that for another evening, hmm?"

Glancing at the glass display counter, I eyed the door to the back room. It was the same room where we had magically visited Bogie earlier in the morning, and I expected it to burst open at any moment.

"He's not in there," Hob said, snapping me from my daze. "You needn't worry. Bogie's on an important errand, payment for suffering such a painful loss at the hand of the Wild Crows, and he won't be back for several days. So, relax, Lucas Silver. Revel in your victory."

"But why did we have to play this game?" Jasmine asked.

Hob opened his mouth and then swallowed in confusion. "I, of course, needed skilled warriors and adventurers—"

"And you picked *us*?" Vanessa interrupted with a boisterous laugh.

"It worked, did it not?" Hob exclaimed. "You defeated Foyos, prevented the Orc Slayers from triumph, and grew together as a Band. I couldn't have asked for a more successful group of Champions."

"Well, next time, I suggest you use people who *volunteer* and not force someone against their will," Vanessa said, glaring at Hob.

"Ah, but you see, no one volunteering actually understands what they're getting themselves into. So it's better to handpick a Band than to wait for just any yahoo who happens to show up on my doorstep unannounced," he said. "I sense a bit of frustration and agitation from you, Ms. Crowe. Did you not enjoy yourselves on your Quest?"

"*Enjoy* ourselves?" she spat.

Our Quest had been super hard, sure, but how could I say I didn't have any fun? We had gone on the most amazing adventure. This was turning out to be the best summer vacation I had ever had, and it was only the first day.

"I had fun," Miles announced, and Jasmine nodded in agreement.

"Okay, yeah, it was really cool," she admitted. "It's just way confusing, and I have a *lot* of questions."

"And the answers will be available to you shortly," Hob explained. "Now is just not the appropriate time to discuss it."

"Going to the mall with my friends is fun," Vanessa clarified.

Hob blinked at Vanessa, his eyes narrowing. "The mall will open again tomorrow, young lady, and your friends will forgive you for your absence, I am certain of it. But you have defeated a chimera. And a witch. You have fought monsters, explored a magical, mystical world, developed quite a reputation as skilled warriors—and now the four of you are Bronze Level Champions."

"Bronze Level Champions?" Miles asked. "We are?"

With the scuffing sound of creaking wood, Hob backed his chair away from the table. "Come, come, take a look."

Waving for us to join him, he hurried over to where the four unusual chests had been lined up beneath the window—the ones labeled with each of our names. Almost immediately, the wild feathered eyeball tied in the window began snarling viciously overhead.

"Now, now, Garasculous," Hob chided, fishing a ring of old, rusty keys from his pocket and fitting one into the keyhole of the footlocker with my name on it. "These are no longer intruders but honored guests. Save your hissing for someone else."

The eyeball instantly fell silent, its feathers sagging like wilted flowers. Shimmering light poured out from the opened footlocker, and I spotted a pile of familiar items. A folded stack of clothing—trousers, a button-down shirt, and a traveling cloak, all appearing as though they had never been touched— my leather Dispenser pouch and, resting on top of the pile, my Advancement Medallion sparkled, the center stone that had once been milky white having turned a coppery sheen.

"Upon the successful completion of your first Quest, new Champions increase their level," Hob explained. "That is why it is rightly named the Advancement Medallion. One must advance. You've also earned yourself a bit of a reward for vanquishing Foyos."

Jasmine raised an eyebrow. "What kind of reward?"

Gold coins and glittering jewels dripped from Hob's fingers as he scooped handfuls of treasure from the bottom of the chest. "You've each earned an equal share," he said.

"Wow, we're rich," Miles gasped.

Hob gave a light chuckle. "Hardly rich. Gold and rubies don't stretch as far as they did back in the olden days, but I would think it's safe to say you're better off than you were. In the Lower Etchlands, of course."

"What does that mean?" Vanessa asked, greedily eyeing the treasure. "Will it not spend here?"

"I'm afraid not," Hob said with a frown. "It is *magical* treasure, you see. It only works in a different realm."

Miles glanced up from the footlocker. "Where are our Heroes' Devices?"

"Ah, those." Hob sucked in a sharp intake of breath. "Madge had little choice but to bargain with Faylinn, and, therefore, the witch now owns the rights to your Devices." His head wobbled, and he made a few strained grunts as he seemed to pick the right words. "It will be tricky, but I'm sure there's a paragraph somewhere in the Questmaster's Guide I can reference to my advantage. But it will take some time to pore over."

"Questmaster's Guide?" Miles practically started hopping up and down with excitement. "Is that like a special version of the Field Guide?"

"Enough of this for now," Hob said, snapping the lid closed and snuffing out the glorious glow of gold and jewels. Glancing down at his wrist, he checked the time. "My goodness, you really should be getting back. I managed to create alibis for each of you, but I wouldn't press your luck."

My head was spinning. I felt like I had just endured another whirlwind conversation with Madge Crockery. I kept thinking about what had happened during the game and also of all the things I could buy with my portion of the treasure. Better armor. A nice sword.

"Is my car still parked outside?" Vanessa asked, moving to the door and grasping the knob.

"Should be," Hob said. "Unless you parked it illegally."

Vanessa seemed a little uncertain, but then she glanced at Jasmine. "Come on, Harvester, I'll give you a ride. And we should probably stop and get some dinner too. Who wants cheeseburgers?"

"Oh, man, please," Miles said, nodding eagerly.

"I'm in," Jasmine said. "Lucas, aren't you coming?"

I had yet to walk toward the door. "What was the matter you wanted to settle with me?" I asked, turning to face the old wizard.

Nibbling on his lower lip, Hob frowned for a moment but then brightened. "Good thing you reminded me. First, let me say that I was absolutely impressed with how you played the game. You overcame quite a few obstacles, as did the rest of the Wild Crows. I don't know if you noticed, but your Creepers didn't show up at all during your battle with Foyos. *That* is cause for celebration." Dipping his hand into his pocket he pulled out an envelope with my name scribbled on one side. "I felt simply horrible for causing you to miss your train. I'm afraid it left hours ago. I tried delaying it as best I could, but that takes all sorts of complicated magic."

"You tried stopping the train with a spell?" Miles's eyes widened with wonder.

"Sort of," Hob admitted, waffling with the answer, "but as I said, it's complicated. If Bogie wouldn't have been so stubborn, the two of us could have managed it, but that fool hardly budges during a match. It's like trying to drag an elephant with dental floss. Anyway, it doesn't matter. I took the liberty to transfer your ticket, Lucas."

"You did what?" I asked, taking the envelope from Hob.

"With the Crowes still tied up in meetings for the next couple of hours, I don't see why you wouldn't be able to hop aboard for a later departure. Perhaps Vanessa could drop you off at the terminal as well?" Hob glanced over at the others.

The train ticket looked identical to the one I had purchased the day before, only this one had been set to depart at 9:05 p.m. on the Carrington Express. I had a whole hour to make it there in time. My hopes of slipping away unnoticed had gone up in flames, but New York was a big enough city that a kid like me could disappear forever.

"I won't rat you out, Lucas," Vanessa said, letting go of the doorknob. "I think you've earned that much from me, but I'm not driving you. If you really want to go through with running away, you'll have to walk to the train station yourself."

"You don't really *want* to leave, do you?" Miles swallowed.

"Yeah," Jasmine added. "Who am I going to hang out with at the aquatic center once you're gone?"

I smirked. "I thought you were kicked out of there for the whole summer."

"I was," she said. "But you don't really think that will stop me, do you?"

Running away had always been my plan, even if it did seem daunting. Besides, after proving I could survive being attacked by monsters out in the wild, exploring one of the biggest cities in the world should be a piece of cake.

"Lucas, look at me," Vanessa said. "I meant what I said back in the cave. No one is going to force you to stay. Honestly, I don't think anyone could force you." She laughed. "But I think you belong here. With us."

I swallowed, something tugging at my throat. I looked down at the gold foil on my train ticket, the candlelight illuminating the tagline.

YOUR LIFE IS YOUR ADVENTURE,
BUT WE CAN HELP YOU ON YOUR WAY.

Taking a deep breath, I grasped the envelope with both hands and ripped the ticket into several pieces. I had spent a big chunk of my life savings on that ticket, and now I was throwing it away. But I could live with the loss, especially now that I had a chest filled with golden treasure and, more important, a trio of best friends who felt like family.

"Who knows?" I said. "Maybe if we're really bored, we can all meet up at the curiosity shop again."

Nobody said yes.

But nobody said no, either.

ACKNOWLEDGMENTS

First and foremost, I have to thank my amazing wife, Heidi, and my children, Jackson, Gavin, and Camberlyn. Writing a book like this demanded a lot from all of us and you were definitely my Band of Champions. Thank you to my Shadow Mountain team—to Chris Schoebinger for his vision and expert advice in helping craft this story into something so much more; to Derk Koldewyn for taking on this editing project without knowing what to expect from my mad, mad ways; to Owen Richardson, the mastermind behind the cover—you never disappoint and I'm your biggest fan!—to Richard Erickson for the clever details sprinkled throughout this book; and to Lisa Mangum for being there at the beginning as the idea of Champion's Quest first sprouted its roots.

Thank you to my awesome agent, Shannon Hassan, I wouldn't be where I am in my writing journey without your support and expertise. To Michael Cole, Jennifer Judd, and Kevin Lemley for being my beta readers on such short notice. And to Tyler Whitesides, Stanton Allen, Brad Baillio, and Carson Younker, for letting me join your group. What started out as "research" for a writing project transformed into some wild, dice-rolling adventures!

Lastly, a huge thank you to my readers! I still have to pinch myself sometimes when I think about how I get to share my stories with you. You're like family to me and I promise—if you keep reading, I'll keep writing!

READY TO PLAY

CHAMPION'S QUEST

AGAIN?

You're in luck!
A new adventure is starting soon.

CHECK OUT FRANKCOLEWRITES.COM

- Discover interesting facts about Hob & Bogie's Curiosity Shoppe
- Find discussion questions about Champion's Quest
- Read new Questing tips from the author that just might save your life

P.S. We think Frank L. Cole might be a wizard.